“I hate dou

She flung the words at him.

He stared at her for a long moment before speaking. “Are you telling me you had the same dream I did?”

“Corridors, doors, a special place and you waiting behind a shining door. Taking me in your arms. Holding me. The feeling...” She sighed and shook her head.

“The feeling we belonged together,” he said quietly.

Tara drew in her breath. “Exactly.”

“You and I were certainly close enough to be on the same wave length while we slept.”

“But... the dream we shared came true.”

His smile broadened to a grin. “We dreamed of what we both wanted. At least I did.”

Despite herself, a smile tugged at the corners of her mouth. She’d wanted him every bit as much.

“Making love was inevitable, dream or no dream.”

Dear Reader,

Spellbinder! That's what we're striving for. The editors at Silhouette are determined to capture your imagination and win your heart with every single book we publish. Each month, six Special Editions are chosen with *you* in mind.

Our authors are our inspiration. Writers such as Nora Roberts, Tracy Sinclair, Kathleen Eagle, Carole Halson and Linda Howard—to name but a few—are masters at creating endearing characters and heartrending love stories. Their characters are everyday people—just like you and me—whose lives have been touched by love, whose dreams and desires suddenly come true!

So find a cozy, quiet place to read, and create your own special moment with a Silhouette Special Edition.

Sincerely,

The Editors
SILHOUETTE BOOKS

SE-RL-3

DIANA STUART

Out of a Dream

Silhouette Special Edition

Published by Silhouette Books New York

America's Publisher of Contemporary Romance

Special thanks to Faith and to Ellin.

SILHOUETTE BOOKS
300 East 42nd St., New York, N.Y. 10017

ISBN: 0-373-09353-5

First Silhouette Books printing December 1986
Second printing January 1987

America's Publisher of Contemporary Romance

Printed in the U.S.A.

Books by Diana Stuart

Silhouette Desire

A Prime Specimen #172
Leader of the Pack #238
The Shadow Between #257

Silhouette Special Edition

Out of a Dream #353

DIANA STUART

lives in the Hudson River Highlands and has been publishing gothic and adventure romance novels since 1973. She's a nurse and is fascinated by Indian culture. She is a native Californian.

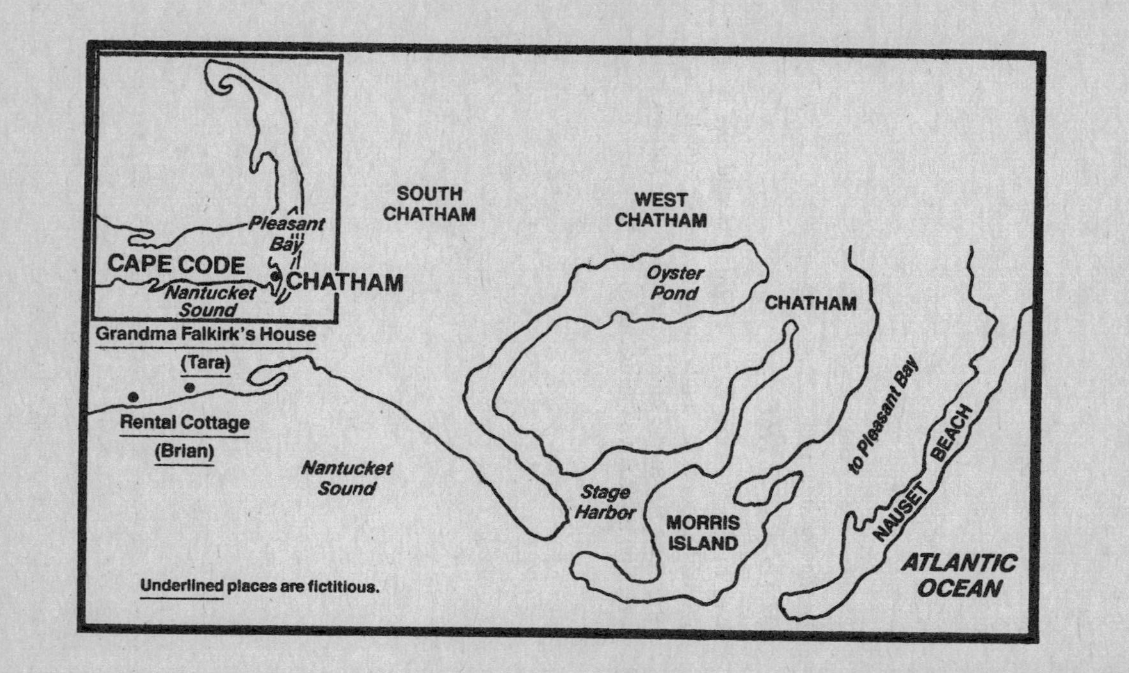
CAPE CODE
Pleasant Bay
CHATHAM
Nantucket Sound
SOUTH CHATHAM
WEST CHATHAM
Oyster Pond
CHATHAM
Grandma Falkirk's House
(Tara)
Rental Cottage
(Brian)
Nantucket Sound
Stage Harbor
MORRIS ISLAND
to Pleasant Bay
NAUSET BEACH
ATLANTIC OCEAN
Underlined places are fictitious.

Chapter One

But Tara," Karen said in her let's-be-reasonable tone, "Leda Umak is licensed by the State of New York as a teacher of meditation and psychic phenomena. She's not some old-time Gypsy gazing into a fake crystal ball."

Tara Reed looked at her sister. Pregnancy seemed to agree with Karen. Her hair formed a blond aura framing a luminous face and her blue eyes gleamed with excitement. It had always been hard for Tara to deny her twin anything. She took a deep breath, knowing she couldn't walk through that door and face a parapsychologist.

Their reflections showed in the windowed top of the side door to Leda Umak's white frame house—Karen shorter than Tara by half a head, her heart-shaped face pleading. Tara's own oval face mirrored her unwillingness to go along with her sister's wish. She brushed a lock of brown hair from her forehead as she tried to summon up a believable reason for not entering the house.

"Why are you so nervous?" Karen demanded. "Don't scowl at me, I know you are. You keep pushing at your hair like you always do when you're on edge, and your eyes are turning positively yellow."

Tara looked into her sister's eyes, as guileless a blue as they'd been a year and a half ago when she and Abbott had come to tell Tara they were getting married....

No! she scolded herself. The past is past. Don't dig up old emotions.

"I'd rather not go in, Karen," she managed to say. "Why don't I wait for you in the car?"

"My reading won't be any good if you don't come with me. Leda said with twins it's better if both are there."

"That's silly. We're fraternal, not identical twins, and we've never shared unspoken thoughts or anything of the sort. In fact, the notion of visiting this woman at all is foolish. If you'd told me ahead of time where we were going I wouldn't have come."

Karen made a face at her. "You're as bad as Abbott. I thought *you'd* understand. After all, you were the one who had those weird dreams that summer at the Cape."

Tara did her best not to show her upset. Those dreams were something she never spoke of, and she didn't understand why Karen should bring them up now. Yet she didn't want to distress her sister. Karen's feelings were hurt all too easily. But the dreams meant Mike, and thinking of their younger brother, dead sixteen years, still made Tara's throat ache.

Karen pounced. "You're afraid to meet Leda, that's why you're acting like this. And it's because of those dreams, isn't it? Don't you think you should face the fact Mike is dead and nothing can bring him back?"

Tara clenched her teeth to hold back an involuntary cry of protest. Don't mention his name, she wanted to cry.

Don't make me remember. But Karen didn't understand, couldn't understand. She hadn't shared the dreams, couldn't know how cruelly her words cut into Tara's heart. She must try to humor her twin, knowing Karen didn't mean to hurt her.

Tara forced herself to shrug. "If you insist on wanting me in there with you, I'll go, but I still think it's ridiculous."

Leda Umak was short and plump, with graying hair and a pleasant face. Her navy blue skirt and white long-sleeved shirt were certainly businesslike. Even the large gold ankh dangling from a chain around her neck couldn't be considered overly esoteric. She hung their coats on a brass rack and seated Karen and Tara in matching wing-back chairs in what looked like an ordinary living room—except for the round table directly in front of them. It was draped with a wine-red cloth, and a pack of tarot cards lay faceup on it.

Tara glanced at the brightly colored top card, a robed and crowned woman seated between two pillars, one black, one white, with a crescent moon at her feet. The High Priestess was printed at the bottom. What on earth am I doing here? she asked herself.

Leda seated herself behind the table in a straight-backed chair and smiled at the twins. A genuine smile, Tara decided reluctantly.

"I'm so pleased you were able to come with your sister," she said to Tara. "It will make all the difference in both your readings."

"Oh, but I don't—" Tara began.

"Why don't you start with me?" Karen put in, effectively cutting off Tara's words. "I can't wait to find out if this is a girl or boy." She patted her rounded abdomen.

Leda nodded at Karen. "Hold your hands out across the table." When she did, Leda clasped Karen's hands in hers, briefly closing her eyes. After releasing her hold she looked through the tarot deck before removing one card from it. "This is the Queen of Wands. This card is your significator, she represents you." She handed the rest of the deck to Karen. "Please shuffle these while you meditate on what you wish to discover."

Harmless, Tara assured herself. Nothing but fortune-telling. Whatever sex she predicts for the baby will stand a fifty percent chance of being right.

After Karen had cut the cards three times to the left, Leda dealt ten of them faceup into a pattern she called Celtic and studied the layout for long moments. Despite herself, Tara grew tense as she stared at the strange and gaudy symbols on the cards.

"Your question has to do with unforeseen perils," Leda said to Karen. "Those who opposed you in the past have suffered while you have had good fortune and success."

Karen darted a glance at Tara.

Meaningless, Tara told herself.

"The future's not as clear-cut," Leda went on. "There's misfortune ahead, which can only be averted if you choose a harmony of inner and outer life, a responsibility of giving as well as taking. If you're able to accomplish this, the rewards you seek will be yours."

"What about the baby?" Karen asked.

"A boy. I felt his aura when I touched your hands. A healthy boy."

Karen nodded, as though Leda's words confirmed her own opinion. She turned to Tara. "Your turn with the cards."

Tara shook her head. "I don't want a tarot reading." Or anything else, she meant to add, but Leda was already reaching across the table toward her and, unwilling to seem rude, Tara let her hands be clasped in Leda's. The wait seemed endless, and Tara's nervousness multiplied until she felt she'd have to pull her hands away and rush out of the house. Finally, Leda opened her eyes and released her hold.

"Why, you're a sensitive yourself!" she exclaimed delightedly.

"No," Tara protested. "Oh, no." She put up a hand as if to prevent Leda from going on.

"How exciting!" Karen exclaimed. "What else?"

"I had some very clear impressions, unusually clear," Leda said. "A house. A man. Hanging over both, a tree, an oak tree wound about with mistletoe, so much mistletoe that the oak suffers from the parasite. And then the misty feel of dreams, one dream overlapping another. Very strange, I've never received anything like it before. It's almost as though the two dreams were one." She stared at Tara. "Perhaps you know what it means."

Tara, her heart hammering in her chest, couldn't speak. She shook her head, rose and, grabbing her coat, ran blindly for the door, knowing she had to get away from Leda Umak before she heard any more, knowing she'd heard too much already.

There was no place to flee except to Karen's car. Tara sat hunched in the front seat, trying, without success, to block the past from her mind. Her little brother's seven-year-old freckled face, topped by carrot-colored hair, flashed into her mind as clearly as if she'd last seen him yesterday instead of sixteen years ago.

She was back in Grandmother Fallkirk's tall gray-shingled house in Chatham, on Cape Cod, and it was summer. Eleven-year-old Tara was lying in the big double bed next to the still sleeping Karen, her heart thumping as she tried to shut away the scary dream she'd had. The plaintive cry of gulls soaring above the beach just below her own window seemed to come from another world.

The dream had started in an ordinary way. She and Karen had been on the tennis court, playing against their thirteen-year-old cousin Hal and the friend he'd brought to the Cape, Darryl Donovan. The boys were ahead as they always were; so far they'd beat the twins every time they'd played. In the dream Mike was watching from outside the fence, his blue eyes darting from the twins to the boys and back, following the ball.

"You can beat 'em, Tara," Mike called to her. "I dreamed you did."

"Okay," she called back as she picked up the ball to serve. "Okay, Mike, if you can dream it, I can do it."

Tara and Karen took the match, two to one. Mike cheered and Tara turned to grin at him. As she did, a spiral of darkness, like a black whirlwind, closed over Mike and spun him out of sight. Tara had gaped, too stunned to scream, but the others went on talking as though nothing was wrong....

Tara sat up in bed and folded her arms across her chest. It would be a dream come true to just once win a tennis match from Hal and Darryl, but she didn't want the rest of that dream to ever, ever come true. Not that they ever did. She sighed in relief at the thought.

Karen yawned and stretched. "Hey," Tara told her, "I had a strange dream. It started like we were playing tennis...."

Why did I tell her? Tara asked herself, shivering as the March wind insinuated its chill breath into the car. And why did Mike repeat his dream to Hal? If only we'd had enough sense to keep quiet.

For the dreams had been the same. The tennis match, the conversation, were identical—except he didn't see the terrible whirlwind. And when they played the next day, nearly everything happened just as it had in the dream. She and Karen beat the boys two to one. Of course, no nightmarish dark spiral appeared to take Mike. Tara had been silly to worry about such an impossible thing.

She and Mike dreamed once more before Hal and Darryl left to go back to Pennsylvania. The second double dream had been a pleasant one about fishing with Uncle George. Both she and Mike had related the particulars—where they went, who caught what and how many—she to Karen and Mike to Hal, before the trip. Again, things turned out exactly as in the dream.

This time Karen told everyone. Tara was already unnerved by having two dreams come true, dreams that weren't even hers alone, and she felt like a freak. Mike thought it was fun and wanted to plan with her ahead of time about what to dream. Tara couldn't forget the dark ending of the first dream, however, and she couldn't enter into his enjoyment. Mike didn't worry about anything; he'd been such a happy-go-lucky kid.

Maybe in time she'd have gotten used to having the same dreams Mike did, or perhaps it never would have happened again. She didn't have the chance to find out. Tara clenched her fists in an effort to keep any more of the past from surfacing. She'd never told Karen the real horror and had only been able to hint at it to her parents long afterward.

How had Leda Umak sensed those dreams?

Karen pulled open the door on the driver's side and slid behind the wheel. She looked at Tara with raised eyebrows. "You can be really weird, you know that?"

"Did you tell her about the dreams?" Tara demanded.

"Certainly not. You shouldn't be so touchy. I think she's marvelous. What about the man she predicted for you? Have you been holding out on me?"

Tara shook her head impatiently. "That's just fortune-telling mumbo jumbo."

"If you don't believe any of it, why did you run away?"

"The dreams belong in the past. I refuse to dwell on ancient history."

Karen eyed her speculatively and Tara stared back, telling herself firmly that Abbott Dade was in the past, too. She was completely over him, and the fact that he'd never told her he was seeing Karen until he and her twin decided to marry no longer had the power to hurt her.

"All those tanned and terrific California males and you're not interested in any of them?" Karen's tone suggested it was hard to believe. "I don't see why I have to pry everything out of you."

Tara shrugged. She wasn't ready to trust another man. Maybe she would never be, but that was none of Karen's business. "Tans are overrated. So are California men."

"As closemouthed as ever, I see. Don't think I'm going to let you get away with it. Leda said a man *and* a house. Fess up—you're living with someone, and you think it'll shock me."

"I live alone in an apartment. And I happen to like it."

Karen shrugged and totally changed the subject. "Abbott wants a boy," she said after she started the car.

"And you?" Tara was glad to change the topic of conversation.

Karen didn't answer until she pulled into the street. "This son and heir bit was all his idea. It isn't that I don't want to have a baby exactly, but I didn't want to have one yet." She glanced at Tara. "You're probably biting your tongue to keep from saying that six months along is too late to have second thoughts and I should have decided one way or the other before I got pregnant."

Something of the sort was indeed running through Tara's mind.

"You don't know how Abbott can be," Karen went on. "When he wants something, I might as well be a hostile witness he's cross-examining for all the heed he pays to *my* wishes. Never marry a lawyer."

Tara didn't reply and after a bit Karen laughed lightly. "Don't take me too seriously. After all, I *am* pregnant and intend to have this child. In fact, I'm taking you to a baby shower luncheon in less than an hour."

"Karen, I'm really tired," Tara said. "A classic case of jet lag. Would you mind if I took a nap instead?"

"I was planning to show off my successful twin—some of my friends don't even know what a design engineer does—but I suppose most of them will see you at the party I'm giving this weekend. So, you're excused." She smiled at Tara. "I can see where a baby shower wouldn't exactly fascinate a career woman. I wish you didn't live so far away, though. Whatever possessed you to take a job in California?"

"They made an offer I couldn't resist." Tara kept her tone light. Was it possible Karen didn't realize how eager she'd been to get as far away as she could from the happy newlyweds? Only in the past six months had enough time passed that she felt able to face Karen and Abbott's marriage at close range.

"I rather miss the East, though," she added. "I think you have to first experience California at a very early age to feel at home there when you're a bit older. But I do enjoy my work."

"I remember how you always longed to be creative. I suppose design engineering is, in its way." Karen sounded doubtful.

"As creative as I'm likely to get," Tara agreed ruefully.

Later, alone in the Dades' new ranch-style home, Tara tried to relax with a long, hot bath, then slipped into a short green robe. The sheer cotton was actually a cover-up meant to be worn over a swimsuit and was entirely unsuitable for

New York's Westchester County in March. She'd better do some shopping in the next few days. In Sacramento, March was spring, and she'd forgotten how cold it could be in the East.

She stared into the bathroom mirror. "Be honest," she asked her green-eyed reflection. "Would you have come to see Karen if Abbott had been home and not away at a convention?"

Tara couldn't find the answer. Opening the bathroom door, she stepped into the hall and stopped short.

"Oh!"

His blond hair tousled, Abbott stood framed in the doorway of the master bedroom, suit coat and tie off, his shirt half-unbuttoned, he was seemingly as surprised as she was.

"Tara! I thought it was Karen in there."

"You—you're home four days early aren't you?" Recovering from her first shock at seeing him, she began to realize how revealing the green robe was and wished she had a towel to hide behind. There was nothing to do but make the best of it. "If you'll excuse me—" she began, intending to slip past him to her room and get dressed.

He caught her arm as she went by. "You haven't changed, Tara." His brown eyes swept over her.

Whatever she'd felt about him in the past had disappeared, and now she was embarrassed and annoyed at his insensitivity. She tried to free herself from his grip only to have Abbott pull her closer and, before she realized what he intended, he was kissing her in a far from brotherly manner.

After her first startled moment of disbelief, Tara struggled to get away from him. The last thing in the world she wanted was to be in the arms of her sister's husband. She felt nothing but a searing anger that he'd dare to touch her.

"Well!"

At the sound, Abbott's arms dropped and, freed, Tara whirled to face Karen, still in her coat, standing in the hall.

"No wonder you didn't want to come with me," Karen cried, staring at Tara. "I felt sorry for you here all alone and came back to—" She bit her lip, her eyes shifting to her husband. "You planned this, didn't you? You knew Tara was here, so you came home early from your damned convention so the two of you could—" She broke off again. "You both planned it!" Her voice rose.

"Karen, listen to me," Tara said, fighting a sinking feeling that no words she might come up with would soothe her twin.

"No!"

Abbott took a step toward his wife, and she held up her hands. "Don't you touch me," she cried.

"Calm down," he ordered. "Nobody planned anything. You're making something out of nothing."

Karen flew at him, striking his chest with her fists. "You're lying. I hate you, hate you—" She burst into hysterical sobbing.

Abbott held her away from him, his aquiline features twisted with distaste. "You're making a scene. Stop it!"

"Karen, please listen," Tara begged.

"Go away!" her twin shrieked at her. "Get out of my house. I never want to see you again."

Tara edged past her sister and Abbott and hurried into her bedroom, knowing from past experience that once Karen worked herself into a rage, there was no reasoning with her. While she pulled on the first clothes she set her hands on—jeans and a dark blue sweatshirt—her mind whirled as she tried to decide what to do next.

She couldn't stay here. Pack and leave? Yes. Go to Kennedy and catch the first flight west even though she had five days left of her vacation? Tara shook her head. She didn't want to go back to Sacramento so soon. What she really wanted was to flee to someone warm and comforting who'd tell her she wasn't to blame.

Tara, despite her misery, smiled one-sidedly. Her father's current job assignment had taken him to New Zealand and her mother had gone with him. They were certainly too far away to console her, even given the unlikely chance she'd involve them. If only she hadn't worn that flimsy green robe. Why hadn't she retreated into the bathroom and wrapped a towel around herself once she saw Abbott?

Tara tightened her lips as she flung clothes into her bags. Stop feeling guilty! Abbott had no right to grab her and kiss her even if she'd come out of the bathroom wearing nothing. After all, she'd thought she was alone in the house. Could he really be so egotistical that he believed she'd welcome his caresses when he was married to her twin? Tara grimaced. Even if she still was carrying a torch for Abbott—and she wasn't—she wouldn't have allowed him to touch her once he was Karen's husband.

He was truly a selfish, insensitive clod. She'd realized that a year and a half ago and was glad she'd found out before she married him. It was too bad Karen was stuck with him. Tara sighed. She could hardly blame Karen for jumping to conclusions. What a scene for a pregnant wife to come home to: her husband embracing her twin sister.

Thank heaven I kept my rental car, Tara said to herself as she juggled her two bags to open her bedroom door. When she passed the master bedroom she couldn't help overhearing the raised voices inside.

"I'm beginning to think I married the wrong twin!" Abbott shouted.

Tara winced, fled down the corridor, through the living room and foyer and out the front door. What a terrible thing to say. Karen would never forgive him.

She'd never forgive Tara, either.

By two in the morning, Tara felt as though she'd been driving forever. Maybe it was from lack of sleep but the once familiar route to Cape Cod seemed strangely alien. It seemed as though she was traveling through a foreign country to an unknown destination.

What mad impulse had led her to head for Grandma Fallkirk's house in Chatham? Her grandmother had died ten years ago. There was no one in the house. It had been left jointly to her and Karen, but they only used it in the summer, and with good reason. Summer was the season to be there. March was cold on the Cape, cold and stormy.

No tourists would be in Chatham. The only people there would be those sturdy souls who lived in the village the year round. Tara nodded. That suited her fine for she didn't want to see or talk to anyone. The beach would be deserted. Cold or not, she could walk along the sand and be alone with the sea gulls.

She was going to the house because it was isolated, because no one would bother her, and because she needed time before she faced her job in California again, time to recover her equilibrium. She'd often wondered how she'd feel and act when she saw Abbott again, but never in her wildest imaginings had she anticipated what had actually happened. How could Abbott be such a fool?

It was after four in the morning when Tara reached the door of Jake Logan, the Fallkirk house caretaker. She apologized profusely for waking him at such an early hour, listened with half an ear as he told her how to adjust the heat and finally took the key he handed her and drove on to the house.

It was a Victorian three story, shingled with weathered gray cedar like most Cape Cod houses. A round tower thrust above the roof to the left and a covered porch spanned the front facing Nantucket Sound. Tara pulled into the back driveway and got out of the car, hardly noticing the March wind whipping her hair across her face as she breathed in the scent of the ocean, a sea smell that meant childhood, sun and summer.

Inside, she frowned when she detected the musty odor of an unlived-in house and told herself she must air the place out later in the day. Musty or not, the house seemed to fold itself around her protectively, and she relaxed a little, suddenly conscious of muscles aching from the night-long drive from New York.

I'll go to bed and sleep all day, she promised herself. When I wake up I'll feel better.

Once she'd located sheets and blankets and made up the big, carved walnut bed in the second-floor room she'd always shared with Karen, Tara found herself so keyed up she knew she wouldn't be able to fall asleep.

Raising a window shade, she stood in the darkness of the bedroom, hugging herself against the chill, while she stared down at the deserted beach. In the gray predawn light she saw waves lashing the shore, foaming high onto the sandy beach.

Cold and windy, with rain predicted, she remembered from the last weather report she'd heard on the car radio. She didn't care. She'd found refuge.

A flicker of motion up the beach caught her eye. Something, someone was moving slowly along the water's edge as though strolling on the sand on a summer's day.

Damn. She'd expected to be alone on this stretch of beach for, the last she'd known, all the houses to either side were summer rentals.

The figure stopped directly in front of her house to look out over the water, close enough now to confirm her suspicion. A man. She wondered if he might be a local who only occasionally walked along this beach, but she didn't think so. Year-round residents weren't inclined to stroll on the sand before dawn on a cold March morning.

He'd be a tourist. Some health nut who'd be so unfailingly cheerful he'd make her regret she'd given up cigarettes and therefore couldn't blow a little smoke his way in retaliation. Or a lonesome soul who'd work to cultivate her acquaintance. Or, worse, a man like Abbott who thought he was irresistible to women, no matter how he treated them.

She didn't have to speak to him if he happened to cross her path in the next few days. Whoever he was, she'd ignore him completely. No man was going to interrupt her retreat.

About to move away from the window, Tara stopped when she saw the man turn toward the house. He looked up. At her window?

A shock ran through her, though there wasn't enough light to distinguish his features, much less tell whether he'd seen her. Yet something told her he knew she was there. For a long moment she couldn't move as she sensed she and the dark figure on the beach were linked, and that some vital yet intangible message had passed between them.

Chapter Two

Tara yanked down the window shade, her heart hammering in her chest. She flipped on the bedroom light, seeing her reflection in the mirror over the marble-topped dresser, her hazel eyes wide and startled. What on earth was the matter with her?

Leda Umak's voice echoed in her mind. "A sensitive." Ridiculous. Of the twins, Tara had always been the down-to-earth one, Karen the creative sister. Karen's delicate water-colors of flowers and birds showed her artistic talent while Tara's attempts at creativity had only provoked Karen's laughter.

Somehow she had to convince Karen the scene back in the Dade house had been a gigantic misunderstanding all around. Especially now, with Karen pregnant and their parents in New Zealand, they needed to be close.

The man on the beach had nothing to do with Tara Reed. It must be all the upset today. Leda, then Abbott, then

Karen's rage had been so traumatic emotionally that her perceptions were altered. How could it be possible to feel a linkage with another person, a total stranger whose features she hadn't even clearly seen in the early shadowy light? Why, she wouldn't be able to recognize the man if she met him.

He, of course, had felt nothing. He couldn't even have known she was standing in the dark of the upstairs window. She was going to put the incident from her mind once and for all, just as she had the dreams. Until Karen and Leda had revived her memory of them.

Maybe that's what had triggered her reaction, remembering the dreams and being here in the house where they'd occurred while she was exhausted physically and emotionally.

She'd read about perfectly normal people having hallucinations when they'd been without sleep for days. Her lack of sleep on top of jet lag might account for what had just happened—no, just *seemed* to have happened. Perhaps there hadn't even been a man on the beach!

Tara flipped off the light and cautiously raised the shade again. The beach in front of the house, and as far as she could see to either side, was totally empty.

Okay, you've had a hallucination. Go to bed, sleep. When you wake up you'll be back to normal and can start planning what to do about Karen.

Tara woke still caught in a dream world of images that shifted shape before she could quite comprehend their forms. She stared up at a ceiling that wasn't the one she expected to see. It wasn't midnight blue with the constellations starred in silver, a leftover from the former tenant of her Sacramento apartment. Yet the ceiling was familiar. She recognized the cracks by the corner that formed a large T.

Grandma Fallkirk's house in Chatham. She was on Cape Cod. She'd driven here last night. Tara sat up groggily and eased from the bed toward the windows where she pulled up one of the shades. Late afternoon sunlight slanted across the water and dampened sand. The predicted rain had apparently come and gone, though the wind was still blowing.

A lone sea gull walked at the water's edge with one gray wing hunched as though fending off the wind. She saw nothing else on the beach. No one else.

As she was dressing in jeans and T-shirt, she realized she was ravenously hungry and there was no food in the house. By the time she'd shopped for groceries, fixed and eaten a meal of scrambled eggs and toast, the blue shadows of early evening lay along the sand. Turning the heat down and leaving a few windows open to air out the house, Tara, wearing an old blue jacket she'd found in a closet, headed for the beach.

She crossed the low dunes, noting the clumps of sea grass were last season's brown with no new green shoots showing yet. The wind had lessened but the chill of winter lingering in the salt sea air made her huddle into the jacket. Looking south, she saw the long finger of Momomoy Island pointing into the sound. The pewter water looked cold and uninviting.

A few gulls scavenging at the waterline scattered at her approach, lifting into the air and flying north up the beach. One flapped awkwardly along the sand in the opposite direction, never becoming airborne. After a moment she realized it couldn't fly and when it settled down several yards away, she saw the left wing, apparently injured, was askew.

That's the same gull I saw earlier, she decided, remembering the bird with the hunched wing. Oh, the poor thing. I wonder if anything can be done to fix the wing? The gull doesn't act as if it would let anyone get very close. Does it get enough to eat? Maybe if I fed it, the gull would get used to me and I could figure a way to take it to a vet.

Tara hurried back to the house. Recalling how the gulls she'd encountered in her youth seemed to eat anything and everything, she grabbed several slices of bread and opened a package of ground meat, taking half. To her disappointment the gull was nowhere to be seen when she got back to the beach.

"Okay, Larry," a man's voice said softly. "Here's supper."

Tara stared all around, seeing nothing in the fading light until she finally spotted red hair above a sand dune where the dried grass swayed in the freshening breeze. It was a deep auburn red, a glorious color—if you happened to like red hair on a man. She didn't.

She started to turn away, then stopped, knowing she'd never rest until she found out if whatever he called Larry happened to be her gull. Moving quietly, she skirted the dune.

The gull spotted her first, fixing her with a beady yellow eye before turning back to stab at chunks of fish with its long, slightly hooked bill. The auburn-haired stranger crouched near the bird, smiling a little as he watched it eat.

"Keep going, Larry," he said. "Wolf down that fish before your thieving mates home in on us."

Despite his crouch, Tara could see he was a big man, his massive shoulders covered by a faded red sweatshirt. Okay, the gull's taken care of, time to go home, she told herself. She didn't move.

He might be the man she'd seen on the beach last night; how could she tell? Maybe if he stood up. Tara cleared her throat. "Why do you assume the bird's a he?" she asked.

He jumped to his feet and whirled to face her. The sea gull squawked in fright, flapping away.

"Now see what you've done!" His voice was deep and accusing.

On the front of his sweatshirt, Harvard was spelled out in white letters. Abbott's school. Had they both majored in arrogance there?

"Your jumping up scared the gull. I had nothing to do with it," she said indignantly.

"What did you expect me to do after you sneaked up behind me?"

"I wasn't sneaking. I was looking for the gull."

He glanced around and her gaze followed his. The bird was back attacking the fish again, gulping morsels that looked too big to go down his throat.

"Apparently Larry doesn't scare as easily as you do," she commented dryly. "And why Larry, of all names?"

"Short for *Larus argentatus*, the herring gull."

Tara could tell a gull from a tern or a cormorant but that's as much as she knew. She gazed up at him, unable to read his expression in the gathering dusk. He wasn't quite six feet, she decided, but the breadth of his shoulders made him seem taller as he stood unmoving, his gaze intent on her. Tension filled the space between them until Tara, aware of her increasing pulse rate, broke the link by looking away.

No doubt about it, he was an Abbott type, enjoying how he'd put her down with his show of knowledge, and already sure she must be interested in him.

She certainly wasn't. The only thing that kept her here was the gull's welfare.

"I thought maybe I could entice Larry with food, capture him and take him to a vet to see about that injured wing," she said.

"I've gotten close enough to take a good look at it. I'm no bird expert, but whatever hurt the wing happened a while back and it healed in the wrong position. I called the local vet, and he said there's nothing he or anyone else can do about a malformed wing."

"But the gull will never be able to fly again!" Tara said regretfully.

"Larry's coping." His tone was cool, disinterested.

How could she expect someone who was clearly as insensitive as Abbott to understand? Was this the man she'd seen on the beach?

Yes, something inside her insisted. You know he's the one.

How silly. She didn't know anything of the sort, though she hoped there was no more than one man likely to intrude on her privacy.

"Good evening," she said abruptly, turning from him to head for the house. She didn't hear his answer, if he gave one.

That's the end of that, she told herself. If I see him again he'll get no more than a casual wave.

The next morning, Larry was beachcombing along the waterline when Tara appeared. He eyed her with his unblinking bird stare but didn't flap away. She returned to the house to bring him some food, which she scattered on the damp sand between them. He ate the ground meat first and had started on the bread when a flock of gulls appeared and swooped down to snatch morsels and fly off with their booty. All the bread disappeared before the surprised Tara could move.

"Some friends you've got," she said.

Larry examined the sand carefully for any stray crumbs, then began to preen his feathers. Watching him, Tara realized how beautifully marked a gull is—the silver-gray white-tipped wings, the black-and-white barred tail, white breast and head, bright yellow eyes, beak, legs and webbed feet.

A herring gull, "Harvard" had called him. *Larus argentatus.* Argent meaning silver? "Larry Silver," she said, smiling. "There, you've got your full name."

The gull cocked his head at her, swiveling it a moment later to stare along the beach. Tara looked, too.

A man jogged along the water's edge toward them, his auburn hair glowing in the morning sunlight. Larry squawked and flapped his wings, the deformed one dragging in the sand.

"You may be welcoming him, but I don't intend to," Tara muttered to the bird. To retreat into the house would make it seem she was afraid to stay. Since she'd planned to jog for twenty minutes anyway, she'd start now. In the opposite direction.

Tara ran toward him, determined that no matter what excuse he might use to try to get her to stop and talk, she'd merely wave and jog on. She found her breathing pattern strangely erratic as they neared one another. What was the matter with her?

He appeared to be about thirty, and was a man who women would look at twice, she'd give him that. Bright-blue eyes and blunt, rather rugged, features with a strong, square, no-nonsense chin. He wore the Harvard sweatshirt again and—her eyebrows rose—jogging shorts.

She felt chilly even in jeans, T-shirt, sweater and jacket. Maybe she'd lived in California too long. "Harvard" obviously wasn't affected by the definitely cold March wind. His bare legs pumped up and down, their fuzz of auburn hair doing nothing to hide the strong muscles in his massive thighs.

Stop staring at him, you idiot! she ordered.

They were almost ready to pass. Tara braced herself for his pitch. Even if he mentioned the sea gull she wouldn't so much as pause.

His arm went up, acknowledging her presence, then he was past her, his pace unflagging. Tara waved back, losing her stride for a moment as she struggled with her disappointment. She'd been all set to refuse to talk to him and he'd hardly glanced her way!

She really wasn't looking her best. The jeans she wore were her rattiest, and the old blue jacket she'd salvaged from the entry closet was meant for someone several times larger, besides having brown paint stains smeared across the front and a ripped sleeve. Not that she cared what he thought of her appearance.

Tara jogged ten minutes before turning for the ten-minute run home. As she passed the beach houses, she watched for one that was no longer shut up for the winter. Seven places west of hers, she saw smoke coming from the chimney of the last in a row of identical summer cottages. She caught a glimpse of a car pulled in behind the cottage.

That must be where he's staying, she thought. Chatham has so much beachfront I wouldn't have seen him twice in two days—maybe three times—if he wasn't nearby. Too close.

By noon the skies had clouded over and the wind off the sound whipped a thin drizzle against her windows. Tara reminded herself that gulls were used to wet and cold so Larry Silver wouldn't be in any distress. A rattling coming from the top of the house sent her into the attic, where she found a loose shutter banging against the shingles with every gust, and she managed to secure it with a piece of wire.

The dim and dusty attic, smelling of old wood with a faint overlay of moth balls, held childhood memories of happy times when she and Karen and Mike had played here under the eaves on rainy days, the three of them feeling snug and cosy while the drops pattered on the roof. How Mike had hated to be the baby when they played house and dressed in the old clothes from the trunks.

Sometimes Mike and Tara changed roles and he got to be the father. Karen, though, wouldn't play at all if she couldn't be the mother.

Now Karen was going to really be a mother and seemed none too sure that's what she wanted. Tara sighed. She'd have to call Karen and try to talk to her. Not quite yet, though. Not enough time had passed for Karen to cool down completely.

As she started for the stairs, Tara noticed a strangely shaped object covered with plastic sheeting sitting atop an old, warped table. Gently lifting off the plastic, she stared in amazement at a conglomeration of bolts, bits of colored glass, dried seed pods and feathers affixed to a chunk of weathered planking. Her sculpture!

Grandma Fallkirk must have stored it up here years ago. Tara had been eleven when she created what she thought then was a masterpiece. Today she knew they called such things found-object sculptures, but all she'd realized at the time was that she'd put the bits of glass and the other pieces together in the way it seemed they were meant to go.

"Yes," Grandma had said, "I can see you're trying to show how you feel about Chatham summers. A good start, child."

Tara wondered if her grandmother's words meant she liked it. Karen had certainly been less than enthusiastic.

"What's it supposed to be?" she demanded later, snickering.

"Well, sort of the seashore and the ocean and—and, I guess, like when summer's ending." Tara found it hard to express what the sculpture meant to her: the house, Cape Cod, the sadness of having vacation over and leaving.

Karen laughed derisively. "This thing? It's nothing but pieces of junk and some weeds."

Karen's laughter had changed the sculpture in Tara's eyes, making it ugly and ridiculous, an inept and clumsy attempt next to Karen's exquisite watercolors.

Now Tara held her childhood creation in her hands and realized for the first time that perhaps her grandmother *had* meant she liked it. Why else would she have stored it away so carefully?

Downstairs, Tara set the sculpture on an oak plant stand and stood back to examine it. The base was a chunk of gray planking she'd found washed up on the shore. From this rose a large iron bolt, possibly cast off a ship. Feathers and red, green, blue and white sand-scoured bits of glass were woven into dried grass wound around the bolt. Along the plank, two rusted iron bolts held wild rose hips, with seed pods from Queen Ann's lace, mixed with pieces of shells, scattered around and between. Though glue and wire held everything in place, she'd worked hard to conceal the wire, and now she was surprised at how well she'd succeeded.

Maybe the sculpture was inept, but she found she enjoyed looking at her creation and decided not to return it to the attic. She found some yellowed paperback mysteries in the bookcase, so ancient that she couldn't remember whether she'd read them or not, and settled onto the couch, planning to spend the afternoon reading.

A whodunit set in San Diego looked most promising. She opened the book and read the beginning sentence.

"Hamilton Driver ran a worried hand through his untidy red hair as he eyed the long-legged blonde seated in the client's chair next to his desk."

"Harvard's" hair was a deep chestnut-red. Why had she thought she didn't like red hair on a man? To touch such a radiant color would warm her fingers. He couldn't be as insensitive as he seemed because he'd been feeding Larry and he'd cared enough to call a vet about the gull's wing. Abbott would never even have noticed the bird, much less tried to help him. She may have misjudged "Harvard." The next time they met she'd be a trifle friendlier.

Tara's eyes shifted to the window. Still raining. She ought to drive over to Main Street and buy herself a decent jacket. Besides its other drawbacks, the blue one wasn't very warm. After she finished shopping she could have her dinner in town....

She chose the Cottage Lantern Inn because the small restaurant looked informal enough for her jeans and sweater. Many of Chatham's other eating places were closed until the season began in June.

The counter was full. Tara hung her new gold jacket on an oak rack, headed for the tiny dining room to the right and stopped short. Only one of the five tables was occupied, and by "Harvard," who was looking at her with what appeared to be a marked lack of enthusiasm.

Well, she wasn't happy to see him, either, but she wasn't going to retreat. She'd murmur a quick greeting and then seat herself as far away from him as possible.

"Hello, 'Harvard,'" Tara said, as she neared his table. Though she hadn't intended to look directly at him, their eyes met and held.

How blue his were, like a bright October sky. Words from an old song came to her.

...eyes of blue, that may be as true
As the starry light of a summer night...

"Won't you have dinner with me?" he asked.

The flat tone of his voice showed a lack of interest, she decided, and obviously the invitation was a courtesy he felt he had to extend. That was fine with her, for she had no interest in dining with him, either.

"Thank you," she said, "but I—"

"It'd sure help my aching feet," a woman's voice said from behind Tara. She turned and saw a middle-aged waitress, order pad in hand.

"I got both the counter and the dining room tonight," the waitress went on. "This time of the year they don't hire much help on account of we usually don't get much business."

"Harvard" rose and pulled out a chair for Tara. She shrugged and sat down. His fingers brushed across her back as he released the chair after sliding it in and her breath caught as his brief touch reverberated along her nerves.

Okay, so he was an attractive man and she reacted to him. Might as well admit it. But she was *not* going to get involved, no matter how potent his appeal was.

"Harvard" looked up at the waitress. "What's good tonight, Wilma?"

"I had the lobster quiche," she said. "It was real tasty."

He raised his eyebrows inquiringly at Tara.

"I'll try the quiche," she said to Wilma. "Separate checks, please."

"Harvard" frowned, then shrugged. "Make that two quiches."

Tara, braced for an argument about the checks, relaxed a little. No, he really wasn't much like Abbott, after all. Just the same, this was the last time she'd be trapped into a situation where she couldn't avoid him.

Brian did his best not to stare at the woman across the table from him. He'd both wanted her there and, at the same time, hoped she'd refuse to sit with him. Damn it, he'd come to the Cape to get away from his problems, not entangle himself in new ones.

She was nothing like Ursula, and he'd known that from the moment she'd startled him in the dunes. For one thing Ursula wouldn't allow closet room to clothes such as she'd had on, much less actually wear them. This woman, though, made her clothes seem unimportant.

It was strange, that night she'd come to Chatham. He'd seen the car drive up to the house while he was walking east along the beach. When he'd come back, though no lights were showing, he'd felt compelled to look at the house, at one upstairs window in particular. Somehow he knew a woman was there and that she was staring at him, offering him—what?

Her hair was a clean, shimmering brown, and the gold turtleneck sweater she wore turned her hazel eyes golden. She was undeniably attractive but he'd known more striking women, Ursula for one. Yet this woman had some special essence, one that drew him despite his determination not to become involved. As though she were a female moth releasing an irresistible pheromone and he was the helpless male moth who had no choice but to come to her.

Why was he thinking such nonsense? He had plenty of other choices and from now on he was going to stay as far away as possible from her.

"I really shouldn't call you 'Harvard,'" she said after Wilma had served their salads, "but I have no other name for you."

"Brian," he said, hearing the reluctance in his voice, as though giving her his name meant surrender.

"Mine's Tara."

No last names. That suited him. If anything should happen between them, and he intended to make certain nothing did, it would be a passing fling between strangers. The

New York plates on her car meant she was only a visitor to Chatham, as was he. Once they went their separate ways, they'd never see one another again.

He shouldn't see her again as it was, shouldn't have invited her to his table. And he ought not to be wondering how that soft, inviting mouth of hers would feel against his.

Damn it, he wanted her more than he could ever remember wanting any woman. Why did she have to appear at the worst possible time in his life?

Chapter Three

The next morning was spring-warm, the sky a lazy blue with wisps of clouds on the horizon. Who says March is dreary on the Cape? Tara thought as she finished washing her breakfast dishes. This day is made for the outdoors, a day to put problems aside and enjoy the sun and sand. A day for just being.

A picnic would be perfect. The problem with picnics was they weren't much fun alone. Of course Larry Silver would be more than happy to share her picnic with her. First, though, he needed his breakfast. She'd saved the leftovers from last night's meal for the gull, plus the rest of the ground round, so she brought the food with her as she left the house.

Yes, Larry was the perfect choice for her picnic companion. Better than Brian and the complications that seeing him again might cause.

Because both she and Brian had their cars last night, it had been easy to say a quick farewell after dinner and head home. At least *she* went home. He might have gone anywhere. Perhaps he had friends in the area, though she didn't think so. He seemed to be in Chatham for privacy and solitude, just as she was. That suited her fine. She had enough problems.

The sun shimmered on the water, enticing Tara to take off her shoes and go barefoot. But when she tested the water with her toes, she retreated hastily to the warm sand. The day might promise spring but the North Atlantic, belying its sunlight glitter, was as cold as winter.

Tara strolled east, inhaling the briny tang of the sea and enjoying the warmth of the sun on her face and bare arms. Finding no sign of Larry, she turned and walked west. When she was almost even with Brian's cottage, the sea gull flapped into view, his injured wing dragging in the sand. A line of gulls, perched atop an overturned rowboat a few yards away, waited and watched.

"Oh no, you don't," she muttered at them. "You've all got two good wings—go find your own food."

From the corner of her eye she saw movement by the cottage. I hope Brian doesn't think I'm here because of him, she thought. If I don't look in his direction he won't have to acknowledge seeing me, and we won't have to be polite to one another when we'd both rather be alone.

As if driven by something other than her own will, her head swung around until she faced the cottage. Brian stood barefoot on the steps, wearing jogging shorts and a blue T-shirt, hands on hips. An anticipatory tingling fluttered in her stomach when she saw him.

"I fed Larry this morning," he called to her. "Save your food for his lunch."

"If I can figure out how to give it to him and not every other gull in sight at the same time."

"We can take him across to Nauset Beach to have lunch with us."

We? she wondered. Us? She tried to ignore the thrill that shot through her when she thought of sharing the day with Brian.

No, she told herself, I won't go with him. I'll say no right here and now.

"You can't get to Nauset Beach without a boat," is what she found herself saying instead.

Brian descended the stairs and walked toward her. "I've rented a motorboat. They didn't have the sailboats ready yet."

So he was a sailboat person, as she was. Tara smiled at him, warming to the idea of picnicking on the strip of barrier beach separated from Chatham by a narrow channel. She'd lived in the East most of her life so she knew the day was unusually warm for March and that true spring was at least a month away. All the more reason to enjoy the day to the utmost while it lasted.

What was one day? In two more she'd be gone and she'd never see Brian again. There was surely no harm in spending today with him. What could be more casual than a picnic?

"I'll bring our lunch," she told him.

Admit it, Brian said to himself as, with Tara aboard, he guided the motorboat into the channel between the barrier beach and Chatham. You rented this boat knowing damn well you meant to ask Tara to go with you. All that philosophizing about getting away by yourself was so much talk.

Today was one of those rare, perfect days, meant to be shared. His two weeks here were close to ending, so why not spend the day with her? There'd be no time for his attraction to her to get out of hand. He'd be gone first.

Tara, seated at the bow, wore jeans with a deep-green T-shirt that matched the color of her eyes. Observing how the shirt also outlined small, perfect breasts, he decided attraction was too mild a word for what he felt at the moment. Never mind, he could handle it.

Larry flapped up from the bottom of the boat to perch sternside near Brian, one bold yellow eye fixed on the picnic basket at Tara's feet.

"You'll have to wait like the rest of us," Brian told him. The gull squawked a protest and Brian smiled ruefully. At least Larry would eventually get what he wanted. He knew *he* wouldn't.

Tara seemed as wary as he of any entanglement. He'd even been afraid for a moment or two she was going to refuse to come with him to the barrier beach at all. She'd obviously weighed the pros and cons and he had a feeling the pros had barely won.

What was she doing on the Cape in March? He didn't like to ask since he felt a tacit understanding between them that there'd be no personal questions. He'd never know where she lived and worked unless she volunteered to tell him. He didn't think she would, any more than he meant to talk about himself.

"We're going to have the barrier beach to ourselves," Tara said. "I've never seen it deserted like this. The Cape's so crowded in the summer."

He nodded, his pulse rate going up when he thought of being alone on a deserted beach with Tara. Throttling down the motor, he edged slowly toward the shore, then shut it off when the channel bottom grew shallow.

Tara, her jeans rolled to her knees, slid over the side into the water and began to pull the boat in. He flipped up the small motor and joined her, the shock of the icy water on his legs contrasting agreeably with the heat of the sun on the rest of his body. Together they beached the boat.

Tara scrambled to the top of the nearest dune, shading her eyes with her hand as she looked at the ocean. He stood watching the sea breeze whip her shoulder length hair about her face while the sun turned the strands to gold. She wore no makeup and her natural loveliness transfixed him.

"Come on up," she called. "It's so clear I think I can see Nantucket."

At the top of the dune the air was cooler, smelling strongly of the sea. Two sailboats, one with yellow sails, the other with red, scudded west toward Hyannis. Farther out, a dark freighter trailed smoke across the pale blue of the sky. Tara pointed south, and he strained to see the gray smudge she thought was Nantucket Island.

"Could be a low-lying fog bank," he said, grinning.

She frowned at him.

It was on the tip of his tongue to ask her if she'd ever been to Nantucket, but he stopped himself in time. No questions. Keep away from the personal.

"Heavens, I forgot about Larry," she said.

"He's guarding the picnic basket in the boat."

Tara turned to look and their eyes met. Trapped in the green depths of hers, Brian felt his resolve drain away. He took a step toward her. She made an inarticulate sound, turned quickly and slid down the dune to the inner beach.

So you thought you could handle it, Brian muttered to himself. Ha! At least she made herself clear. She expects hands off, so let's keep things that way.

Tara took a deep breath, letting the air out slowly, then another, trying to relieve her breathlessness before Brian joined her on the beach. For a moment atop the dune she'd thought she couldn't control her urge to let him touch her, the need to feel the hard length of his body against hers.

It won't happen again, she assured herself. I absolutely do *not* want to become involved with him and I won't.

Seeing Brian sliding down the dune toward her, she walked to the boat to retrieve the picnic basket.

Larry had abandoned the boat for the water. Tara, watching him, shook her head. The deformed wing didn't fold properly and tipped him to that side, making him float askew.

"Larry could never survive in a rough sea with that list," she told Brian.

"He's too smart to risk it. I think he realizes his limits. Here, let me take the basket."

They started north up the beach and after a few minutes Larry joined them, squawking noisily as he waddled behind.

"Hey," Brian protested, "you'll have every gull within hearing distance coming by to see what's up. Cool it."

"Larry really recognizes us, doesn't he? Maybe we're doing the wrong thing by feeding him and making him dependent on us. After all, I'll be leaving in a couple of days." She glanced at Brian.

He frowned. "I won't be around much longer, either, but Larry's not a pet; he's a wild gull. Don't forget he survived the original wing injury without us. He'll be okay."

Tara wasn't so sure. Gulls mewed overhead and she glanced up at four birds wheeling and dipping above the barrier beach. Larry was at a disadvantage when it came to competing for food. Would he be able to get enough to eat?

As for Brian, she'd guessed from the beginning his stay at Chatham was only temporary. Since she wasn't remaining here herself, why did she have this sudden aching sense of loss?

"This looks like the ideal picnic site," Brian said, halting.

He'd stopped in a small cove where scattered clam shells showed the high tide markings on the damp sand. The barrier dunes rose on three sides around them.

Tara nodded. "Such a secret cove makes me wonder if pirates anchored here in the past. This seems the perfect choice."

"Pirates did pull into Pleasant Bay in the old days," he said, "and they'd have had to use this channel to get to the bay. Maybe we're standing on buried treasure; who knows?"

"Darn, I forgot my shovel." She grinned at him.

"We could use clam shells."

"At that rate it'd be June before we got deep enough to find anything."

"Would that be so bad?" Brian spoke softly.

Tara was amazed at how much the idea appealed to her—spending day after day of sun and sea and sand with Brian.

Today is a onetime experience, she warned herself. A day's picnic isn't a commitment any more than one warm day makes it spring.

Yet she couldn't shake the growing conviction she'd been meant to come to Chatham. Had it been fated that she and Brian would meet? She hadn't intended to have anything to do with him, but here they were together for the day.

Leda Umak had foreseen a house, a man.

No! I don't believe in fate, Tara admonished herself. I don't believe in fortune-tellers' predictions.

"I used to make things from clam shells," she said, resolutely changing the subject. Bending over, she gathered a handful of shells.

Brian spread out the old quilt she'd brought along and set the picnic basket down on it. Tara gathered a small pile of shells and pieces of shells, and knelt beside it.

"The Cape Cod Indians were fond of clams," she said. "With all the seafood available here it's no wonder the Pilgrims found so many tribes on the Cape."

"One of the Cape Indians even had the dubious honor of being the first in New England killed by a European."

Her brows puckered, then her face cleared. "I remember! My grandmother told me that Champlain sailed into Stage Harbor and landed in what's now Chatham where he and his men had a skirmish with the local tribe." She sighed. "It's a shame our ancestors couldn't find a way to live in peace with the Indians instead of doing their best to exterminate them."

"War's always been easier than peace."

"Why is it so hard for people to get along with one another?" she asked, looking up at him.

Brian crouched beside her, bringing his face dangerously near hers, and Tara turned hastily to the clam shells and began arranging them in a pattern. Out of the corner of her eye she saw Brian sit on the sand and fix his eyes on the Chatham beach across the channel from them as if deliberately demonstrating how harmless he was. She watched him surreptitiously as her fingers absently moved the shells.

In all her twenty-seven years she'd never been so aware of a man. Sunlight glinted in the deep red of his hair and turned the lighter hair of his forearms and legs red-gold. His jogging shorts left little to her imagination and she swallowed, forcing her attention back to the shells.

Without thinking she'd formed two triangles lying on their sides, interlocked at each apex. Brian, she saw, had turned to look at what she was doing. Tara swept the shells back into a pile and stood.

"I'm getting hungry," she said more brightly than she felt. "How about you?"

As she began unpacking the basket and putting the food onto the quilt, Larry waddled up and she had to toss him part of a tuna sandwich to keep him from poking his beak into their lunch.

"At least we won't have any leftovers," Brian pointed out as he bit into one of the egg salad sandwiches. After the second bite he smiled at her. "You put sweet pickle relish in—just the way I like egg salad. How'd you know?"

"Looked in my crystal ball." Immediately Tara wished she hadn't said those words because they brought Leda Umak to mind. Her predictions had partly come true in that she'd come to stay in a house, and Brian was very clearly a man, not to mention one she found it difficult to stay away from.

"In answer to your question a while back," Brian put in, "you and I are strangers, and we're having no trouble getting along with each other."

"That's not exactly what I meant."

"I can only extrapolate from the available data."

She started to reply, then gasped as Larry plucked a half-eaten sandwich from her hand and flapped across the sand with it. "You thief!" she accused.

"Gulls can't help stealing, it's their nature." Brian, who'd eaten two sandwiches and drank two glasses of lemonade, lay on his side, one hand propping up his head. "You can't change what's in the genes. Unless you're a research geneticist, of course, and so far I don't think they've tackled sea gulls."

"Okay, so I'll forgive him." Tara finished her lemonade and got up to crumble the leftovers by the waterline for Larry.

When she turned, she found Brian had come up behind her. Again their eyes met and she found it impossible to look away. His eyes were blue flames of desire, sparking an insidious glow inside her. She saw his hands reach for her and she swayed toward him, unable to fight any longer against the urgency of her need to have him hold her.

Then she was in his arms, pressed hard against him, aware of nothing but him. His lips came down on hers in a kiss that flared through her like wildfire. She clung to him, buffeted by the enthralling needs of passion, lost in a warm, whirling wonderland of erotic witchery.

No man's touch had ever affected her so acutely. The sorcery of his first kiss cast a spell she couldn't shatter. She could only wish for a talisman to make the kiss last forever.

Larry's furious squawking brought her back to earth. Brian lifted his mouth from hers, his breath rasping as they both looked for the gull. All that could be seen of Larry was his barred tailfeathers sticking out of the picnic basket. She twisted away from Brian and hurried to the trapped gull.

"Any bird stupid enough to climb into a picnic basket deserves to stay there," Brian growled.

"You were just telling me how smart he was." Tara still felt so shaken and breathless she was surprised at her even tone. She managed to work her fingers on each side of the struggling gull, grasp his body, ease him out and set him on the sand.

After one final, loud complaint, Larry began to preen his ruffled feathers.

Brian glared at the gull, unable to forgive him for the interruption. Tara's enticing taste was still on his lips. He couldn't control his need to touch her again, to feel the softness of her body against him and the arousing warmth of her mouth under his. He reached out to grasp her shoulders and pull her to him.

Tara backed hastily away.

For a few moments he couldn't mask his disappointment and feeling of loss. Then he slowly came to his senses. She was right. Another kiss would inevitably lead to more involvement. Just what he didn't need, what he'd made up his mind to stay away from.

"You're going to hear the grand-daddy of all excuses," he said wryly. "I didn't mean to kiss you."

Tara took a deep breath. "Neither did I mean to let you."

He smiled one-sidedly. "I can forgive you if you can forgive me."

She smiled in return, but the smile was forced and he knew the picnic was over.

It was the weather, Tara tried to tell herself as the boat chugged back to the mainland. She'd been seduced by the beauty of the day and the surroundings into forgetting her vow to stay free of involvement.

Once back home and alone, though, she caught herself leaning against the window frame, staring dreamily out at the blue water of the sound as it darkened in the early evening and reliving the moments in Brian's arms. She ran her tongue over her lips, trying to bring back his intoxicating taste, a taste that, come to think of it, had held a slight flavor of pickle relish. She smiled, remembering how he'd enjoyed her egg salad. She wasn't the world's most talented cook and the compliment had really pleased her. What else did they share? The kiss: they'd certainly shared that!

Enough. Why, you'd think she'd never been kissed before. The trouble was, she hadn't been—not the way Brian had kissed her.

Tara tightened her lips in annoyance. If she was going to behave like a moonstruck young girl, there was only one solution. Catch the next flight to California so she wouldn't be tempted to see Brian again.

Immediately, all the reasons she couldn't flashed into her mind. Larry. What would happen to the sea gull? Despite Brian's assurances, she didn't believe Larry would survive without help.

I'll put him in a box and take him over to the caretaker. I know Jake will feed him and watch over him.

Your return ticket won't let you leave early.

Call and get it changed to an earlier flight.

I'm not ready to leave.

You're as ready as you'll ever be. You can't stay here forever.

The airline was able to put her on an early morning flight two days from now. Fine, she assured herself. I'll pack, get a good night's rest and leave as soon as it's light.

She couldn't fall asleep. Every time she began to relax, Brian's image slipped into her mind, and banishing him from her thoughts brought back the tension. After tossing and turning for hours, she drifted off only to be jolted by a tremendous crash of thunder.

Tara leaped out of bed and ran to the window, pulling up the shade just as a wicked slash of lightning forked into the sound. In its vivid glare she saw gigantic waves lashing the beach. Rain hammered the window pane. Between roars of thunder, she heard the wind howl as it attacked the house. The attic shutter, loose again, slammed against the house with each gust. She hugged herself against the chill, listening.

She should have realized the unseasonal warmth presaged a storm. There'd be no use in trying to fix that shutter now. The wind would tear it out of her hand. But since she'd never be able to sleep in this racket she might as well stay up. She'd go downstairs and turn up the heat while she was at it, for the house was really cold. Turning away to find her slippers, Tara suddenly froze.

Larry! Where was he? The other gulls would have sensed the storm long before it began and would have found refuge. Larry might have sensed the storm, but he couldn't fly to safety.

Biting her lip, Tara threw on jeans and a sweatshirt. She ran downstairs, grabbed the old blue jacket from the closet and hurried to open the door. The wind plucked it from her hands and slammed the door all the way open against the house. As Tara struggled to shut it, wind blasted inside, tossing the pages of a newspaper she'd been reading into the air before scattering them over the floor.

When she finally managed to close the door, she plunged into the storm, fighting against the wind. She ducked her head to try to keep the battering rain from her eyes as she took advantage of each lightning bolt to look around for Larry.

Icy water plucked at her feet, and she realized with a shock that storm-driven waves were topping the dunes. "Larry! Larry!" she shouted desperately into the wind, over and over, aware her calling was useless but unable to stop.

She didn't know when she began to cry, tears mingling with the rain and the sea spray on her face. She only knew she was exhausted from battling the wind and struggling to keep the water from pulling her feet out from under her. She'd have to give up and return to the house.

"Larry!" she shrieked in despair as another searing green-yellow flash split the sky. Her heart leaped in unbelieving joy as she caught sight of something white bobbing up and down on the turbulent waters ahead of her.

It must be Larry; an uninjured gull wouldn't have been caught by the storm. She had to get to him. With his damaged wing keeping him off balance in the water, he'd never survive in this stormy sea.

Tara lunged for the gull, lost her footing and fell headlong. Waves slammed into her. She fought to get her head above water. Choking and sputtering, she tried to scramble to her feet but the water sucked at her legs, drawing her back under. Desperate, she struggled to the surface and gasped air, fighting to stand erect.

Numb with cold, she stumbled toward safety, battling the waves. She thought she heard a cry and sobbed as she tried and failed to locate the gull.

Chapter Four

A voice shouted Tara's name, and a hand gripped her arm, yanking her forward. Lightning illuminated Brian's drenched face.

"I can't find Larry," she gasped.

"I've got him," Brian shouted over rumbling thunder. "Come on!"

He pulled her with him until they were free of the surging icy water. Through the darkness, light glimmered from her house and Brian helped her toward it. By the time he flung open the door, Tara was barely able to stagger inside. She stood shivering while he forced the door shut against the cruel thrust of the wind.

Brian extracted a bedraggled Larry from under his arm and, dumping kindling from a wooden box near the unlit fireplace, put the gull inside the box.

"Is he all right?" Tara asked through chattering teeth.

"In better shape than you look to be." Brian swiped at his dripping hair and shrugged off a sodden jacket. "You need to get out of those wet clothes right away."

Before she could will herself to move, he scooped her into his arms and started for the stairs. Except for her father when she was a child, no man had ever carried her, and she not only felt protected but relished the sensation. Halfway up the stairs, while she was fighting her urge to cuddle, a violent thunderbolt startled her into clutching at Brian. Seconds later the house was plunged into darkness when all the lights went out.

"Damn," Brian grunted. Still carrying her, he climbed the rest of the steps, then paused. "Got a flashlight anywhere?"

She was shivering so hard her voice quavered as she answered. "There's a candle in my room. Second door to the right. Put me down and I'll—"

"You're ready to collapse." He shifted her in his arms, and she realized he was feeling his way by running his shoulder along the wall to his right.

In her room, he set her carefully onto her feet and, following her directions, found the white candle in its iron holder on the old washstand in the corner, then lit it with a match from the box in the washstand drawer. Grandma Fallkirk had believed in being prepared for emergencies.

"Get out of those wet clothes," Brian ordered.

Tara slid out of her jacket. Despite the chills shaking her, she was very much aware of him in this, her girlhood bedroom. What did he intend to do? The room, indeed the entire house, was cold, but the two of them under the covers of the bed could warm each other. She stared at him, wondering if he was thinking the same thing.

Brian drew in a deep breath and let it out slowly. "Put on some dry clothes," he told her. "I'll light a fire downstairs."

Did his words relieve or disappoint her?

He was at the door before she remembered he was as drenched as she and had no dry clothes to put on.

"Brian, there's a cedar chest in the next bedroom with blankets and quilts. And another candle on the stand between the windows. Grandma put them in all the rooms."

He nodded and plunged into the darkness of the hall.

Tara fumbled off her sweatshirt and jeans with trembling fingers and, too cold and exhausted to make the trip to the bathroom at the end of the hall for a towel, wiped her skin and hair as dry as she could with an ancient terry beachrobe from her closet.

I'll turn up the heat the minute I go downstairs, Tara assured herself, then shook her head and groaned. If the electricity was off, so was the furnace.

In her mind she pictured Brian's fire: flames licking at the split oak logs and radiating a wonderful, blessed heat she couldn't wait to savor. Thrown across her pillow was the mid-thigh striped T-shirt she'd slept in. Hurriedly she pulled it over her head, slid her feet into slippers and wrapped herself in the arrow quilt hanging over the bed's iron footboard before picking up the candle to light her way downstairs.

For a while Tara could concentrate on nothing but getting warm as, sitting on the raised hearth, she soaked up every available ray of heat. Brian, with a blanket draped over his body Indian-fashion, padded barefoot back and forth carrying wood from the shed off the kitchen to the fireplace. Finally, Tara took note of his stockpile of logs.

"You've got a two-day supply there, at least," she said.

"Seasoned wood burns fast, and there's no telling how long before the electricity comes back on." Brian dusted his hands together and sat beside her. "Feeling better?"

As she started to nod, she remembered the sea gull and looked around but didn't see the box Brian had put him in. "Where's Larry?"

"I covered his box and carried it to the kitchen so he'll sleep."

"He wasn't hurt?"

"Larry's fine. Gulls don't get soaking wet like we do."

They were all safe—she, Brian, and Larry. Safe and warm. Tara hugged herself under the quilt, surprised at her sense of rightness about the three of them here in Grandma Fallkirk's house. It felt as though they belonged together.

That was ridiculous! She sat straighter, careful not to look at Brian, who was sitting too close to her.

"You took a crazy chance running out into the storm like that," he told her. "Didn't it occur to you I'd look after Larry?"

Tara stiffened. "Why should I think that? I hardly know you."

"You saw I was feeding him before you started."

"You also told me he could take care of himself," she accused.

Brian shrugged and his blanket, an old cotton one as faded a red as his Harvard sweatshirt, slid off his bare shoulders, dropping in folds around him on the bricks of the raised hearth. His tanned torso gleamed in the firelight, the whorls of his chest hair shining gold. Flames flickered in his blue eyes. An almost tangible aura of virility pulsed from him, flowing around her, enticing her. She willed herself to look away but could not.

Everything faded from her consciousness except Brian. Touching her tongue to her suddenly dry lips, she watched breathlessly as desire sparked in his eyes and softened his mouth. The memory of his kiss flared in her mind. Without her willing it, her body leaned to him, expectant.

He blinked, mouth hardening, eyes shifting from hers. "I'm hungry," he said, a slight huskiness in his voice.

For an instant, starved for his touch, she mistook his meaning.

"Any food in the house?" he went on.

Tara, feeling as though Brian had actively pushed her away, grasped her quilt about her and stood up, controlling her urge to tell him to go home and fix his own meal. The windows rattled as a gust of wind battered the house; obviously he had to stay here until the storm's fury abated.

She tried for a casual tone. "I'll see what I can find."

He stood, folding over his blanket and tucking it around his waist. She couldn't help thinking that he wore nothing underneath. His hands grasped her shoulders, pressing her down onto the hearth again.

"Rest," he said. "I'll fix us something."

Why argue? she thought. The fire was warm and she was tired. If he wanted to wait on her she might as well relax and enjoy it. Since she didn't seem to be able to trust her reaction to him, she'd welcome the barrier the act of eating would put between them. Anything to keep him occupied and apart from her because this situation—the two of them sheltering together from the storm—was potential dynamite. She'd already discovered her own fuse was much too short.

I can't risk touching her, Brian told himself as he buttered bread in the kitchen by the candlelight. She's already responsible for a major neurochemical disturbance in my hypothalamus. If I hold her in my arms again...

He held his hand above the bread as he gazed into space, remembering her softness against him when he'd kissed her on the barrier beach. He felt his body react and muttered a curse. You'd think he'd never had a woman before.

In a sense, he hadn't. Not a woman like Tara. There was an elusiveness about her that intrigued him while at the same time he was aware of what seemed to be an understanding between them. The rightness of being in this house with her circulated through him with each beat of his heart. Larry shifted and Brian glanced toward the box. Even the gull was somehow involved, he thought.

He hunched his shoulders against childhood memories of the time he believed he could look inside his mother's head and sense what she felt, always after she and his father had quarreled. He'd hated knowing her pain; he'd fought to blunt his sensitivity and had finally succeeded. Had he really had this ability, or was it all childish imagination?

Brian shrugged. He certainly had no such ability now, nor did he wish to. In his profession it would be a disaster. He was fantasizing about possessing Tara, that's all. Despite how much he wanted her, he knew better than to get involved with any woman at this point in his life. His mind must be conjuring up this psychic nonsense to justify his need for her.

Make the damn sandwiches and stop thinking, he chided himself. Eat, maybe get some sleep. The storm can't last forever, and once you're out of Tara's house, stay away from her. In two days you'll be gone; in two months you won't be able to recall her name.

Brian slapped peanut butter onto the bread and reached for a jar of strawberry jam. He paused, hand outstretched. Looking at it another way, why not take advantage of this time with Tara? Why not make love with her? He'd never see her again. No complications. He didn't know her last name, and she didn't know his. Neither of them lived on the Cape. They'd never meet again.

He sighed and shook his head. Already she was far more than a casual itch that needed scratching. He couldn't risk the chance she might become important to him. After the complications caused by Ursula, he damn well didn't need another woman fouling up his life.

He carried a tray into the living room with two and a half peanut butter and jam sandwiches on it, plus two stemmed glasses three-quarters filled with milk.

"I'm surprised you found that much," Tara said. "I'm about out of everything."

"I left the liverwurst and the bread heel for Larry. He's sure to wake up hungry."

Tara's smile lit her face in the way he'd come to notice and watch for, and he wondered how long it would be before he forgot that smile. Deliberately turning away, he searched for a place to put down the tray. Seeing a small table, he reached for it with one hand. A piece of driftwood on the tabletop wobbled precariously, and Tara jumped up to catch the wood before it fell. Her quilt slipped to the floor.

Her thigh-length striped shirt clung to her curves so snugly he was certain she had nothing on underneath and his breath caught. Her face flushed under his gaze but she didn't retreat.

Clutching the driftwood to her like a talisman, she said, "I made this when I was eleven." She sounded as breathless as he felt.

Setting the tray on the table, Brian forced himself to focus on the wood. At first glance he saw an iron bolt affixed to the driftwood, with feathers, grasses and bits of colored glass strewn over and around both the bolt and the wood. After a moment, he discerned a pattern to the apparently random placement of the decorations, and he frowned, intent on pinning down the elusive feeling the pattern evoked in him.

Suddenly a door seemed to open inside his head, and he tensed as he sensed an emotion not his, an alien picture in his mind.

"Summer's over," he muttered. To his relief the door closed and his mind was once more all his own. He glanced at Tara.

She stared at him in shocked surprise. Had she experienced what he had?

What had happened? Tara wondered apprehensively. For an instant there'd been a flow between the two of them as though they shared unspoken feelings. She'd be crazy to believe such an unlikely transfer, but how else could Brian have possibly known what she, at eleven, had called her sculpture? Even Grandma Fallkirk hadn't seen right away what she'd meant to capture with her bits and pieces. Yet this man, a stranger, knew immediately.

Tara shivered. Setting the driftwood on the table beside the couch, she picked up the quilt and draped it over her shoulders. Brian made a lucky guess, she told herself firmly.

"I must have said the wrong thing," he muttered.

He looked so upset she overcame her unease to reassure him. "You startled me because you gave my sculpture the same name I did when I first put it together."

He clenched his jaw, his tension obvious. Hesitatingly she reached to him, her fingers grazing his forearm.

He took a deep breath, visibly relaxing, and put his hand over hers. "You were good at eleven—you must be great by now. Do you still work with found objects?"

Tara shook her head. "I'm not an artist. My sister—" She stopped abruptly, aware it was dangerous for her to tell this man about her life.

Too much had already passed between them. She pulled her hand from under his. He was now, tonight, but he wasn't tomorrow, he wasn't in her future. She had to be careful not to give any more of herself to him.

Yet his praise warmed her more than the fire. His understanding of what she'd done and his appreciation of her talent gave her an inner glow. No one besides her grandmother had ever liked her creations.

"Peanut butter's my favorite sandwich," she said, eager to switch to a safe subject. "Even if you happen to be the kind who doesn't put butter on the bread first."

Brian grinned. "Gourmet cooks like me never forget to put butter on first."

They ate on the floor in front of the fire. Brian had carried quilts and blankets down from the chest upstairs and spread one out for them to sit on. He'd even brought the pillows they'd need for sleeping here, in the warmest spot in the house. She decided not to pursue that thought any further at the moment; his nearness made her edgy enough without borrowing trouble.

She'd noticed at their picnic he was a graceful eater. Some men weren't. Watching his strong, tapered fingers set his empty glass on the tray, she wondered if he could be an artist. Perhaps a musician, a pianist. Would he tell her if she asked?

It was safer not to know. To keep him as much of a stranger as possible even though she was beginning to feel she'd known him forever.

From another life, a psychic might say. No, she wouldn't get into unknown waters. She had faith only in the tangible.

Brian was all too tangible, and that was the trouble. Her fingers remembered the feel of his fire-warmed skin, and her lips knew the shape of his mouth. How could she possibly bed down in front of the fire near him and not touch him?

He cleared his throat. "The storm's put us in a provocative situation." He paused, waiting for her response.

Tara gave a terse nod, thinking it had to be the understatement of the year.

"There's no point denying we're attracted to each other." He half smiled.

No point at all. He was what Yvonne, her co-worker in Sacramento, would call a hunk. Any woman would notice him. What she felt could be totted up as a healthy female's response to a virile male. Nothing more. She ought to appreciate his cool appraisal of their position instead of being annoyed that he could be so calm and collected when the restraint she'd imposed on her own emotions was driving her frantic.

His eyes flicked over her face and down to where her quilt separated to reveal the fullness of her breasts under the clinging nightshirt. When his hands started to reach for her, she felt her nipples contract with need. Hastily she drew the quilt closed, and his hands dropped to his sides.

He was not quite as collected as he pretended, which made the situation more dangerous. Still, they were two mature adults who ought to be able to overcome a mere physical attraction neither of them wanted to consummate.

What would happen if they failed? If *she* failed? No, she wouldn't even think about that! There was a bond between them, and had been from the moment she'd first seen Brian on the beach. She mustn't let anything more happen, for then she'd never be able to forget him. Never.

Brian returned the tray and dishes to the kitchen. The lightning and thunder had moved on, but rain slashed viciously at the windows, and the wind's cold fingers thrust around the frames to chill his bare feet. After making sure the gull's box was in a protected nook, he hurried back to the warmth of the living room.

Tara had spread several blankets atop the quilt on the floor by the hearth, and he helped her unfold others for a covering. He smiled when he noticed she'd placed the pillows as far apart as the quilts allowed, as if a few inches would decrease their desire.

He hadn't managed to finish his carefully planned talk on how honorably he intended to behave; he'd damn near lost control when her nipples peaked for him. She was temptingly lovely, a woman any man would lust for.

Whatever the hell had happened when he thought he'd linked with her over the sculpture? He'd try his damnedest to keep that from happening again. Best to keep his hands off her, even if he couldn't control his thoughts.

He added fresh logs to the fire, then snuffed the candles while Tara eased under the covers. After settling himself into the nest of blankets and quilts, he glanced at her and saw she'd turned on her side away from him.

He lay on his back watching the play of light and shadow from the firelight on the ceiling. The faint scent of smoke brought back the memory of the outdoor campfires of his childhood, and the last great camping trip with his father.

"You're a bright boy," his father had told him by the fire. "You need to discover what you're best at doing, and when you do, don't waste your time like I did. Go straight to the top. Be somebody!"

He'd loved both his parents and, as a child, couldn't understand why they'd quarreled so incessantly. Now he realized it might have had something to do with the fact that, though his father made a comfortable living, he wasn't "somebody."

Now that his father was dead, his mother refused to remember the fighting. He'd come to realize they'd loved each other in their way but had never resolved their differences.

Was it possible for a man and a woman ever to resolve their differences? Certainly he and Ursula had never even come close. The bitterness of their divorce so tainted his memories of her he couldn't recall if he'd really loved her at the beginning, or if he'd only been trapped by his lust. Never again, he vowed silently.

Beside him Tara shifted slowly and carefully. Even her breathing sounded measured, as though she felt she needed to keep a low profile to avoid arousing him. Hell, the very fact she lay next to him was arousing enough, but he'd made up his mind not to so much as touch her.

"I've never yet attacked a woman in her sleep," he murmured reassuringly. "I'm not planning to start tonight."

She didn't answer. Time passed, and Tara shifted restlessly beside him.

"Do you believe people have psychic abilities?" she asked finally.

The question took him aback. "Let's say I'd need more proof than I've so far seen," he said after a moment. "Why?"

"I just wondered. Your answer beats around the bush. Are you saying you sort of believe?"

He saw she'd turned onto her back, staring not at him, but at the ceiling. "I'm a pragmatist, and I don't take much on faith," he told her. "While there've been some interesting experiments, I find them inconclusive."

"Do you think the possibility exists?"

"A reluctant yes."

Tara sighed.

"Does my answer disturb you?" he asked.

"Not exactly. If I'm honest with myself, I guess I feel about the same as you do. Just as reluctantly."

He wanted to find out why she'd started the conversation. Had she sensed the silent, inner exchange between them over the sculpture? Another part of him shied away from asking for fear of what she might tell him. To share with Tara could only lead to unwanted involvement. Or worse—it might lead to a repeat of that inner contact.

"You need to rest," he said softly. "Don't fret over what can't be solved, and don't pose problems with no answers. Clear your mind. Relax. Go to sleep."

She turned her head and looked at him, firelight flickering in her eyes. She was so close. So desirable. His breathing accelerated. He heard the rasp of air in his throat as he fought against his urge to gather her into his arms.

Tara longed to reach out to Brian and shelter in the warmth of his embrace. How strange to feel that safety and danger lay in exactly the same place.

We could share a good-night kiss, she told herself. One kiss.

That's not all you'd wind up sharing, another part of her warned.

She sighed again and turned away from him. She *was* tired, and she *did* need sleep. Clear your mind, Brian had advised. If she stopped thinking of him, maybe the rest of her would stop wanting him. She'd try the breathing exercises for relaxation that she'd learned in her meditation class....

Tara ran naked along a corridor, the lush tan carpeting caressing her bare feet. She breathed in a faint sea smell mingling with the jasmine scented air. To either side of her, closed doors led to many different rooms, but she knew none of them were meant for her. The joyous anticipation of reaching the room where she belonged quickened her breath.

"Ta-a-ara." Her name echoed down the corridor, speeding her pace, for she knew who called her.

She was an invited guest in this place that had no name. She wasn't afraid because nothing would harm her. Her fingers brushed against velvety gray walls pulsating with welcome. Because *he* waited here the wonder of love flowed as smooth and sweet around her as honey on the tongue.

Only the two of them existed in this special place, created for them alone. It had always been here, but until she found *him* she couldn't enter. Now the way was open to her, and it would always be waiting for her.

"I'm almost there," she told him silently, feeling how his eager impatience matched her own.

There was her door, his door, their door at the end of the corridor. Theirs was the golden door of promise, of fulfillment, of happiness. As she flew toward it on winged feet, the door swung open, and she slowed to savor the sight of the man who stood with his arms outstretched.

His hair glowed red, a warm beacon to welcome her. The blue of his eyes invited her to enter the heaven created when they embraced. His beautiful strong body waited to offer the ultimate pleasure he alone could give her. She belonged here with him as he belonged here with her.

Tara melded into his arms. He gathered her to him, and the door closed, shutting them away from everything but each other.

They lay entwined on soft robes with his warm lips nibbling at her throat, at her ear, at her mouth, teasing and promising. She ran her fingers through the silky thickness of his hair and along his broad shoulders, exploring the smooth warmth of his skin. Desire coiled, waiting, inside her, but there was no hurry. Time had stopped.

His mouth possessed hers, tenderly, tasting and caressing. She felt his excitement. She knew her own and couldn't tell one from the other. Her lips parted beneath his and their kiss deepened.

"Brian," she murmured.

Chapter Five

Brian waited for Tara behind the shining door, aware of her running along the corridor. His restless impatience made him call to her because there were so many other doors between them. He feared she might choose the wrong one.

At the same time he was certain she'd come only to him; she knew he waited here in their special place. He'd never seen the room before, but he belonged here. Not alone. He and Tara, together.

When he opened the door and saw her beauty, the inner radiance that turned her eyes a shimmering shade of green, he forgot his restlessness. If ever a woman was worth waiting for, she stood before him now. Aroused to distraction by the sight of her, by her enticing scent, he held out his arms. There was nothing in his world but Tara.

No words could describe the feel of her hair, her skin, her lithe body. He tasted the soft wonder of her lips and was no longer impatient. Since time didn't exist he was content to savor her slowly. They had forever to make love to one another, a fusing of their bodies while their separate life forces intermingled.

Everything that had come before Tara didn't matter. His life until this moment had been merely waiting. For her. Now each of them would be complete. Complete in themselves and, when they came together, a whole greater than either.

His fingers traced the curve of her breasts, caressing the firm nipples, and within himself he experienced her arousal and pleasure as well as his own. While he discovered her most sensitive places, he thrilled to her eagerness to learn all the secrets of his body.

He felt her blood flowing in his veins, his feelings flickering along her synapses. Her need was his; his desire was hers....

Loving arms enfolded Tara, and warm lips nuzzled her breast. She cradled his head against her, moaning at the sweet agony of his tongue circling her nipples. Through half-closed eyes she saw the play of firelight on the ceiling, and in her mind a question stirred.

Didn't she remember a corridor with a shining door?

Grandma's house had no such door. She was in Grandma Fallkirk's house in front of the fire. In Brian's arms. Where she belonged.

She wasn't dreaming; Brian was arousingly, excitingly real. But hadn't she had a dream...?

His mouth covered hers in a deep, demanding kiss that wiped everything from her mind but the compulsion to respond as she was driven by an urgent summons toward fulfillment. She pressed closer to him, hugging him to her in a frenzy of wanting.

They breathed in unison, rapid gasps of air that mingled as they exhaled. His masculine scent filled her nostrils, and the taste of him tantalized her tongue. Though she didn't recall shedding her nightshirt, her bare breasts still tingled from the remembered touch of his lips and from the provocative rubbing of his chest hair. Flesh to flesh, heart to heart.

And something more, an elusive sensation of inner sharing she'd never experienced with anyone. Almost as though she was inside Brian's mind and he inside hers.

"Tara," he murmured and all the thrilling wonder she felt echoed in his voice.

She ran her hands over the breadth of his shoulders and down his back, aware of the powerful muscles under the sleekness of his skin. She was aware, too, of how her caresses inflamed him. Now, now, her heartbeat insisted. Her nails dug into his back as she tried to urge him closer.

Instead, Brian pulled away slightly and she moaned, first in protest, then in delicious frenzy as he trailed kisses along her abdomen. She arched to him when he approached her erotic center. Then bright waves of sensation battered her, and she gasped his name.

He rose above her, positioning himself. She reached and touched him, and his involuntary cry of pleasure joined hers when he entered her. He eased in and out with an incendiary rhythm that set every cell in her body ablaze. She moved with him, around him, until he thrust deep and hard, faster and faster.

Shining waves broke over her head as she and Brian drowned in a surging storm of rapture, a passionate fury beyond anything she'd ever experienced or even dreamed could happen.

When they ultimately drifted to shore on the gentle aftersurf of release, still in each other's arms, the empathy remained with Tara. She kept her underlying awareness of Brian's emotions, knowing he also understood hers. With such a powerful bond between them, words were superfluous. His fingers caressed her upper arm with feather strokes, and she sighed drowsily, happily.

"I dreamed about this." Brian's voice was a soothing lullaby, and it took a minute before the sense of what he said sank in.

Tara tensed.

"I waited for you in a strange place," he went on, "a room with a shining door."

She raised her fingers toward his face, preventing herself at the last moment from covering his lips to silence him.

"You ran down the corridor to me, ignoring all the other doors." Brian spoke huskily. "Then you were in my arms, and when I woke up, you really were. Dreams *do* come true."

"No!"

Brian eased away, raising himself on one elbow to look down at her. Tara started to sit up, remembered her nakedness and clutched the blanket around her instead.

"What's the matter?" he asked.

She stared at the ceiling. "I don't want to hear about your dream." Her voice rose. "Don't tell me any more."

His hand on her cheek turned her face toward him. "If my dream's upset you I want to know why. If it's something other than the dream, I want to know why, too."

His eyes showed puzzled concern. Tara bit her lip. She couldn't tell him. She didn't even want to think about it.

Brian's fingers brushed a strand of hair from her forehead. "We've shared something special. That's why I ask."

"I didn't want to share a dream!" she cried.

He blinked.

Tara sat up, a blanket clutched around her. "I didn't want to ever have the dreaming happen again. Never!"

Brian sat, too, his blanket falling to his waist. Tara straightened, willing herself not to be further bemused by the magic of his body.

"I hate double dreaming." She flung the words at him.

He stared at her for a long moment before speaking. "Are you telling me you had the same dream I did?"

"Corridors, doors, a special place, you waiting behind a shining door. Taking me in your arms. Holding me. The feeling..." She sighed and shook her head.

"The feeling we belonged together," he said quietly.

Tara drew in her breath. Exactly.

"The night you arrived," Brian said softly, "you stood in your bedroom watching me on the beach. I couldn't see you, but I knew you were there."

She hugged the blanket closer, as if that could shield her from his words. "I shouldn't have come to the Cape," she muttered. "I was here the other time."

"The other time you dreamed with someone? Who was he?"

How does Brian know I dreamed with a male? she wondered, frantically trying to think of a way out. She couldn't bear this discussion of dreaming.

"I can't talk about that. It was a long time ago, I was a child." She shivered.

Brian slid over and put an arm around her shoulders. She stiffened, but he persisted, drawing her closer, stroking her hair. "Don't be upset. I've read about the same thing happening in the sleep labs where they test brain waves. A dreamer sometimes influences other sleepers around him to have dreams similar to his. One explanation is that certain people have more potent electrical fields and affect others nearby." He smiled at her. "You and I were certainly close enough to be on the same wavelength while we slept."

"But the dreams we shared came true."

His smile broadened to a grin. "We dreamed of what we both wanted. At least I did."

Despite herself a smile tugged at the corners of her mouth. She'd wanted him every bit as much.

He leaned to kiss the tip of her nose. "Making love was inevitable, dream or no dream."

Could the double dream actually have been a coinicidence, as he was trying to convince her? They both had denied their need, had tried to ignore their desire as they slept side by side.

"In fact," he went on, "I *still* want you."

A responsive thrill undulated through Tara.

"I told myself I wasn't going to touch you." Brian's tone was rueful. "I reminded myself the last thing I needed was any kind of involvement. It was an uphill fight to convince myself, but once I'd kissed you—zap, all the way down again."

She looked into eyes warmed by desire, pleased his struggle was as unsuccessful as her own.

"I'm going to toss a couple of logs on that fire—" he nodded his head toward the hearth "—then do my best to convince you dreams have nothing to do with refueling ours."

He stood, scorning the blanket while he added the logs. Flames shot up around the new wood, illuminating the magnificent power of his naked body and casting a golden aureole around him. Even as Tara felt the throb of need begin deep within her, she knew this firelit image of him was being irrevocably etched into her memory whether she wished it or not.

Standing with his back to the fire, Brian watched Tara. Her face, upturned to him, was rosy and flushed from lovemaking, but the rest of her was hidden.

"Drop the blanket," he said softly.

Her eyes widened, and the beginning of a frown creased her forehead.

"Please," he added.

Slowly she eased her grip on the blanket, and it slipped from her enticing pink-tipped breasts. He held out his hands, mutely urging her to rise and come to him. She hesitated, then stood up. In his eyes she was unflawed, with a pure and natural beauty from her becomingly tousled hair to her graceful feet.

Tara's gaze traveled over him, increasing his already potent arousal. The curves of her hips beckoned to his yearning hands, but he forced himself to wait because he wanted her to make the choice to come to him.

"This isn't a dream." She spoke breathlessly, her voice and her dilated pupils revealing her own desire, though she didn't move.

"The hell with dreams," he growled, aching with his eagerness to hold her.

"Yes, you're right. To hell with dreams. It's silly to let them bother me." Tara smiled at him, a smile of such utter sweetness and trust that his heart turned over. She held out her arms and walked straight into his.

The feel of her under his hands combined with the scent of her drove him wild. He kissed her hungrily, and her passionate response throbbed through him to increase his urgency. Two impulses fought for supremacy: to lingeringly make love to every inch of her or to possess her with savage intensity. He was dangerously near losing control over the choice. What witchery did this woman work on him?

Smooth skin, soft breasts, warm lips, an alluring body—many women could lay claim to these. None had, nor would ever have Tara's essence, the magic she cast over him by merely being herself. To him her skin was smoother than any other woman's, her breasts softer and her lips warmer. Holding her, he marveled at the beauty of her body. Just looking at her could make him want her.

He'd need hours of caressing her, of making love with her to slake his thirst.

Tara wriggled against him so provocatively he groaned and cupped her buttocks, holding her close, his desire pounding a fiery demand he couldn't ignore.

"Brian," she pleaded, her breath warm in his ear. She said no more, but he suddenly felt he knew her inner need. He knew she was experiencing the same desperate arousal that drove him to frenzy.

Clinging to one another, they tumbled onto the twisted blankets in a tangle of arms and legs. Her mouth, hot and persuasive under his, invited him to possess her further and he abandoned all attempt to go slowly. He thrust into her, hearing her cry of pleasure mix with his own sensual groan.

Caught up in the whirlwind of passion, he lost track of everything but the erotic rhythm of their lovemaking, a rhythm past control. Nothing existed except their timeless union.

The thrill of her release triggered his own, a dizzying spiral that left him replete, content, and reluctant to let her go. He wanted to hold her forever, awake and asleep.

We should talk, he told himself drowsily. We know everything about each other except the facts. Last names. Addresses. But that wasn't important....

Tara awoke from a dreamless sleep. Rain still splattered against the windows and she snuggled closer to Brian's warmth. She had no idea what time it was but the room seemed less dark. The storm would make a gray morning. She yawned, thinking neither the storm not the time really mattered.

Brian murmured in his sleep, and she sighed happily as his hand found the curve of her hip and pulled her against him. His heart beat reassuringly under her ear, making her worries of yesterday, her fear of the dreaming, all of her problems, seem very small and far away. He was here with her and everything else diminished in importance.

She closed her eyes, lulled by the steady beat, feeling secure and content. Halfway to sleep she thought, I don't even know his last name, but it doesn't matter. Later, I'll ask him later....

What was that awful noise? Tara opened her eyes and looked around. She lay in a nest of blankets on the living-room floor in front of a dying fire. Gloomy daylight filtered through rain-washed windows. She remembered a delicious warmth that seemed to be missing and sat up abruptly.

Where was Brian?

Tara stood, wrapping a blanket around her nakedness. The kitchen? Certainly that's where the squawking noises came from. Blanket trailing behind her, she investigated.

Larry Silver, perched on the counter, greeted her with a flap of wings and a loud demand for food.

"You're pretty darned feisty for a bird who was drowning last night," she said to the gull as she gathered the remainder of the liverwurst from the refrigerator. She coaxed him onto the floor and set it out for him along with the last heel of bread.

Brian's clothes were no longer drying on the hearth. He must be upstairs dressing.

He wasn't.

Shivering in the chill, Tara washed and pulled on jeans, a T-shirt and a sweater, then hurried back downstairs, telling herself she should have realized he'd gone out because he'd taken his jacket. He must have left a note and she'd somehow missed seeing it.

She found no note.

He'll be back, she assured herself, slipping on her new gold jacket to combat the cold creeping along her spine. She caught sight of her face in the wavy glass of the walnut eagle mirror in the front hall. Abruptly she turned away from the alarm in her eyes, but it was too late to prevent her from realizing she wasn't sure he *was* coming back.

"Give him time," she muttered, not liking the uncertain tone of her voice.

He wasn't like Abbott, she reminded herself. He was entirely different. She and Brian had shared something special. Brian *would* return.

Tara cleaned the living room, folding the blankets and quilts and taking them upstairs. Eyeing her bed, she decided to strip off the sheets and put them in a laundry bag with the used towels for Jake, the caretaker, to have washed. If she meant to catch her scheduled flight to California tomorrow morning, she'd have to leave for Kennedy by tonight, at the latest.

Brian would be back long before that.

But when she'd finished straightening up the house and washing the dishes, over an hour had passed. This was more than enough time to give him. Tara clenched her fists, fingernails digging into her palms, as the truth jolted through her.

Brian had gone, without waking her and without leaving a note. He'd told her he didn't want involvement. She should have listened to that instead of immersing herself in the other things he'd said—the honeyed words, the sweet talk.

Tears pricked her eyes and she blinked them back furiously. Larry waddled in from the kitchen and fixed her with a bright yellow gaze.

"He left you, too, friend." Her voice broke, and she swallowed against the lump in her throat.

Maybe I'm wrong, she argued. Brian might have run home for a change of clothes and fallen asleep. Neither of us slept much last night. This spurt of hope thrust her from the house and into her car. She drove through the diminishing rain along puddled streets until she reached his rented cottage.

There was no car in the driveway. She jumped from hers and peered through a window into a living room with a cold fireplace, a room showing no sign Brian had ever used the house. He was gone from her and from Chatham as well. Tara buried her face in her hands and sobbed.

Finally conscious of the rain soaking her hair and running in rivulets down her cheeks with the tears, she regained control of herself and got back into her car. The quicker she left the Cape, the better. A man who'd behave like Brian wasn't worth wasting tears on.

Back at Grandma Fallkirk's house, she packed hurriedly, stowed her luggage in the car and returned to smother what remained of the fire and retrieve the sea gull.

"Well, *I* won't abandon you to the cruel, cold world," she announced to Larry, pushing the protesting gull into the box where he'd spent the night. "Jake will take good care of you."

Driving to Jake's, with the box on the seat beside her, she brooded over what a fool she was. Hadn't she learned anything from the fiasco with Abbott? It was easy for her to see, after her eyes had been painfully opened, that Abbott Dade was a selfish, arrogant man who would always put himself first, love himself best. A man who didn't care what anyone else wanted, especially if it interfered with his own plans.

When she'd first become involved with Abbott, though, she'd created her own image of him as warm and loving, ignoring evidence—and there'd been a lot of it—that he wasn't.

Gradually the veneer she'd supplied had peeled away, revealing more and more of Abbott's true personality, but she'd clung desperately to what she wanted to believe until the devastating day he and Karen had come to her with their plans to marry. Even then it had taken months of listening to Karen's complaints about her handsome new husband to understand how completely wrong the Tara vision of Abbott had been.

How on earth could she have been so stupid as to do exactly the same thing with Brian? She really didn't know him. She'd fashioned a Brian sculpture from her own needs exactly the way she'd made the found object sculpture as a child at Grandma's house. A bit of kindness here, a feather of understanding there, a few stalks of empathy, a solid bolt of sensitivity, all glued together with love.

Love! Tara snorted with derision.

Brian had said it all, the truth she'd again been too blind to see. Proximity and desire. He'd clearly warned her he didn't mean to get involved. Why put all the blame on him, when it was partly her fault for not paying attention?

He'd left without a word, though, and she could never forgive him for that, no matter how right he felt it was to sever their tenuous relationship with a sharp, quick cut, using the deadly knife of disappearance.

She didn't know where he lived or worked, or even his last name. Not that she'd ever try to find a man who so obviously wanted no more to do with her.

He'd dreamed with her. That much was true. How could he ignore the closeness that had come from the dream to be a part of their lovemaking? Or was that incredible intimacy just in her imagination? She might well have projected her own emotions onto Brian and convinced herself they shared a bond that only she actually felt.

I won't cry again over him, she told herself firmly. I'll put him from my mind and in a month or two I won't even remember the color of his hair.

Larry squawked and thrust his head out from under the cloth covering the box beside her. Glancing at him, Tara wondered if she imagined the derisive glint in his yellow eye.

Chapter Six

Tara phoned her sister from Kennedy Airport only to have Karen hang up as soon as she heard Tara's voice. When Tara called back, Abbott answered.

"How's Karen?" she asked.

"Still acting like a spoiled child." He sounded sulky.

"But she's all right otherwise?"

"I suppose so."

"Tell her I'll call her from Sacramento."

"I can't guarantee she'll talk to you. I've lost all patience with the ridiculous way she's carrying on over such a minor matter."

Minor matter? Tara rolled her eyes but said no more than goodbye and hung up.

Abbott was behaving selfishly, which was true to form. As Brian had? No, she wasn't going to waste energy thinking about Brian.

Tara sighed. Karen hadn't yet forgiven her—or Abbott, either, from the sound of it. Served him right, but unforunately she had to suffer as well. Of course Karen had been hurt the most, so she could hardly be blamed for still being angry and upset.

Karen will get over this, she assured herself hopefully. Being at odds with her sister gave her a curious sense of guilt as well as making her feel lonely. With their parents in New Zealand, there was no one else to call, and Tara did her best to ignore her longing to pour her troubles into a sympathetic ear.

She'd lost touch with her eastern friends when she moved to Sacramento. To be honest, she'd more or less given them up before that because Abbott had insisted she be constantly available to him. Still, that was no excuse for not forming new friendships in California. She'd remedy that as soon as she could. She'd make women friends. The hell with men.

She'd go out and enjoy herself. A life that was all work was no life. Look what it had done to her! She'd thrown herself into the arms of the first attractive male she decided to trust. You couldn't trust any of them. Why had she been so certain Brian was different? She'd been sure they shared more than a mutual attraction, that there'd been a special bond between them. She couldn't have been more wrong.

"Looks like we'll have clear weather for the flight," the man sitting next to her in the waiting room said.

Tara glanced at him. Dark hair. Pleasant smile. She nodded, then looked away. After a moment she got up and changed her seat. She may not be through with men forever but, the way she felt at the moment, she certainly didn't care to exchange small talk with any of them today.

Spring flourished in Sacramento. On a Thursday morning, the week after her return to California, Tara drove to her job at Delta Two Design. She did her best to ignore the sweet scents from the blossoming plum orchards blowing in the open window of her golden-brown Firebird, imbuing her with their promises of new beginnings. Even the damn car has a message, she thought wryly. Firebird meant the phoenix, a bird eternally reborn from its own ashes.

While I sit among the ashes of my past like Cinderella before she went to the ball. The trouble is I thought I'd met the prince, until I discovered he was just another frog. That's really mixing up fairy tales. Unfortunately, this one doesn't have the obligatory happy ending.

Stop feeling sorry for yourself!

In the Delta Two building, Tara smiled at Yvonne Bowdin as she passed the sales office on her way to her own desk in engineering.

"How about lunch?" Yvonne called to her.

Tara hesitated, but, mindful of her new plan of action—women friends—agreed and went on. For the past week she'd gone out of her way to speak pleasantly to Yvonne and also to Lucy Holmes in bookkeeping. Actually she'd always liked both women, but she'd never made an effort to show it.

Her work had kept her busy while she recuperated from the trauma of Abbott, but that seemed a simple recovery compared to the way she felt now. Since she'd returned from the Cape, a pall of loneliness and despair had settled over her like permanent smog. Work was far from enough to keep her thoughts from centering on Brian and their time together at the Cape. She could only hope the friendship of other women would help distract her.

Night after night, her recurring, unpleasant dreams made everything worse. Tara raised her chin determinedly. She wouldn't bring the dreams to the office with her and deliberately relive them. It was bad enough to have them forced on her while she was helplessly asleep. And Karen still wouldn't talk to her.

No more, she warned herself. Keep your personal life away from your work.

Arriving at the engineering department she greeted Roger Gaines, the only one of the other designers working in the office this week, and tossed her shoulder bag onto her desk.

"The way you slammed that bag down, anyone would think you had a grudge against it," Roger observed. "Was the traffic bad?"

She managed a smile. "No. Actually nothing's wrong."

It wasn't that she didn't like Roger, but she already knew exactly how self-centered he could be and, since her return, she wasn't in the mood to be sweet to him, no matter how boyishly charming he acted.

He looked dubious but merely said, "Since the two of us are holding down the fort for the rest of this week, let's pray we aren't deluged with new orders."

Tara murmured agreement, turned to her desk, sat down and took the top sheet from her In basket.

Catching up on her backlog made the morning pass quickly. When she heard Yvonne talking to Roger, Tara glanced up in surprise.

"Time to indulge the inner woman," Yvonne said to her after blowing Roger a mock farewell kiss. "All work and no food keeps you skinny but grouchy."

Tara wasn't hungry; she hadn't felt hungry since she left the Cape. "Something light," she suggested.

"There's the About Sprouts if you're in a Mother Earth mood," Yvonne said. "Or the Whale and Ale if you crave seafood."

Minutes later Tara was staring down at her avocado and alfalfa sprouts sandwich on stone-ground wheat bread and wondering if she could swallow even one bite.

Yvonne stopped eating her cheese and broccoli quiche to glance at Tara. "Are you okay?"

"Sure. Fine."

"Something wrong with the sandwich?"

"No." Tara picked up one half and bit into it.

"Just getting over a bug, maybe? You look a tad peaked."

"I feel all right."

"I'm glad because I wanted to ask you if you were interested in heading up to Tahoe this weekend, as my guest. There are four of us going from the office. We've rented a condo with another foursome from Frisco. Tahoe's so great and it's not crowded this time of the year."

The last thing Tara felt like doing was spending a weekend in a Tahoe condo with eight people, four of them strangers. Still, what waited for her in her apartment but bad dreams? Lake Tahoe was lovely any time of the year; she could spend most of the day outside. If she couldn't sleep there were always the gambling casinos on the Nevada side, open day and night. Not that she particularly enjoyed gambling, but at least the casinos were brightly impersonal, with diversions such as rock combos and lounge shows.

"I might be able to go, but I'm not sure," she told Yvonne.

"Roger Gaines is one of us. Then there's me and Lucy and Nate Stein from personnel."

"Oh, if it's couples I don't think I—"

"The Frisco group is three gals and one guy so it doesn't come out even anyway, if that matters."

"I'll let you know by tomorrow," Tara equivocated. "Thanks for asking me. It's really nice of you."

Back in the office, she found herself alone in engineering. She knew the other two men were away on assignments, but Roger hadn't mentioned not being in this afternoon. Maybe a new job had come in and he'd gone to do a preliminary review.

Roger was the boss's favorite, the fair-haired boy of engineering. Tara knew, as far as old D.D. was concerned, she was the token woman. She also knew she'd been doing good work and that the other engineers accepted her as one of them. Their approval mattered more to her than the boss's old-fashioned opinion of women as design engineers.

Her thoughts drifted to Yvonne's invitation. Lake Tahoe. She'd be surrounded by fresh water, not the salt spray of the Atlantic Ocean. Strange, that her bad dreams this past week had been about the Pacific when she knew the Atlantic so much better.

And they were also about Brian. She and Brian were splashing through the surf hand in hand, then plunging into the waves, letting go of one another and swimming out and out into the blue-green water. She kept sight of his head, auburn hair darkened by the water, and felt reassured by his nearness. Then, suddenly he was gone. He was under the water and she dived to seek him.

Seaweed clutched her legs with slimy tentacles, and she realized she'd ventured too close to a bed of giant kelp. Where was Brian? Trapped and helpless amid the kelp? She tried to call his name but only bubbles came from her mouth. She swam desperately among the rubbery fronds in a twilight world of green gloom, searching, searching.

Soon she was lost in an underwater kelp forest. She couldn't find Brian; she couldn't even find her own way back to safety. Seaweed tangled around her, holding her prisoner. Brian was lost, she was lost, and they'd never find one another again....

Caught in the remembered pain of the dream, Tara felt tears start in her eyes. She reached for a tissue, impatient with her inability to keep her mind from wandering back to Brian, no matter how hard she tried not to think of him.

"Hey, something wrong?" Roger asked.

Tara wiped her eyes, turning to see him standing just inside the door. "I have an allergy," she managed to say.

"Spring's tough for people with allergies."

Spring's tough for people with broken hearts, too, she thought.

"You must be feeling rotten."

Tara frowned. It wasn't like Roger to be so solicitous. "I told you earlier I felt all right."

"Good." Roger walked over to perch on the edge of her desk. "Because I really want to ask a favor of you. A big favor."

She eyed him warily. "What kind of a favor?"

"Well, after lunch I went in to talk to D.D. and I happened to say a few kind words about you. I told him you were the best in the department when it came to small instrument designing."

Roger wasn't given to handing out plaudits, and she couldn't help but wonder what had prompted this one. "Thanks. At least I think I mean thanks. What brought up my name?"

"A call came in just before noon. By the time D.D. got to me, you'd already left with Yvonne. D.D. gave me the specifics, wanted me to handle it, even told the client I would. I thought it over on my lunch hour, came back and convinced him you'd do a better job, since this is right up your alley."

"What's right up my alley?" She didn't for a minute believe Roger was being magnanimous without his own reasons.

"This surgeon in San Diego wants us to design a clamp for ultra fragile intestines that will hold without crushing."

Tara blinked at Roger, not understanding why he didn't want the job, which seemed like a fairly simple one. Had he heard this particular doctor was a pain to work with? But that could happen with any client and was considered one of the milder hazards.

"So, naturally I told D.D. that Dr. Shute would be happier in the long run with your work rather than mine," Roger went on, "since you're so talented with small instruments."

"Dr. Shute?"

"He's the San Diego surgeon. La Jolla, actually. I hear he's a hotshot, so you'll probably get no end of medical referrals after you perfect his clamp. Ought to be good for your allergy to head south, too."

She almost asked what allergy before she remembered how she'd covered her tears. At the same time it dawned on her why Roger was dropping Dr. Shute in her lap. It must have something to do with the weekend trip to Lake Tahoe.

"I take it this La Jolla surgeon wants a rush order," she remarked.

"How did you guess? He asked that our designer fly down tomorrow and stay in San Diego working with him until he's satisfied with the clamp design. Money seems to be no object."

"But whoever flies south can't travel east."

Roger grinned at her. "Yvonne told me she'd asked you to come to Tahoe with us. Said she didn't think you wanted to go. I do. But, hell, Tara, you really do design little gadgets better than I do, anyway."

"You don't have to flatter me into taking the job. I'd really like to get into medical designing and, as you say, this may be my doorway. I'll be happy to go to San Diego or La Jolla or wherever Dr. Shute is."

"Great! I'll even put a dollar marked Tara in the slots and give you half of any jackpot that comes up."

"You're all heart, Roger."

"Yeah, I know."

In the year and a half she'd lived in California, Tara had never seen San Diego. In a way, she looked forward to the trip as a diversion from her own problems. She got off the jet at Lindbergh Field shortly before noon and followed Dr. Shute's instructions by renting a car and driving directly to UCSD Medical Center.

He'd asked Delta Two's designer to meet him in the operating room at one o'clock and observe the surgery he'd be doing. It was this type of operation he wanted the clamp designed for.

Tara wasn't wild about watching an operation but, if it helped her understand the client's need, she guessed she could stand it. The other thing that bothered her a little was that Dr. Shute had been told to expect Roger Gaines.

D.D. had a strict rule about never leaving messages, other than requests to call back, because, in his opinion, the message was too often forgotten or garbled. D.D.'s secretary hadn't been able to reach the doctor personally. She'd left requests for him to contact Delta Two Design with both his answering service and his office but when Tara had left Sacramento, Dr. Shute hadn't yet returned the call. She disliked being a surprise to him.

Well, if Dr. Shute was biased against women engineers, that was his problem. She might not be as talented as Roger had claimed in his eagerness not to miss the Tahoe weekend, but she was good at her job and confident the clamp wouldn't give her much trouble once she understood what the doctor wanted.

E.B. Shute, M.D. To her the name suggested an older man, fiftyish, with graying hair and a small mustache. He'd be tall and rather thin, and inclined to sarcasm when irritated. Never mind what he was like, she thought. She'd work as she always did, creating the best design possible to meet the client's specifications.

The tang of salt air blowing into her car windows gradually faded as she drove away from San Diego Bay on a freeway heading inland through Mission Valley. She was glad to leave the sea scent behind. She wanted no memory of the Cape distracting her. The car rental clerk had given her directions to the UCSD Medical Center and she concentrated on these.

"They changed the name—it used to be called University Hospital," the clerk had said. "Once you get on the Mission Valley Freeway, on a rise to your right you'll see a tower with UCSD Medical Center on it. Just look for the green signs. They'll tell you where to turn."

Following the green signs telling her how to reach the hospital, Tara maneuvered onto another freeway and up a hill, turning onto an off ramp at the top.

She found the medical center to be the usual collection of old and new buildings, none particularly distinctive architecturally, set amongst semitropical trees, shrubbery and flowers.

After a five minute trek up from a canyon parking structure, Tara found the information desk inside the main entrance and gave her name. She explained about the change in designers and how Dr. E. B. Shute expected her in one of the operating rooms.

"I have Dr. Shute's request here," the receptionist said. "As soon as I change the identification badge, I'll ask a volunteer to show you where to go."

The volunteer, a graying matronly woman dressed in pink whose badge said she was Ruth O'Mara, smiled at Tara. "Dr. Shute is one of our favorites. Do you know him well?"

"I've never met him."

"You'll just adore working with him. He's so understanding. Of course his wife—" Ruth O'Mara broke off, putting a finger to her lips. "Well, you wouldn't be interested."

After taking her up one flight in a crowded elevator, the volunteer led Tara through automatic swinging doors into the operating suite where she left her with a green-garbed technician. Tara, who'd envisioned being behind glass in a viewing area above the actual operating room, found she was wrong.

"Here's a surgical gown that ought to fit you," the tech, a young man named T. Lancaster, told her. "You can change in this dressing room. When you're ready I'll show you how to scrub before we get into the sterile stuff."

Tara emerged in a green cotton shift with a round neck and soon learned T. Lancaster hadn't been exaggerating when he said scrub. Feeling her hands had never been so clean, she followed his example by drying them carefully on what he told her was a sterile towel. After that everything seemed to be sterile: the cap for her hair, the long-sleeved ankle-length green gown he tied for her in the back, the mask, then finally, the gloves.

"Don't touch anything, even your own back or your mask or any exposed skin," T. Lancaster warned. "That way you'll stay sterile."

"You'd think *I* was going to do the operating," she observed, thinking her voice sounded odd coming through the mask. "And I don't think I have any exposed skin left."

"Try and stay out of the way of the doctors, nurses and techs," he advised, indicating she was to go through an archway into the operating room. "When I was learning technique, that was the hardest for me. Every time I got close to the table to see what was going on, someone backed into me or clobbered me with an elbow."

She nodded, figuring she'd better not admit she really had no keen desire to be at the forefront, viewing human insides.

Five figures in sterile green stood grouped around a sheet-draped figure on the operating table. All wore caps, masks and gowns identical to hers and she found it a bit daunting. How did medical people in operating rooms know who was who? Looking at their feet, Tara saw by their ankles and shoes that three were women and two were men.

"Which one is Dr. Shute?" she asked the tech.

"He's not here yet. Dr. White, at the head of the table, is the anesthesiologist, and she's putting the patient under now. There's the instrument nurse on the far side of the table and next to her is a med student. On this side is the assisting doctor and a surgical resident. Not much room for you; you'll have to be careful."

Walking with her to the foot of the table, he introduced Tara. "Ms. Reed is observing so she can design a new clamp for Dr. Shute," the tech added.

The five glanced at her briefly, and the man she took to be the resident winked a friendly dark brown eye.

"Ever see this kind of operation before?" he asked.

Tara thought it best not to mention she'd never seen *any* operation before, so she merely shook her head.

"Dr. Shute's the best in the West when it comes to friable intestines," the resident told her.

Momentarily taken aback, she had to think for a few seconds to realize that friable meant fragile. She'd always supposed all intestines would be delicate, but evidently some were more so than others.

"I understand he needs a special clamp for the, uh, friable intestines," she said and edged closer to the nurse with the instrument tray, hoping to identify what type of clamp the doctor would be using.

"When Dr. Shute does an end-to-end anastomosis," the resident said, "he doesn't want the clamps mangling tissue that's at best marginally viable."

Should she admit she hadn't the slightest idea what he was talking about? Before she could make up her mind, the doctor next to the resident said, "I hear him scrubbing now. Go ahead and begin the incision, Joe."

The resident, all his attention now focused on the patient, asked the instrument nurse for a number seven blade.

Swallowing, Tara stood on tiptoe to watch as the scalpel blade traced a line of red along the bare flesh of a living abdomen. Staring in unwilling fascination as gauze sponges soaked up blood and tiny forceps clamped off what the resident called bleeders, Tara didn't notice Dr. Shute's arrival at the table.

When a voice she hadn't heard yet said, "Good work, Joe," she realized the best in the West had spoken.

She looked at him, knowing she should announce who she was and that she was here instead of Roger before Dr. Shute noticed her and asked what she was doing in the operating room. The back of his green-capped head was to her as he spoke to Dr. White about the anesthesia.

His voice seemed familiar to her for some reason. Who did he sound like? She didn't dare interrupt his conversation and hoped she'd find a chance to say her piece before he became involved in the operation.

He turned so his masked profile was to her as he watched the resident cut through the layer of tissue under the skin. Now or never, Tara thought, annoyed she'd been put in this uncomfortable position by Roger's maneuvering.

She cleared her throat. "Dr. Shute?"

His gaze swung toward her, blue eyes fastening on hers.

"I'm—" She got no further because her throat closed in shock, cutting off her words. She knew those eyes!

But Dr. Shute's initials are E.B., her mind protested inconsequentially.

Unable to move or speak, Tara could only stare as startled recognition flared in his eyes.

"What in hell are you doing here?" Brian growled.

Chapter Seven

With difficulty, Tara conquered her first impulse to rush from the operating room, drive the car to the airport and fly back to Sacramento. Heart pounding in her ears, she forced herself to meet Brian's angry gaze, knowing the only way to keep from going to pieces in front of everyone was to act as though they'd never met.

"Dr. Shute, I'm Tara Reed, the design engineer from Delta Two," she said, amazed she could keep her voice level when she felt she could scarcely breathe. "Sent here instead of Roger Gaines. My home office wasn't able to get a message through to you. I'm sorry."

Watching Brian fight for self-control, she told herself he hadn't suffered through sleepless nights and bad dreams like she had. He deserved the shock. Her own control was tenuous, but putting some emotional distance between them by calling him Dr. Shute had helped a little.

E. B. Shute. What did the *E* stand for?

It doesn't matter, she admonished herself fiercely, wondering if she should offer to withdraw from the operating room.

No! If he wanted to get rid of her, let him say so. She'd apologized for the switch in designers, and she had a perfect right to be here. After all, he was the one who'd set up this meeting. Would he never stop glaring at her?

Brian cleared his throat. "Ms., uh, Reed. We'll talk after the surgery. Please stand over there next to Ms. Kern and Dr. Gunnison." He motioned with his head to the opposite side of the table where the nurse and the medical student waited. "I'll expect you to pay close attention to the instruments I use to clamp the intestines. While I'm operating I'll try to demonstrate what changes I need in the design and why."

For the next hour and a half it was obvious Brian had dismissed not only her but everything else from his mind to concentrate solely on the operation. Determined not to be outdone, she set aside her own emotional turmoil and convinced herself she could watch this without fainting. She found herself impressed by Brian's deftness and, oddly, by his gentle handling of the patient's internal organs.

He talked as he worked, a technical lecture intended, she was sure, for the resident beside him and the medical student she stood next to. It was a courteous gesture on Brian's part to address the student as "Doctor." He was polite to her, as well, when he pointed out the deficiencies of the clamps he used. Not once, though, did he meet her gaze.

Near the end of the operation, as Brian directed the resident in the closing of the incision, Tara had time to remember the chatty volunteer, Ruth O'Mara, and what she'd said about how much everyone liked the wonderful Dr. Shute.

"Of course his wife—" Ruth had begun before belated prudence stopped her. Wife. Brian was married.

Well, what had she expected? His quick disappearance from the Cape certainly meant he wanted no complications.

What had he thought when he first recognized her here in his operating room? That she'd tracked him down for a confrontation? Tara felt herself redden and was glad the mask hid her face. It would be like him to be that arrogant, to think any woman he'd made love to couldn't possibly live without him.

I can't work with him on this instrument design, she thought. I don't want to have anything to do with E. B. Shute, M.D., a man who wasn't even truthful about his first name, much less anything else.

Yet the image of herself returning to Sacramento and telling D.D. to send someone else reminded her of nothing so much as a whipped dog slinking off with its tail between its legs. Tara had been raised to finish what she started. Grandma Fallkirk used to say the only person she couldn't tolerate was a quitter, and she thanked heaven her daughter had chosen to marry a man who felt the same way so her grandchildren would have a proper upbringing.

"Good work, Joe. You go ahead and finish the skin," Brian told the resident.

Tara tensed, her attention fixed on Brian. He looked up, directly into her eyes, then blinked, almost as though he'd forgotten she was in the operating room. She swallowed, her throat suddenly dry as she faced the searching intensity of his gaze.

"Ms. Reed," he said formally. "Please meet me in the cafeteria on the ground floor in half an hour."

"Yes, Dr. Shute." Her tone was equally stiff.

Changing back into her suit of cinnamon cotton twill, Tara tried to organize a plan of action. She found herself seesawing between a final leave-taking with or without a few scathing comments, and a grim determination to stick the thing through. She'd show him by impersonal, businesslike behavior that he meant nothing to her except as a client of her company.

When she found herself adjusting and readjusting the tie of her shirt to make certain it was exactly right, she scowled at her mirror image. Clouded green eyes stared back at her, eyes too clearly showing her confused state of mind.

He'd seen her in old, grungy clothes, so it certainly didn't matter about the tie. In fact, he'd seen her when she wore nothing at all....

Tara closed her eyes so she wouldn't have to see the pain lurking in their depths. Damn it, Brian Shute, she promised herself, I'm going to get even. I don't yet know how, but I will.

She lingered in the dressing room, finally walking out and finding the fire stairs the technician had told her led almost directly to the cafeteria. She hoped she wouldn't arrive there too soon. The last impression she wanted to convey was eagerness. When she walked into the cafeteria ten minutes late, she saw all her dawdling had been for nothing. Brian wasn't in the room. When has a doctor ever seen you on time? she asked herself wryly.

Getting a cup of coffee, she sat at a table and glanced about the nearly empty room. To the south, floor to ceiling glass windows looked out on the next building, which was only one story, so there was still a view of eucalyptus trees beyond and of blue sky. If she were in San Diego for any other reason, Tara thought, she'd be able to enjoy her visit here.

Sighing, she pulled a pad of paper from her bag and began to sketch possible designs for the surgical clamp, keeping her eyes glued to the paper. After a few minutes she grew genuinely engrossed in her sketching as she translated

Brian's operating room comments about the changes he wanted into her designs.

"It's all the fault of those damn shells." Brian's voice, from behind her, made Tara jump and whirl around.

He wore a gray shirt, open at the neck, with charcoal-gray pants and a casual burgundy-colored jacket. He was even better looking than she'd remembered, his auburn hair damp and wavy from the shower he must have taken.

"Shells?" she managed to say, willing herself into calm remoteness.

"On the barrier beach. You picked up shells and used them to make a design." He lifted the pencil from her hands, leaned over and traced two triangles lying on their sides, apexes interlocking. "Delta Two. Your company logo."

He was so close his breath stirred her hair as he spoke, and Tara fought to keep her composure, not trusting herself to say anything.

Brian slid into a chair next to her. He was still too close but at least she could breathe.

She kept her eyes on her sketch pad. "I may have. I don't always pay attention to what I'm doing with my hands."

Brian made such a strange sound she glanced at him in surprise. Had he laughed? Protested? He shifted position, leaned on one elbow and screened his eyes with his hand, making it impossible to read his expression.

"I'm afraid I remember what I did with mine," he said so softly she wasn't quite sure she'd understood his words, and for a moment she didn't grasp his meaning.

No! She wouldn't let him bring her back to their time together at the Cape. Tara sat straighter, saying nothing.

After a few moments Brian also straightened in his chair. "I certainly didn't know you worked at Delta Two," he said briskly. "I must have noticed the logo when I looked at the design brochures of various companies, subconsciously remembered your shells and chose Delta Two."

"You can always choose another company." If only she felt as cool as her voice sounded. Anger, sensual memories, and, despite everything, desire, boiled together inside her in a witch's brew.

She couldn't stop herself from glancing at him and saw with dismay the circles under his eyes. He looked tired and, for a tension-filled moment, she fought her urge to reach out and brush her fingers soothingly over his eyelids, to cradle his head against her breasts and whisper that she, too, had suffered sleepless nights without him.

How could she be such an idiot? No doubt he slept very well unless an emergency kept him up. Slept with his wife.

"You're married." The words came out of her mouth totally unexpectedly, totally unplanned.

His eyes widened as he stared at her, then he shook his head. "Not anymore." His tone was caustic. "I'm divorced."

Tara gripped her hands together in her lap to hide their trembling, upset because her heart had leaped at his denial of being married. I don't want these feelings, she thought desperately. I can't bear to have it all start over with this man I don't trust.

Taking a deep breath, she said as firmly as she could, "We met to discuss the clamp design. I've done a few preliminary sketches." She pushed the pad toward him.

Brian couldn't make himself stop looking at her. Tara Reed. A design engineer. He might have known she'd work with her hands, creating. She wore makeup today, a small amount she'd delicately applied to enhance her natural beauty. He actually preferred her with none. Her changeable eyes were more gold than green, and her shining hair was caught into a chignon. He remembered her hair blowing in the Cape breeze and its fragrance in his nostrils when he held her....

He remembered too damn much for his peace of mind. No other woman had ever given him sleepless nights. And then there'd been those depressing seaweed dreams.

If he followed his instincts he'd take her in his arms, here and now. He'd forget the unhappy ending at the Cape, and he'd say the hell with everything else.

And wind up without her again?

He forced his gaze away from her and onto the sketch pad she'd thrust at him, wondering how he was supposed to concentrate on clamps when she was close enough to touch. In the O.R. he'd been shocked into near catatonia by her eyes looking at him over the mask and for a moment or two he thought he must be hallucinating from too little sleep and too much thinking about her.

He'd had a devil of a time blanking his mind to focus on the surgery, with both anger and desire simmering under the professional detachment he'd summoned to get him through the operation. He was still angry, and he still wanted her.

"Did I come close?" Tara asked.

"Close?" he repeated.

"To what you want."

She was everything he'd ever wanted. Bemusedly he watched her forefinger point to one of the clamps she'd sketched.

"You seem to be studying this one," she said. "Are there any changes you'd suggest?"

Pull yourself together, Shute. Shape up. So your subconscious, against all odds, found her for you again. So what? She doesn't seem any too eager to fall into your arms. You got her message it was over, didn't you? The lady's only here on business, as she's already reminded you.

Brian forced himself to examine her sketch, his attention sharpening as he saw how close she'd come to what he'd envisioned. Almost as though she could see inside his mind. If she altered the angle a centimeter or so it looked to him as though she might well have the clamp he needed.

Okay, tell her and get this over with. Get rid of her. Who needs more pain?

"No, this won't do at all," he found himself saying. "None of these is right."

Tara blinked. "Maybe I misunderstood what you said in the operating room."

"It seems you did. I don't have time to go over it all with you again now. We'll have to set up another meeting." He mentally reviewed his schedule, cursing silently when he realized not only was he already behind on office hours but his evening was tied up with the hospital ethics committee meeting he'd promised to chair.

Tomorrow was almost as bad. She'd have to meet him for breakfast after he made early hospital rounds and before his first case.

"We'll have breakfast together," he announced.

Again she blinked. "I'd hoped to get back to Sacramento—" she began.

Brian slammed his fist on the table, sending the coffee she hadn't touched slopping over the brim of the cup, the sudden explosive gesture startling him as well as Tara. He hadn't realized he was so tightly coiled.

"I told your boss I expected his designer to work with me until I was satisfied." His voice was hard, his tone angry.

"Perhaps I'm not the one who'll be able to satisfy you." She spoke coolly.

He stared at her until he caught her gaze. "Oh, I think you can. I expect you to stay in San Diego until we discover whether I'm right. We need more time together so you can be sure of what I want, what I need."

Tara glared at Brian. If he was so damn put out about her being here, why was he prolonging her stay? Why not admit they couldn't work together and dismiss her? If anyone had the right to be upset, she did.

Don't think of him as Brian, she warned herself. Think of him as E. B. Shute, M.D., a client of your company. You're here on business. Put personal issues aside.

"Where do you want me to meet you for breakfast?" she asked resignedly.

"I'll pick you up. Where are you staying?"

She didn't want to tell him. "I prefer to meet you."

"We're wasting time. Where are you staying?"

Annoyed, Tara dug into her bag to locate the slip of paper with the name of the hotel where D.D.'s secretary had made a reservation. Finding it, she thrust the slip at him.

"Town and Country. Does it suit you?"

"I wouldn't know. I drove directly here from the airport." She heard the antagonistic, challenging note in her voice and wished she was better able to camouflage her annoyance. She didn't want him to think he affected her in any way whatsoever.

"If you took the freeway through Mission Valley you passed the Town and Country. I'll pick you up there at eight-thirty tomorrow morning."

She didn't want to ride in a car with Brian. She intended to avoid being alone with him. "They must have a coffee shop," she said. "Couldn't we just meet there and save time?"

Brian's scowl was positively threatening. "Whatever happened to 'the customer is always right'?"

"Client. We don't call them customers. Since you're a doctor I know your time must be limited."

He nodded curtly. "If you insist on breakfast at the hotel, I prefer the dining room."

"I'll be waiting for you there." Tara reached for her pad but Brian anticipated her. Tearing off the sheet with the sketches, he folded it, thrusting the paper into his pocket before handing her the pad.

"Why would you want those?" she protested. "You said they weren't right."

"A client's privilege, unless I'm mistaken."

"Well, of course, but—"

"Until tomorrow morning, then." Brian rose, holding out his hand.

Tara stood and reluctantly gave him her hand, expecting him to shake it. Instead, he raised her hand toward his lips and for a breathless moment she thought he meant to kiss it.

"Your hands are more talented than mine," he told her, clasping hers in both of his. "You create."

Flustered, hoping he couldn't tell how acutely his touch affected her, Tara groped for words. "But you—you're a healer."

Brian shook his head. "I cut away diseased organs, repair and sometimes replace them so they function better. Surgeons are glorified mechanics."

She was so taken aback by this cynical description she couldn't think of a reply. He still held her hand, his fingers warm and alive over hers, and she thought inanely that his touch could heal her.

Then she remembered he'd caused the problem in the first place. Tara wrenched her hand away, put the sketch pad in her bag, then held it defensively over her chest.

"Thank you for the breakfast invitation," she said, struggling for a distancing tone. "I'll have other sketches to show you by then."

He nodded. When he made no further move, she walked away from him toward the door, every inch of her body aware of his gaze following her.

In her rented car, Tara collapsed in the driver's seat and sat staring through the windshield at nothing. To think that Dr. Shute was Brian! And that she'd unwittingly given him the clue to find her by doodling with shells on the barrier beach. It seemed as though they'd been meant to meet again, to complete what they'd begun.

What *was* she thinking? Nonsense, that's what. Okay, so they'd met again. Had he apologized for leaving the Cape so abruptly? No. Had he given any kind of an explanation? No.

Watch it, friend, she warned herself. Complete your design to his satisfaction and get out of his territory. Before it's too late.

Tara started the car, returned to the Mission Valley Freeway and located the Town and Country Hotel. After registering, she dropped off her luggage in a room that opened directly to the outside like a motel. She then left the sprawling complex and, following the desk clerk's directions, found the Fashion Valley Shopping Center. Strolling along its open-air mall in the soft warmth of the late afternoon, she fought the temptation to look for a new outfit.

Did she want it to impress Brian at breakfast tomorrow? Tara frowned at the thought, dismissing the entire notion until a lime-green sweater in Robinson's caught her eye. It was cotton, casual in the relaxed southern California style, and yet elegant. It was also expensive.

The other suit she'd brought with her was jade colored. The sweater would complement its color and look stunning with the suit. Much better than the white shirt she'd planned to wear. And she had several other outfits at home the sweater would go with.

You're buying it for Brian, she accused herself. Don't rationalize.

As she handed the salesclerk her charge card, Tara was still arguing silently with herself. So she wanted to look her best tomorrow. What was wrong with that?

Tara woke early the next morning from a troubled sleep. She showered and then, in her robe, tried to work on sketches for the clamp but crumpled up each attempt in disgust. Those first few she'd done on the sheet Brian had kept still seemed to her the closest to what he'd outlined in the operating room. Maybe she'd have a better idea of what he wanted after they discussed the clamp at breakfast.

She certainly didn't intend to discuss anything else except that. She'd allow no involvement other than their professional one. She wouldn't let herself respond to a look or a touch, a phrase or the tone of his voice.

Tara glanced at her watch. Six-thirty. Too early to get dressed. Neither *The New Yorker* nor the design engineering journal she'd brought with her to read appealed to her at the moment. Maybe she ought to dress anyway and go for a walk. It might decrease the tension she felt building with every second that brought her closer to seeing Brian again.

As she started to rise, she heard a tapping at her door and her breath caught.

"Who is it?" she demanded, afraid she knew.

"Brian."

Tara tried to calm herself but there was nothing she could do to slow the trip-hammer beat of her heart. Telling herself she wasn't going to let him in, she tightened the belt of her wraparound blue robe and walked quickly to the door. As if of their own volition her fingers released the night lock and opened the door.

Brian stepped inside and closed the door behind him. A reddish stubble shadowed his cheeks and chin, and his eyes looked hollow with exhaustion.

"I've been up most of the night doing emergency surgery on a shotgun wound to the abdomen," he said, dropping onto the edge of the unmade bed. "I was driving past here on my way home and decided to stop on the chance you were up and wanted to eat breakfast now."

"I think you need sleep more than anything else," she protested.

His eyes traveled from the V of her robe down to where it ended at mid-thigh, and his gaze lingered there for a moment. He sighed. "It's too late to try to sleep." Reaching into his pocket, he pulled out an electric razor. "If I can borrow a plug and a mirror, I'll make myself a bit more presentable."

She gestured toward the mirror over the chest of drawers, gathered her clothes and headed for the bathroom to dress, wondering how she was going to keep her distance when Brian had already turned this encounter into something far more intimate than a business meeting.

When she came out, dressed except for her shoes, Brian wasn't in sight. Had he left? she wondered. Then she saw him, his razor still in his hand, sprawled across her bed, sound asleep.

Little as she wanted him in her room, she didn't have the heart to wake him. Now what? she asked herself. She could stay here and watch him sleep—a dangerous choice, since her impulse already was to ease off his shoes and cover him with a blanket. Or she could leave and eat a leisurely breakfast, letting him sleep for an hour or so, and then bring food back for him.

The second choice was obviously the sensible one. What if he roused when she tried to cover him? What if he reached for her, pulled her onto the bed with him, holding her close, capturing her lips with his? Tara's knees went weak thinking about what would happen after that.

Why did she want this man so much? He was wrong for her. He'd hurt her already; he'd only hurt her again. Yet if she stayed in the room with him somehow or other she'd wind up in his arms. She wouldn't be able to help herself.

How innocent he looked sleeping. Her fingers yearned to touch him, to push the strand of auburn hair off his forehead, to trace the outline of his lips, to feel his skin, vibrant with life and infinitely arousing.

She took a step toward the bed.

Chapter Eight

Tara stood next to the bed frowning down at Brian's sleeping figure. He not only shouldn't be in her hotel room, he shouldn't have come back into her life at all. She'd cover him with the extra blanket and leave to have her breakfast. If he woke before she returned, he'd have to guess where she was.

How uncomfortable he looked, with one leg hanging over the side and not even a pillow under his head. It seemed as though he'd been so exhausted he'd gone to sleep sitting up and fallen over onto the bed without waking. At least she could take the electric razor from his lax grip.

As Tara leaned over the bed, a shrill sound startled her. Seconds later, just as she realized he must be wearing a beeper, Brian sat up abruptly, dropping the razor as his hand reached toward his belt. She moved hastily away from the bed.

He pressed buttons on the two-way communicator he removed from his waist and the beeping stopped. "Dr. Shute," he said into it.

"Call UCSD Medical Center I.C.U. stat." The female voice was distorted by static.

Brian shut off the gadget and, as he reached for the phone on the nightstand, his gaze caught Tara's.

"I have a feeling that gunshot wound's gone sour," he muttered, punching phone buttons.

Listening to his end of the conversation with the hospital, she deduced he was right.

Brian hung up and got to his feet, combing through his hair with his fingers. "Sorry, I have to run." He started for the door, stopped and returned for the razor. "Tonight's the first chance I'll have to see you again. Dinner?"

"Well, I—"

He gave her no chance to accept, refuse or equivocate. "I'll pick you up here about six." At the door he turned and smiled at her. "I like you in green."

Tara stood for a long moment staring at the door he'd shut behind him. As a client of her company he had the right to set their meeting time but what right did he have to tell her what color to wear? If she'd brought any more clothes with her she certainly wouldn't wear green tonight, just to spite him. As it was, though, she had no choice but to wear this suit.

Since she had the entire day to herself she decided to put on jeans and a T-shirt and go sightseeing. She re-dressed slowly, thinking that at this rate she'd never get back to Sacramento.

Relax and enjoy, Tara told herself, eyeing the colorful brochures on the dresser. Treat this as a paid vacation and discover the fascinations of San Diego such as Balboa Park, Sea World, the San Diego Zoo and Old Town.

Old Town was the closest and sounded interesting. After breakfast she followed the directions, crossing over the Mission Valley freeway and threading through narrow streets to where, in the 1820s, the Spanish-Mexican pueblo of San Diego had begun. She parked the car and walked between golden-flowered hibiscus bushes toward the plaza where the first families of the pueblo had built their homes.

The bright primary colors of Mexican weaving and pottery hung in front of the many small shops along the way, tempting her to shop and browse. She went on, bemused by a breeze carrying the sweet scent of orange blossoms and charmed by the old adobe buildings. She paused before a still gracious house labeled Casa de Bandini and, reading further, discovered it was the site of Ramona's marriage.

Helen Hunt Jackson's romantic tragedy, *Ramona*, was based, she knew, on real lovers. Doomed lovers. Had orange blossoms scented the air when Ramona wore her bridal dress? Surprised at the ache in her throat, Tara shook her head and turned back to the shops. She was certainly no Ramona. She had no belief in the myth of only-one-man-in-the-world-for-me. And if she *did* believe in it, the last man she'd choose would be Brian.

The sooner she left San Diego, the better. She needed to get back into her familiar work routine, back to her real life. From the very beginning everything with Brian had been a fantasy, brought on originally by that visit to the parapsychologist Leda Umak and reinforced by her memories of dreaming at Grandma Fallkirk's house. And when she and Brian had dreamed together by the fire of making love, their coming together had seemed fated.

The fantasy should have ended as Brian intended, with no goodbyes, with them never seeing each other again. Meeting Brian here was a fluke. It shouldn't have happened and had absolutely nothing to do with fate bringing them together again. She did *not* believe in fate.

She could hardly accuse him of deliberately keeping her here against her will when it was obvious he was an extremely busy surgeon who was doing his best to fit her into his crowded schedule. Dinner tonight was a business meeting to discuss the clamp design. She'd be prepared. With luck, they might agree on a design before the evening was over and she could fly back to Sacramento and get to work on the prototype. Any subsequent problems could be worked out over the phone or by mail.

Realizing she'd been standing and staring without really seeing a gold-colored tin reproduction of an Aztec sunburst displayed in a shop window, Tara sighed and walked on, determined to put everything from her mind except enjoying the day.

After a leisurely lunch in the outdoor garden of one of Old Town's Mexican restaurants, she returned to the Town and Country to work on new ideas for the clamp. She'd bought a lovely pale yellow peasant blouse, hand-embroidered with golden flowers nestled among green leaves. She laid it out to put on after her shower, then changed her mind. The blouse's low scooped neck might suggest she had something in mind other than designing surgical instruments; the green sweater from Robinson's looked more businesslike with her jade suit.

She was dressed and ready to go by five-thirty and decided she had time to call her sister in New York. Abbott answered.

"Karen's sleeping," he said. "I'd rather not wake her."

Alerted by the tenseness in his voice, Tara asked, "What's the matter with her?"

"This morning she had some contractions and called me, hysterical, insisting I had to rush home and take her to the hospital. The nurse there told her she wasn't in labor, but you know Karen. She wouldn't believe anyone but her own doctor. He was in the delivery room, and when he finally examined her, he said she was having something called Braxton-Hicks contractions. Many pregnant women have them, and they're perfectly normal. He said she was definitely not in labor, she should go home, and that she wasn't going to deliver for a couple of months."

"How upsetting for her!"

"I didn't exactly enjoy myself either. I had no idea pregnancy would turn Karen into such a shrew."

"Pregnancy takes two," Tara reminded him, then hurried on before he could react. "Do you think Karen will talk to me if I call back tomorrow?"

"Frankly, no. I've never seen her so unreasonable, which is what I've been trying to tell you. She's behaving as though she walked in on an orgy instead of a brotherly kiss."

Brotherly kiss! Abbott certainly had a convenient way of altering the facts to fit his own purposes.

"Did she get my letter?" Tara asked.

"If she did, she didn't mention it to me."

"I'll write her again. Will you tell her I called and asked about her?"

"When she's in a better mood, yes."

Tara stared at the phone after she'd hung up, wondering how long it would take before she and Karen were on good terms again. Maybe once the baby came her sister would forget her jealous anger.

Brian arrived a few minutes after six. When she heard his knock, Tara immediately stepped outside, sketch pad nestled in the depths of her shoulder bag.

"Are you a good sailor?" he asked as he handed her into his maroon Porsche.

The memory of crossing to the barrier beach in the motorboat with Brian and the sea gull flared in Tara's mind before she could prevent it. He'd kissed her on that beach for the very first time....

Too bad it hadn't been the last, she told herself crossly, annoyed that she'd remembered. She glanced sideways at Brian.

"Why do you ask?" Her tone held a touch of hostility.

Brian settled into the driver's seat and buckled his seat belt before answering. "We're dining on the Reuben E. Lee, and she's afloat in the bay off Harbor Island."

Tara, reminding herself that this evening's dinner was a business meeting, forced courteous interest into her reply. "Sounds interesting. What kind of a boat is it?"

"A riverboat, a replica of a stern-wheeler."

"Replica? Do you mean restored?"

"No. They built the boat as a restaurant and had it towed to the present location. It's never been used as a boat, never will be."

"A fake."

He slanted a glance at her, and she realized her tone might have been a touch sharp. Why couldn't she keep away from the personal?

"That's rather a harsh indictment of the poor old Reuben E., considering the food's quite good."

But it's not real, she was tempted to say. Like everything else we've shared.

By the time he pulled the Porsche into the restaurant parking lot, she'd discovered the very ground they drove on—Harbor Island—was artificially constructed from fill. Another falsity. Maybe if I close my eyes, she thought half seriously, none of this will be here when I open them, Brian included. I'll be staring up at my star-spangled ceiling in Sacramento, waking from a dream.

Brian's hand on her arm as they climbed the gangplank onto the boat, though, was all too real. His touch sent tingling messages along her nerves, messages she'd rather not receive. Tara pulled away when they reached the door. Inside, Brian murmured to the maître d', who nodded and gestured to the stairs.

At the top, Tara faced a second dining area and hesitated, wondering why the maître d' hadn't come along to seat them. Brian touched her elbow, guiding her toward a large table running across the rear of the room, a nearly full table, with only two vacant chairs.

Before she had time to ask any questions, Brian was seating her in one of the empty places while greeting the others.

"This has to be a first," the graying man to Tara's left said. "We all made it—and on time, too."

"Rick Manning," Brian told her. "Rick, this is Tara Reed."

"My pleasure," the older man said.

Tara was introduced to the other eleven people at the table and, in the process, gathered from their remarks that they were doctors from Brian's medical group, their wives, and in one case, husband.

Before she'd quite adjusted to the idea this wasn't to be a private business dinner for just the two of them a beeper went off, and Dr. Manning reached for his waist. After listening to the two-way, he excused himself and rose.

"I spoke too soon," he said ruefully as he left the table.

His wife leaned across the empty seat, a tanned, attractively fortyish woman wearing dark blue and diamonds. Tara tried to recall her name. Rita?

"I'm so glad Brian brought you tonight," she said.

"Thank you." Tara could have kicked him for involving her in this. Why on earth had he?

"Rick said Brian had sworn off women forever but I knew that was so much nonsense." She smiled at Tara but her eyes were watchful, assessing. "What a charming suit, my dear."

"Thank you." What in heaven's name was she going to say to Rita Manning? The truth was rather involved.

"Do you live in La Jolla?"

"No. Sacramento."

"Oh, you're visiting Brian, then."

"As a matter of fact, I'm assisting him with a project. We really don't know each other well." The words sounded lame in Tara's own ears, and she could hardly blame Rita when the older woman's smile turned knowing.

A waiter rescued Tara, offering champagne from one of the bottles in the nearby bucket.

"You should have told me," she hissed at Brian after she'd swallowed several healthy sips.

He shrugged. "This dinner was scheduled, and I didn't like to think of you alone in that hotel with nothing to do while you waited for me to get around to a meeting with you."

"When *will* we meet to discuss the design?"

"I'm not on call tomorrow. Unless you object to doing business on a Sunday."

"I don't object. I'd like to get back to Sacramento as soon as I can."

"Your place or mine?"

Her eyes widened, annoyance flaring when she saw his lips twitch as he subdued a grin.

"If you mean your office, fine." She kept her voice even, unconcerned. "What time shall I meet you there?"

"I can pick you up."

"I prefer to drive myself so I can go on to the airport."

"What if I'm not satisfied?"

She tightened her lips. "I believe I have the design worked out. If I ever get a chance to show it to you."

He didn't speak for long seconds and his eyes, shadowed by fatigue, held hers, isolating the two of them. Was it pain that clouded his gaze? For one impulsive instant she wanted to soothe away his hurt with gentle, comforting caresses. Then he blinked and the moment was gone.

"Tomorrow," he said. "Ten o'clock. Fiero Surgical Group on Pearl Street in La Jolla." He turned to speak to the woman on his other side, an attractive blonde who'd been trying to attract his attention.

Tara, sighing at her foolishness in thinking Brian needed any comfort from her, sipped her champagne and looked out the restaurant windows at the view. The setting sun tinted horizon clouds with a palette of pinks and oranges, reflecting in the water of the bay where the white sails of small boats flitted like cabbage butterflies across lazy blue-green waves.

"Rick is dying to try out our new cabin cruiser by sailing to Catalina," Rita said from Tara's left. "Some of us meet over in Avalon Bay every summer and we have a ball. Maybe you can persuade Brian to come along with us this year."

"I really don't think—"

"Oh, don't say no. We have such fun. Brain's never joined us because Ursula hated boats. *You* don't, I hope."

"I like boats and sailing but I—"

"Wonderful. We'll look forward to entertaining you in Avalon. Brian needs to get away; he's been so grumpy since he returned from his so-called vacation in the East. Rick says Brian's working too hard. That's no good, you know, especially for a surgeon."

Deciding Rita wasn't about to let her talk long enough so she could be set straight, Tara smiled noncommittally, then turned to look at the menu a waiter had placed in front of her.

As the evening passed, lights blinked on across the water in San Diego, their reflections sparkling in the bay like Rita's diamonds in the lamplight. While she ate, Tara, conscious of every move Brian made, tried to ignore her body's tingling awareness when his fingers touched hers as he passed her the butter, when his arm accidentally brushed against hers, when their glances met.

She loved the abalone she'd ordered, but her increasing tension made swallowing difficult and, after eating a few bites, she put down her fork and excused herself from the table. Taking a short respite in the women's room, she reminded herself sternly that she meant nothing to Brian and, damn it, he meant nothing to her. So what if there was still chemistry between them, at least on her side? She certainly wasn't going to let it influence her.

On the way back she passed Rita, who was leaning over another table talking to the couple there. As she paused to allow a waiter to pass her, Tara couldn't help overhearing part of what Rita was saying.

"...doesn't have Ursula's flair, of course, but maybe it's just as well. Too rich a diet causes indigestion in the long run, and Brian could do with a little plain fare."

Tara returned to her seat, realizing Rita meant her. Plain fare, was she, compared to the glamorous ex-wife? No doubt that was Brian's opinion, too. She wasn't even worth saying goodbye to back on the Cape, and he'd been ordering her around since she'd come to San Diego as though she was nobody of any importance in her own right.

To him, obviously, her time had no value compared to his. Even if he *was* paying her company for her presence, he could make requests instead of snapping out orders. How thoughtless he'd been to invite her to dinner without telling her they'd be joining his associates. The more she thought about it the angrier Tara became.

Brian ruffled through the pathology reports on his office desk, initialing each one after glancing at it. Last night had been a disaster from the moment they set foot on the gang-plank. He should have warned Tara they were meeting his group for dinner. True, if he'd said so in the beginning she probably would've refused to go, but if he hadn't been so damn tired he would've at least thought to mention it at the restaurant door.

He couldn't very well beg off from the dinner but why hadn't he been able to dismiss his foolish obsession of wanting her with him? Was he turning into a masochist?

As the evening wore on, she'd gotten gradually cooler and more distant. She was barely speaking to him by the time coffee was served. Her chill demeanor in the Porsche as he'd taken her back to the hotel had practically given him frost-bite. She was out of the car and into her room before he'd unbuckled his seat belt.

Every time he so much as touched Tara's arm he was reminded how badly he still wanted her, but he'd had no plans last night to risk his hands-off policy by kissing her good-night. She'd made it very clear both at the Cape and here that she didn't want to get involved.

If his flat-out exhaustion hadn't blurred his mind, he'd have had the sense to avoid her until today. He'd really crashed once he hit the bed last night so now, with a few hours of sleep behind him, maybe he could think rationally again.

She'd betrayed him once; she'd do it again. She was just like Ursula. He'd okay the design and send Tara packing. Prevention was the best medicine.

The intercom pinged. He frowned. Rick was taking patients, not him, and he'd asked the Sunday morning receptionist to pass Tara on through to his office. Why was she ringing him?

"What is it, Consuela?"

"There are some people here from Channel Seven News who want to interview you," Consuela said. "Something about Steven Palomar."

The gunshot wound. Palomar had been a prime-time singer in his day and getting shot by his ex-live-in evidently made him newsworthy again. The policy for any doctor in the group involved with a celebrity was to give a single statement to the media when asked, but only if it didn't violate patient privacy. Brian glanced at his watch. If he hurried he could make a brief comment and get rid of them before Tara showed.

"Send them in," he told the receptionist just as the door to his office opened.

Tara stood in the doorway looking crisp and efficient in a tan suit and white shirt. He got to his feet, cursing silently as he felt his pulse rate increase at the sight of her.

"I'm a few minutes early," she said. "I couldn't believe it when I saw people in the waiting room—you actually have Sunday morning office hours!"

"Not me, not this Sunday. The guy on call—Rick Manning this week—sees a few patients. It's easier to bunch everyone up from ten to one here where their records are than to have people straggle into emergency rooms all over the city."

"I suppose so." She pulled her sketch pad from her shoulder bag. "Shall we get started?"

"Tara, there's one slight hitch. First I have to—" The knock on the door interrupted him.

"All right to come in?" The man who spoke pushed the door open without waiting for Brian's response. He was tall, dark and had a very white, even-toothed smile. A stocky man with a videotape camera eased past him into the office.

"Pete Ulrich, Channel Seven News," the tall man said with the breezy confidence of one who knows his face is seen daily in thousands of homes. "Bob Quincy with the camera. You're Dr. Shute."

Brian nodded. "This is Tara Reed," he said.

Pete Ulrich put out a hand and shook Tara's while he spoke to Brian. "We appreciate you seeing us, Doctor. We're planning a five-minute segment about Steven Palomar's life and times, and we want to tape a short interview with you about the operation you performed and his medical condition. Okay?"

"I'll tell you what I can without violating Mr. Palomar's right to privacy."

"When an ex-lover fills your belly full of shotgun pellets in front of six other people, you ain't got much privacy to lose," Pete pointed out. He glanced at Tara. "Is she your assistant, Doctor?"

"She's assisting me on a project, yes. Designing a clamp to be used in cases such as Mr. Palomar's."

"Maybe we'll work that in. All right with you, Ms. Reed?"

Brian watched conflicting emotions flick over Tara's face, but she finally nodded.

As soon as the camera began whirring, the questions began. The interview was brief and to the point, concerned with the surgical procedure and the prognosis—always tricky with a perforated intestine.

"I'm sorry for the delay," Brian told Tara when the local news crew had gone.

"I certainly never expected to be on TV," she said, smiling a little. "You're full of surprises. I hope that was the last one, though. I'd really like to get on with this."

So she could get away from him, just as she'd done at the Cape. Not a hint of apology from her, either. Brian tried to push aside his annoyance as she sat in the chair on the other side of the desk and opened her sketch pad.

"I did these drawings yesterday. They're all variations on those you took with you the other day. If I'm missing some vital point, now's the time to tell me." She spoke briskly, all business.

Damn her. Why did she have to come back into his life? He glanced at the sketches. He didn't like any of them as well as the first she'd done.

"I'm afraid none of these are right." He couldn't control the anger edging his voice.

"Why not?"

"The blade's too serrated, for one thing."

"In the first sketches, I didn't—"

"We're discussing the ones in front of us." He knew he was being unfair but holding onto his anger was the only way to block the wild surge of desire pounding through him.

Tara took a deep breath and his gaze clung to the rising curve of her breasts.

"Will you please go over your requirements one more time, Doctor?" Her voice was as chill as liquid nitrogen.

He started to speak, stopped, rose to his feet, sweeping the sketch pad from the desk as he rounded the corner and reached for her, pulling her up from her chair and into his arms.

"You know damn well what I require," he growled before his mouth closed over hers possessively.

Chapter Nine

Tara, caught by surprise, had no chance to rebuff Brian's embrace as his lips, warm and demanding, covered hers. Before she could summon any resistance, a wave of erotic excitement swept away her will. Brian's kiss was all that she remembered. Her lips clung to him, and one arm crept up until her fingers caressed the silky hair at his nape while the other slipped around his body to hold him close.

She wanted to stay in his arms forever, wanted the kiss never to end, wanted him....

His body pressing hard against her told her his need matched hers. His hands sliding urgently along the sides of her breasts betrayed his longing to touch her more intimately, and she gloried in the knowledge.

The renewed marvel of his taste on her tongue, his scent in her nostrils, the feel of his body under her hands intoxicated her. Everything fled from her mind except the joy of being in Brian's arms and sharing the wonder of passion with him. The way he'd left her at the Cape, his behavior here in San Diego, her determination never to involve herself with him again—all were forgotten. Nothing else mattered but the magic of their embrace.

A torrent of desire surged through her body, turning her knees to limp seaweed. She moaned, arching to him. His inarticulate reply, deep in his throat, sent a thrilling shockwave along her spine to lodge deep within her. He wanted her. . . .

Yes, her body throbbed, yes, yes, yes.

Yes, her mind echoed unreservedly.

"No!" Brian said hoarsely, tearing his lips from hers and shoving her away from him. "Damn it, no. I'm not going to get into that mess all over again."

She stared at him with anguished disbelief, her body still yearning for him, tears threatening. Is that what he thought of their coming together on the Cape?

"Once was more than enough," he muttered, turning from her.

A hot flare of anger burned away her tears. Tara retrieved her sketch pad, picked up her bag and turned to face him.

"You can find yourself a new designer," she snapped. "I never want to set eyes on you again." Whirling, she stalked to the door and left his office, shutting the door sharply behind her.

Since she'd checked out of the Town and Country before driving to La Jolla, Tara drove directly to Lindbergh Field. After returning her rental car, she called D.D. at home, still seething with fury.

"I'm sorry to bother you on a Sunday," she said, "but I wanted to let you know I'm returning to Sacramento without finishing the job here."

D.D. tried to say something, but she cut him off, knowing she had to convince him of the impossibility of working with Brian before D.D. plunged into one of his the-client-is-always-right homilies.

"Dr. Shute doesn't like my designs. He doesn't like me and the feeling is certainly mutual. I can't possibly work with him and so I'm—"

"Hold on there, Tara," D.D. insisted. "Do you realize your call is the second one I've had from San Diego here at home today? Now I don't know just what the problem is. Apparently you managed to antagonize Dr. Shute in some way—"

"*I* antagonized *him*? You don't understand—"

"My dear young woman, will you kindly allow me to finish?" D.D.'s tone had taken on an edge.

"Sorry," Tara muttered. She knew better than to keep interrupting D.D. She was allowing her anger to cloud her judgement.

"Dr. Shute called me less than fifteen minutes ago," D.D. went on. "He informed me that despite your antagonistic attitude, he wants to continue working with you. He considers you a talented designer, and he's certain anyone else we might send wouldn't be as empathetic when it came to the 'feel,' as he put it, for the instrument he wants."

Tara swallowed, unable to think of an acceptable reply.

"Well?" D.D. demanded, characteristically not waiting for her response. "You've dealt with problem clients before, Tara, and you usually charm them. I've never known you to give up and I'm sure you won't now. I expect you to stay in San Diego, to calm down and put any personal feelings aside. What difference does it make whether you like Dr. Shute or not? He's our client until he's satisfied with our finished product, and it's your job to be courteous while you work with him. Don't you think I'm right?"

In most cases, he probably was. She certainly had no intention of revealing to D.D. that, to her, Brian was a special case.

"Yes, of course," she mumbled reluctantly.

"That's the Delta Two spirit. Remember, the harder you try to please Dr. Shute, the quicker you'll be able to get back home to Sacramento."

A wry smile twisted her lips as she imagined her boss rubbing his bald spot as he always did when he was trying to convince someone to view things his way. Little did D.D. realize nothing she'd done up to now had seemed to please Brian Shute. She doubted that anything she managed to do in the future would, either.

"I'll give it a few more days, if you insist, D.D.," she said, "but I don't believe—"

"I'm sure you'll come up with exactly what the good doctor wants, Tara."

Fat chance, she thought. And good doctor, my eye. Brian might be a hotshot surgeon, but otherwise he was as insensitive and arrogant as they came.

"I'll do my best," she said, knowing that in her boss's eyes any other attitude would be inconceivable.

While she waited at the rental car counter she pictured Brian's smug satisfaction at getting his way. Damn him! Why did he want her around? To torment and humiliate her? He won't get the chance, she vowed. Not again.

Driving along the freeway from the airport she ignored the pleasant warmth of the day as she struggled to keep from reliving the moments in his arms, dwelling instead on the abrupt, embarrassing finale. How could she have been such a fool? She knew very well she couldn't trust him.

When she reregistered at the Town and Country, the clerk at the desk handed her a folded slip of paper with her key.

"When he phoned here the gentleman said to be sure you got the message the same time as you signed in," the clerk told her.

Tara knew before she unfolded the note who the gentleman had been. Gentleman? Ha!

"Call me," the message read, followed by a number, then "Brian."

She crumpled the slip of paper in her hand, wishing she could toss it into the trash can and forget him and his orders forever. Unfortunately, she couldn't. Not quite yet.

In her room, she took her time unpacking and settling in before she finally sat on the edge of the bed and smoothed the wrinkled paper she'd tossed alongside the phone. The sooner you get this over, the sooner you'll get away from him, she reminded herself. You have to begin sometime and it might as well be now. She picked up the phone.

"Tara?" Brian's voice was emotionless.

"Yes. You left a message for me to call you." She kept her tone stiff and formal.

"I—" he hesitated, then continued. "I apologize for the scene in the office. I believe you're the right person to design what I want, and I hope you'll continue to work with me despite what happened."

She sat back farther on the bed, searching for the right words. Though he'd forced her to stay by calling her boss, his apology disarmed her slightly. Before she'd decided how to reply, he went on.

"Can we call a truce? No mention of the past, including this morning, nothing personal between us. Purely business."

"That suits me," she told him coldly.

"Good. We'll take another shot at it right away then. I won't keep you away from your home office any longer than necessary."

"Today, you mean?"

"Yes. If you don't mind, that is. I don't often have this many free hours at my disposal."

He sounded stiff, too. Could she bear to see him again so soon? Did she have any choice?

"You're quite right," she told him. "I *would* like to complete the design, and the sooner the better. Where shall I meet you? At your office?" She was proud of the evenness of her voice, considering that his office was the last place in the world she wanted to go.

"I'd be happy to pick you up—"

"That won't be necessary," she put in hastily and firmly. "I prefer to drive myself. In fact, I insist on it."

He was silent a moment before he spoke. "The most convenient place for us to get together is where I am now. I'll give you the directions. You don't object to working at my house, do you?"

A slight mocking note had entered his cool, professional tone, causing Tara to bite back her automatic refusal. If he thought she was too afraid of him to risk coming to his home, he was badly mistaken!

"Whatever is convenient for you will be satisfactory to me," she said. "Business is business no matter where it's conducted."

And there'll be nothing else *but* business between us from now on, Dr. E. B. Shute, she added silently as she hung up after writing down his directions.

Edwin? she mused while she drove north toward La Jolla. Elmer? Or something really strange like Englebert? The *E* could stand for a biblical name, maybe Ezekiel or Elijah. Not that she cared. To her it stood for Enemy.

Tara wasn't surprised to find he lived on the shore, but discovering his house was a small, older bungalow did make her alter her preconceptions. She'd expected him to own one of those soaring modern homes on the La Jolla bluffs, not an unpretentious cottage whose exterior needed a fresh coat of paint. In fact, she was amazed to realize such homely places existed at all in the rarefied air of wealthy La Jolla.

The brine scented breeze off the Pacific cooled the heat of the sun on her head and her bare arms. Tara stood by the steps leading up to the front porch and stared out to sea, watching a boat with a yellow sail tacking toward shore, while closer in, a catamaran skimmed along paralleling the beach. Sun sparkled on blue water, though just beyond the boats a gray line of fog hovered offshore. Four sea gulls probed for food in a tangled mass of seaweed at the waterline. If only she could relax and stroll along the beach instead of having to climb those steps and face Brian again.

"Mesmerizing, isn't it?" Brian's voice said from above her.

Tara looked up. Brian stood at the top of the stairs, barefoot, wearing cutoffs and a faded green T-shirt, sunshine highlighting his auburn hair with tints of gold. Her stomach fluttered, her heart pounded and she cast about for something to say, anything, to stop her unwelcome reaction.

"Are those herring gulls, too?" she asked, hating the slight breathlessness to her voice and devoutly hoping he hadn't noticed it.

"They're called California gulls. If you look closely you'll see a black band on their lower bills that herring gulls don't have." He hadn't taken his eyes from her. "What did you do with Larry?" he asked.

"I left him with someone who'll take care of him." She couldn't seem to move, couldn't stop looking at him.

He nodded brusquely and turned away, breaking the spell. Tara began to climb the steps to the porch. Already he'd broken his promise and mentioned the past, but she was also guilty of backsliding. One sight of him and where was her well-justified anger? What had happened to her determination to remain cool and detached?

The interior of the house seemed shadowed after the bright sunlight. Cushioned rattan settees and chairs furnished the living room, and through an arch to the right she caught a glimpse of a far from modern kitchen. An open door to the left led into a hall, probably to the bedrooms and the bath. She doubted there could be more than two bedrooms.

"This is an old-fashioned place," she said. "Homey."

"You sound surprised."

"Well—La Jolla..."

"There aren't many of these original old bungalows left. I enjoy this one and wish I owned it. Leon refuses to sell, though. I'm lucky he even consented to rent it to me."

Okay, she thought, we've gone through enough preliminaries. Let's get down to business. She seated herself in a chair near a bamboo coffee table and reached into her bag for the sketch pad and a pencil.

Brian removed a well-folded sheet of paper from his back pocket. "I've been studying those sketches of yours I kept—the ones you did at the hospital—and I believe you caught what I want on your first try."

She stared at him. That's what she'd thought at the time, but he'd insisted the designs weren't right.

"May I look at them again?" she asked, reaching for the paper.

Their fingers brushed as he handed over the sheet and she was proud of the way she ignored the electric tingle sparking along her nerve endings. With a little effort she *could* control her response to him.

"Which design?" she asked, glancing at the three possibilities she'd drawn, then spreading the paper out on the coffee table and looking at him.

He sat cross-legged on the floor by her feet and bent his head to study the sketches. He was so close she could feel the warmth from his body against her legs. He felt too close.

I refuse to move away, she told herself. I won't do anything unless he touches me. Then I'll let him have it!

"You might have to alter the angle a centimeter or so," he said, his forefinger indicating one of the designs.

She leaned forward to see better. "Which way?"

He plucked the pencil from her fingers to show her, his arm grazing her thigh.

Is he doing this on purpose? she asked herself, annoyed when her breath caught at the brief contact. Deciding he was truly engrossed in the clamp design, she gave him the benefit of the doubt.

Beside her sketches she saw the interlocked triangles—the Delta Two logo—that Brian had drawn on the paper when they were in the hospital cafeteria. How ironic she'd unwittingly given him the means to locate her and how doubly ironic his subconscious had tricked him into finding her again after he'd tried to lose her for good. What treacherous games the subconscious played.

Here they were together once more at the edge of another ocean, sand, gulls and all. No, not quite all. This time there'd be no dreams to unite them, and once he okayed her design she'd never see him again. Wasn't that what she wanted?

Tara straightened abruptly. "Let me redo the one you prefer, increasing the angle slightly," she said, reaching for the pencil, "and you can tell me how it looks to you."

Some time later, with discarded sketches littering the table and the floor nearby, Brian finally held up one design and nodded.

"I think this is what I want," he told her, "but I'd like to sleep on it. Okay?"

"The decision's yours." Tara put down the pencil and flexed her cramped fingers. "The prototype shouldn't take more than—"

"I don't want to hear about the prototype at the moment. I need a break. Let's take a walk on the beach and discuss that later."

Tara hesitated but finally shrugged. Walking on the beach was certainly innocuous enough, and she really did feel the need for some exercise. She'd almost been able to relax and lose herself in her sketching but her underlying awareness of Brian had kept her tense.

"Those shoes aren't made for walking in the sand," he observed, flicking a finger against the two-inch heel of one of her sandals before rising to his feet.

A quiver shot up her leg as though he'd touched her instead of her shoe. "Bare feet are the only really appropriate footwear for sand," she countered—smoothly, she hoped. She had hose on and would need privacy to remove them.

As if reading her mind, Brian gestured toward the door to the left. "The bedrooms are through there. The second one is the guest room."

Tara hadn't meant to glance at Brian's bedroom when she passed, but she couldn't resist a quick peek. A deep blue spread covered a king-size waterbed. Above the bed hung a large oil painting of an old abandoned building at the water's edge, its outline blurred by the gray fog that dominated the picture. A haunting sense of familiarity made her stare at the painting. Yet at the same time she knew she'd never seen the building before.

You will, a voice inside her said softly. *Sadly*.

Tara blinked, then shook her head and hurried on down the hall. What was the matter with her? Being with Brian seemed to affect her adversely all the way around. A brisk walk would help relax her tense muscles, while the sea air would blow such nonsense from her mind.

"I think in another life I must have been a beach bum," Brian said to her later as they strolled south along the ocean's edge.

Tara stepped over a strand of drying kelp, the damp sand cool underfoot, and glanced curiously at him. "Do you believe in previous lives?"

He shrugged. "Not really, though I try to keep an open mind. What I do know is I never get enough of the beach."

Noting the dark circles below his eyes, she said, "Maybe you're working too hard."

He shrugged again, not answering.

"There's so much seaweed on the beach today," she said after a minute. "Is it always like this?"

"There's usually some but lately we've had more than normal washed in from the kelp beds north of here." He paused, watching a wave curl around his feet. "Maybe that's why I've been having dreams about being tangled in seaweed." He moved on, kicking aside a clump of kelp.

It doesn't mean anything, Tara assured herself. *So he dreamed about seaweed. So what? Your seaweed dreams were nightmares. Why would super surgeon Dr. E. B. Shute be having bad dreams? Just because you once shared a dream with him . . .*

No! She stopped herself. *Even thinking about shared dreams is dangerous.*

"What *does* the *E* stand for?" she blurted in a desperate attempt to change the subject.

He stared at her for a moment, then shook his head, smiling a little. "That's my secret, one nobody's guessed yet."

What kind of a name would he refuse to admit to anyone? Edsel? Elgar?

"I like your name," he went on. "Tara. It fits you."

"My middle name's Agatha," she said, laughing. "Does that fit me, too? My twin's named Karen Althea, and neither of us uses our middle names unless we're forced to."

"A twin." He stopped and eyed her speculatively. "To my way of thinking, one of you at a time is more than enough."

"Oh, we're not identical." As she spoke she poked at a kelp strand with her bare toes. She stooped to retrieve a mummified sand dollar and arranged it at one end of a chunk of driftwood. "Karen's a pretty and petite blue-eyed blonde, so you can see we don't look alike at all."

"Any other siblings?"

Tara shook her head, increasingly involved in what she was creating. As she foraged along the water's edge for flotsam, adding it to her collage, she went on talking about Karen, scarcely aware of how much she was telling Brian in answer to the questions he interjected.

"So Karen's husband dated you before their marriage?" Brian asked finally, and Tara suddenly realized she'd revealed far more than she'd meant to about her family and herself.

She nodded, not looking at him, resolving to keep her mouth shut from now on, feeling he'd taken advantage of her concentration on the collage to probe her past. What business was it of his?

"I admire what you've made," he observed after a moment. "Even if it does remind me of those damn dreams I've been having."

She blinked, not understanding.

"Your seaweed collage." He nodded his head toward her creation. "It gives me the clear sensation of being trapped underwater. You're very talented. Have you done any more found-object sculpturing? I'd be interested in buying one if—"

"No," Tara said hastily, upset by his mention of the dream. "No, I don't do sculptures. Karen's the one with artistic talent. She paints really charming watercolors. I'm just an engineer."

"I can't imagine you creating anything I'd label charming—you're better than that. What you've done on the sand here is almost frightening in its intensity."

What was he saying? His blue eyes were so intent on hers she found it difficult to look away. "But this—the seaweed and flotsam—is just doodling," she protested. "Fooling around."

He scowled at her. "Don't denigrate your talent. If you're not doing something with it, something beside design engineering, I mean, you should be."

Warmth flooded through her as she realized he really meant it and honestly believed she had creative talent. He truly admired the collage at their feet. Gazing down at it, she saw how, without thinking, she'd put the anguish and terror of her seaweed nightmares into what she'd made. While she studied it, a wave pushed in to lick at the edge of the wood.

In a few minutes it would be washed away, like everything left at the ocean's edge. As impermanent as human emotions. Tears stung her eyes, not for the loss of the collage but for what she'd thought she and Brian had once had within their grasp.

This morning had shown her the physical attraction between them was stronger than ever. Was it possible for them to try to regain the elusive bond they'd begun to forge at the Cape?

She shook her head. What folly to think along those lines when he'd made it clear he wasn't interested, not just at the Cape but again this morning.

Tara whirled and began to run along the wet sand, unaware of the water splashing her skirt as the waves flowed around her feet, aware only that she had to get away from Brian before she made a fool of herself again.

Chapter Ten

Brian ran through the edge of the surf after Tara, his anger increasing with every stride. When at last he caught up with her, he halted her flight by grasping her arm, forcing her to stop.

"Is that how you react to everything?" he demanded. "By running away like you did at the Cape?"

"You're hurting me!" she gasped, jerking her arm free.

He glared at her, clenching his fists to control the urge to grab her by the shoulders and shake her until her teeth rattled. Why did this woman have such power to infuriate him?

"Answer the question!" he rasped.

"I don't know what you're talking about." Her face was flushed, her voice breathless, her eyes metallic gold.

"No? Next I suppose you'll tell me you weren't the one who packed up and left in such a hell of a hurry you didn't have time to bother with a note."

Her eyes widened. "Me? *You* left first!"

"That's a lie."

Tara scowled, hands on her hips. "When I woke up you were gone. No note. I went over to your—" She paused and took a deep breath before continuing. "It was close to two hours later when I left. You had plenty of time to come back if you intended to."

Brian blinked, his rage abating as he weighed her words. "Was it that long? I went to get food for our breakfast. I wanted to surprise—" He shook his head. "Forget it."

"Two hours to buy food?" Her voice was cool but the grim lines of her lips had softened.

He spread his hands. "The first couple of stores weren't open. Most of the streets were flooded and then the car stalled. I couldn't get it started. Even if I'd been near a phone I couldn't have called. I didn't know your number or your last name. I had to walk miles in that damn rain, and when I did get to your house it was locked and you were gone."

Tara bit her lip. "You came back?"

He gripped her shoulders. "How could you think I wouldn't?"

"Neither of us wanted involvement." The metallic sheen faded from her beautiful eyes as she spoke, leaving them the green-gold of an evening sea.

Everything about her was beautiful. He longed to crush her in his arms as he had this morning in the office, feel the incomparable thrill of her response. Yet he knew this wasn't the time. Not while there were doubts between them. She'd only run away again. He wanted her, God, how he wanted her, but she was right: he *didn't* want involvement.

His hands fell to his sides. "I would never have left like that," he said softly. "Without even a goodbye."

Tara folded her arms and looked away from him, out to sea. "If I misjudged you, you were wrong about me, too. I didn't leave the Cape until I was certain you were gone."

The ocean breeze teased strands of her hair, making him remember its silky softness against his cheek. He lifted his hand, hesitated and gently let it drop. Wait, he urged himself.

"Yes," he admitted, "we misjudged one another."

"And now?" She kept her face turned seaward, and her voice was so low he scarcely heard her.

He glanced about, seeing a jogger approaching from the north, three teenage boys tossing a Frisbee on the sand behind them and a woman holding a toddler's hand heading for the water. No privacy.

"I think it's time to return to my place," he told her.

She slanted a look his way. "Just to retrieve my shoes," she said. "I must get back to the hotel."

He knew she'd be wary. It was just as well. He needed a couple of hours to sort out what he felt.

"Fine. I'll pick you up there at seven and we'll have dinner."

She faced him at last, eyebrows raised. "With your surgical group?"

"Only the two of us."

"It really isn't necessary to—"

"It's absolutely necessary. We've more or less settled on the instrument design, but we haven't settled anything else." He reached for her hand but she evaded him.

"Race you to your house," she challenged, sprinting away.

He laughed as he sped after her. How like Tara, consistent to the end, doing her damnedest to evade him and the powerful attraction that drew them together.

It was bound to be a losing battle.

* * *

Tara put on the peasant blouse she'd bought in Old Town with the cinnamon twill skirt, wishing she had more of her wardrobe here to choose from. She wanted to look her best this evening because it might well be her last with Brian.

Who was she kidding? He hadn't sounded as though he meant it to be their final time together. And if she said she hoped they'd never meet again after tonight, she'd be a liar.

Could she believe what he'd told her? That he thought she'd left him at the Cape? There was certainly no need to make up the story if it wasn't true. If she'd trusted him more, if she'd waited at Grandma Fallkirk's house longer, what might have happened?

Tara shook her head. The past was over and done with. Neither of them had been trusting then. Would it be any different now?

She leaned toward the mirror to apply a faint brush of golden eyeshadow and stared at her reflection long and hard. If Brian's ex-wife is a glamor girl, as Rita Manning had hinted, what does he see in me? she wondered.

At the Cape, Brian had told her she was beautiful but Rita's words echoed in her head: "plain fare."

Maybe she was building too much on the basis of this dinner invitation. Maybe he just wanted to say goodbye gracefully.

Had she overdone the eyeshadow? Karen would tell her no, but then Karen had been insisting for years that she didn't use makeup effectively. "A dab here, a flick there. Tara, the secret is to use exactly enough. You put on too little, and that's almost as bad as too much."

But when she let Karen make her up, Tara didn't feel like herself, no matter how much better her twin told her she looked.

Tara wiped off some of the eyeshadow and sighed. She'd never be haute couture, with or without makeup.

Brian drove east in the soft warmth of the evening, on and on until Tara began to wonder where they were headed. Not that she cared. She was hypnotized by the motion of the car and the lights ahead of them on the freeway, but most of all by his presence next to her. They were together without the fog of misunderstanding that had shrouded them both with anger and hurt ever since their parting on the Cape.

Anything might happen if she dared to let it. But could she risk being hurt again?

"Where are we?" she asked.

"Passing through La Mesa. That hill of lights ahead to your right is Mount Helix. The restaurant's just beyond, according to Rick's directions. I've never been there." He lifted one hand from the steering wheel, and his forefinger brushed across the back of her hand. "I wanted to take you to a place I hadn't been before—where neither of us has ever been before."

She nodded. He sought a new beginning, untainted by any memory. But was it possible? Perhaps, since anything seemed possible with this man whose lightest touch triggered her need for him.

The small restaurant was uncrowded, possibly because it was a Sunday night. That much she noticed. Otherwise, her attention focused entirely on Brian.

"Night after night I've dreamed of you," he told her as they sipped wine. "Dreamed of trying to find you but because I was tangled in seaweed—"

"No!" she cried, raising her hands as though to ward off a blow. "I don't want to hear."

His surprise gave way to an understanding smile. "I forgot you're sensitive about dreams and dreaming." His hand covered hers, warm and comforting. "I won't mention it again."

Tara tried to return his smile, tried to dismiss the frightening surmise that they'd dreamed together again. No, she was seeing dragons where none existed.

"Tangled in seaweed?" She did her best to speak lightly. "Sounds Freudian—tentacles of the past and all that."

"Like an octopus?" He shrugged, removing his hand from hers. "You may be right."

I've hit a sensitive spot, Tara realized. Cover it over or dig it up? she asked herself. She'd nattered on about her life earlier today but she knew almost nothing of his. Was he referring to his broken marriage? If they were really starting over, the less concealed between them, the better.

"Divorce is a painful process," she commented, leaving the choice to him of whether to pass or discuss it.

"California calls it a dissolution. Mine was messy by any name."

She waited, wondering if he meant to go on. His eyes no longer sought hers. He stared beyond her as though seeing into the past.

"Ursula wanted freedom. I was more than willing to agree to that. She also wanted everything else." His voice was bleak.

After a long silence Tara said, "Rita Manning mentioned how beautiful Ursula was." As soon as the words were out she regretted them. What did it matter how Ursula looked?

"Elegant's a better word. When she discovered I wasn't as malleable as she'd thought, she decided to discard me and content herself with keeping all the assets." He made a brushing away motion with his hand. "I wouldn't have fought her if I hadn't known by then just what lay hidden under that elegant gloss of hers."

Brian's eyes met hers, and Tara saw shreds of bewilderment amid the harshness of remembered anger. "I think I could have understood an affair," he went on, "because of an overwhelming attraction to one other man. Maybe not, but I think so. It wasn't that way with her. Ursula collected men. Any man that took her fancy for the moment." He shook his head. "She didn't seem to have *any* deep feelings. Not for me or for anyone else."

He sighed. "I told my lawyer I wanted to be fair. He insisted she was legally entitled to only half the assets, and I'd be a fool to agree to more than that, especially in view of the fact she still pulled down high fees as a model. So her lawyer and Harvey—he's my lawyer—fought for nine months until I couldn't stand being tied to her any longer. I told Harvey to get it over with as fast as he could, even if he had to give her everything. When the dust settled, I took a short leave from the group."

"To go to Cape Cod," she said softly.

He nodded. "I grew up in Connecticut and we spent summers at the Cape. I wanted—" He broke off, smiling a little. "The last thing in the world I expected was to meet you."

The last thing in the world you wanted, she thought. The last thing either of us wanted at the time.

"Do you suppose Larry misses us?" she asked, hoping to lighten the somber mood that gripped them both.

Brian laughed. "Larry's loyalty fixes on the hand that feeds him, like any proper gull."

All through the meal, though the food was good and Tara did her best to recover the aura of expectation she'd brought into the restaurant with her, the residue of Brian's bitterness tainted the feeling between them.

"I don't want to get into that mess again," he'd said this morning in his office after he'd thrust her away. Now she thought she knew what he meant.

How could he be ready for a new commitment? How could their fragile bond grow and flourish with his past haunting him?

When they returned to the car, Brian didn't follow the signs to the freeway, driving instead along narrow residential streets that twisted as they climbed. The higher they went, the larger the homes became and the more hidden behind shrubbery and trees. At last the road topped the final rise and Brian pulled off into a small parking area.

"We're at the summit of Mount Helix," he told her, easing from the car. He went around and opened her door.

Tara stood in the warm darkness, smelling the sharp odor of eucalyptus leaves and staring down at the lights of San Diego spread below her. At her side, Brian pointed out the brilliant arc of the Coronado Bridge. She watched the blinking lights of a jet coming in to land at Lindbergh Field and thought she ought to be on the next plane taking off. She should leave San Diego before it was too late.

As if reading her mind, Brian said, "I won't have much free time for the next two days. I'm off Wednesday. Stay until then."

Instead of answering she moved away from him, but he followed, guiding her along a path until, to her surprise, they reached a small outdoor amphitheater.

"They hold Easter sunrise services here," he told her, pulling her down to sit next to him on one of the benchlike tiers. He waved an arm at the dark mass of mountains to the east. "When the sun rises above those hills in the misty chill of the morning and the choir's singing—" He stopped. "I can't describe the feeling. It's like a fresh beginning, like the world's reborn. Some Easter I'd like to share the experience with you."

Tara sighed. Would he even remember her by next Easter?

His fingers touched her cheek, gently traced the outline of her lips. She shivered under the onslaught of need his tender caress evoked within her.

"Beautiful Tara," he whispered. "Don't be afraid."

The only thing she feared was losing control of herself. She'd ask him to take her back to the hotel before anything more happened.

"Brian, I'd like—"

His lips closed over hers, shutting off her words. He gathered her to him, one hand entwined in her hair, and she nestled against him feeling she'd come home. Though his kiss was leisurely and undemanding, she sensed the firm rein he held on himself, as though he, too, feared losing control.

"You know I want you," he murmured into her ear, the words and his warm breath sending delicious tremors down her spine. "But you can't know how much."

Could his need match her own? She'd never dreamed it was possible to desire a man so much. Only one particular man—no other would ever do.

So she'd admitted it to herself at last. Brian or no one.

"We need to have time together," he said softly before his tongue flicked along her lips. "Give me the time, Tara."

"I don't know. . . ." Her words were a moan.

"You know. You show me how you feel when I hold you. Come home with me tonight. Stay with me."

His lips, warm against her throat, traveled down, down to the tender skin above her breasts. Desire rayed through her, paralyzing her will.

"I can't think when you kiss me," she gasped.

He raised his face to look at her. In the pale light of the rising half moon his eyes were dark and unreadable, but his harsh breathing gave away his need.

The faint odor of night-blooming jasmine mingled with the scent of his skin. Her tongue still tasted the winelike flavor of his mouth. Under her fingers his hair was curly silk. She longed to blend with him here and now, to stay with him forever.

Except it wouldn't be forever.

Tara eased from his embrace, putting her palms against his chest to hold him away. "You said you wanted to sleep on the instrument design before you decided. I need to sleep on this. Alone."

Under her hands she felt the slowing of his heartbeat as he regained control. "I plan to show the design to Rick and one of the other surgeons in the group and see what they think," he told her, covering her hands with his. "It'll be Wednesday before I have an answer for you. I'll rephrase my request. What if you spend the time until then at my place on the beach? You can have the guest room and do whatever you want. No pressure, I promise. You can set the rules."

She thought of the beach and of sharing the house with Brian and knew she'd enjoy it. But is that all they'd share? She might trust him to keep his promise but what about trusting herself?

If she left the hotel for Brian's bungalow she'd be setting herself up for what was certain to happen when they were alone together. No rule she could ever make would keep her out of his arms.

It seemed clear Brian wasn't ready for any prolonged involvement. He offered no commitment beyond Wednesday. Wednesday would come and go, and it would all be over and she'd go back to Sacramento. Alone.

Short flings had never held any appeal for her, and they still didn't. Even if she were willing to indulge in one, the intensity of her attraction to Brian made her fear what might be a fling to him would be much more to her. Wasn't it foolish to ask to be hurt? The sensible solution was to go back to Sacramento the first thing in the morning and avoid any added pain.

She slid her hands free. "Take me back to the hotel, Brian," she said, her voice not quite steady. "If I decide to come to the bungalow you'll find me there tomorrow. If not, you can call me about the design on Wednesday. In Sacramento."

Chapter Eleven

Tara found the key where Brian had told her to look—under the stone tiki on the porch. The weight of the carved Hawaiian god scowling eternally toward the Pacific resisted her attempt to remove the key, and she felt its angry face expressed disapproval of her coming to the bungalow.

She hadn't meant to do this. She'd checked out of the Town and Country this morning, fully intending to drive to the airport and catch a flight to Sacramento. Why hadn't she?

Tara shook her head as she fitted the key into the front door lock. She could rationalize her behavior and say she stayed to acquire a final okay on the design before reporting back to D.D. However, she didn't believe that for a minute.

Was it because she sought to end this disturbing relationship with Brian once and for all? She didn't believe that either because coming here would end nothing for her.

Okay, so she was here to see what would happen.

Ha! It didn't take her degree in engineering to be pretty darn sure what inevitably must happen.

Why, then?

Because she couldn't help herself, because in her heart of hearts she was an unreasoning optimist and believed, against all odds, in happy endings. Maybe that explained part of it.

You'd do better to heed the tiki's warning scowl, she told herself. You don't belong here.

She'd paid little attention to the guest room yesterday. Now she saw it was sparsely furnished, containing one small chest of drawers, a single bed and a nightstand. With walls painted fog gray and curtains to match, the effect was anything but cheerful. The lone picture on the wall was a print of an old engraving—a mezzotint of a melancholy woman in Grecian draperies gazing mournfully at her reflection in a pool of water.

Tara remembered the oil painting of the deserted building in the master bedroom and wondered if Brian had *any* upbeat pictures in the bungalow. She thought of the bright tin Mexican sunbursts she'd seen in Old Town and wished she had one to hang on the wall here. Strange, when she'd been in the house yesterday with Brian she hadn't noticed the gloominess of the interior.

It didn't matter. She was looking forward to spending the day on the beach in the sun. What time would Brian get home this evening? She'd have to wait and see.

After six, Tara, newly changed from her maillot and beach robe into jeans and a T-shirt, turned on the TV to the national evening news. Curling her feet under her as she made herself comfortable on the settee, she grimaced in disappointment when she saw she'd missed most of the newscast, and the program was about to end with a special report.

"...on Steven Palomar," the newsman finished. Tara sat up and leaned forward.

A voice she recognized as Pete Ulrich's smooth baritone detailed Palomar's life as clips of the singer's early career flicked onto the screen. The concise report ended with the tape of the interview with Brian.

Tara smiled at his handsome and assured image, only to gasp when her face suddenly and briefly appeared before the camera cut back to Brian. She sat staring at the screen after the report ended and the local news came on, still not quite believing she'd actually seen herself on national TV. She'd been so startled she wasn't sure what he'd said about her besides her name.

She could hardly wait to ask Brian if he'd seen the program.

By eight o'clock she gave up planning to eat with him and fixed herself an egg salad sandwich. By ten o'clock she could barely keep her eyes open: she'd not only had a late night on Sunday but hadn't slept well. She crawled into bed in the cheerless guest room at eleven, thinking she'd stay awake and listen for Brian.

The ringing of a phone woke her. Tara groped toward the nightstand, her searching fingers finding only a lamp. She roused completely, realizing where she was. Brian's phones were in the living room and master bedroom. She turned on her lamp and sat up.

The ringing stopped and she heard the murmur of Brian's voice. She checked her watch. Two-thirty. How long had he been home? She'd just about decided to get up when she heard him call to her.

"Tara?"

A moment later he stood in the doorway to her room wearing gray sweatpants, his torso bare. As she met his eyes her heart skipped a beat and then started up faster than ever.

Why had she wondered about coming here when the answer was so simple? She'd come because this was where he was.

Brian strode to the bed and sat on the edge, reaching for her. She flowed into his arms.

"You were sleeping so peacefully I didn't want to wake you," he said into her ear.

"When did you get home?"

"About an hour ago. Now I have to go out again."

"The phone call?"

"Yeah. Motorcycle accident. An eighteen-year-old with multiple trauma and massive internal bleeding." His hand smoothed her hair before his fingers gently turned her face toward him and his lips met hers.

His kiss held a promise that tingled through her body, awakening every cell to anticipatory eagerness. She sighed when he pulled reluctantly away.

"To think I once believed I'd rather be doing surgery than anything else in the world." He smiled ruefully before leaning forward to kiss the tip of her nose. "You don't know how happy you've made me by being here. See you for breakfast about six. I hope."

Tara dozed off and on until five, then rose, showered and dressed in jeans and green sweatshirt. She had coffee ready by six but six o'clock came and went. At seven-thirty Brian called her.

"Tara? I'm hung up at the hospital. I'll have to go on to the office from here. If I'm really lucky I might make it home for lunch. Otherwise, I'll see you around seven tonight." He hesitated, then added, "Please stay."

Was he always this busy? she wondered after hanging up. The hours he worked seemed excessive to her. Did all the doctors in the group work this many hours a week? Rita

Manning had said something about Brian working too hard and she certainly seemed to be right.

Tara enjoyed the morning's warm sunshine on the beach, but by noon the fog rolled in to blanket the coast in a damp and chilly gray mist, causing her to retreat to the bungalow. Brian didn't arrive for lunch, and he wasn't home by seven. When the phone rang at eight she expected to hear his voice and steeled herself to another delay. To her shock it was Abbott.

"My God, Tara, you've really upset us." His tone was accusing.

"Is Karen all right?" she demanded immediately, not quite taking in his words in her anxiety over her sister.

"She hasn't had the baby if that's what you mean, but you could have had the courtesy to let us know where you were and what you were doing. Karen is beside herself."

"What I'm doing?" she repeated. "I don't understand."

"Do you have any idea how much trouble I've had reaching you? I've been trying since last night."

"Look, Abbott, get to the point. If it isn't Karen, why *did* you call me here?"

"Did you think we wouldn't see the newscast?"

Tara frowned. "What on earth does that have to do with anything?"

"'Tara Reed, Dr. Shute's surgical assistant'—does it ring a bell? You might have mentioned you were moving to San Diego and changing jobs. You know how upset Karen gets when she thinks you're hiding things from her."

Tara nodded, remembering Karen's avid interest in her life. "I haven't hidden anything," she said wearily. "I'm still working for Delta Two. Dr. Shute's a client I'm designing a surgical instrument for, and that's why I'm in San Diego. You could have called the office you know."

"That's not what the newsman said. If you're telling the truth it seems odd they'd bother to include you in their program."

"For heaven's sake, Abbott, you know how the media shape words and circumstances to suit themselves. I just happened to be in Brian's office when Pete Ulrich came by to tape the interview."

"Brian." Abbott's tone was triumphant.

"Is it a crime to call a doctor by his first name?"

"Karen feels strongly you're up to something and, much as I hate to go along with her unsubstantiated whims, this time I agree with her. After all, you *are* staying at his house."

"What business is that of yours? Or Karen's?"

"It's my business when you make her go to pieces like this. Especially now. She insists on talking to you."

"Tara?" Karen sounded both tearful and annoyed. Hearing her twin's voice made Tara temporarily forget the reason for the call.

"Oh, Karen, I'm so glad to be talking to you. How are you? Is the pregnancy okay? When—?"

"I'm all right, I suppose, no thanks to you. I can't imagine why you had to be so secretive. This affair with Dr. Shute must have been going on before you visited here. I told you I suspected you were hiding something then, and now I know you were. Just like Leda Umak said—a man. A house and a man. You're living with him. In San Diego. How long has it been going on?"

Tara tried to wipe away the resentment that always surfaced when Karen pried into the intimate details of her life. If her sister ever needed to be humored, now was the time.

"I'm at his house, yes, but I'm not living with him. I just met the man." Well, not exactly, she admitted to herself, but somehow she couldn't tell Karen about the time in Chatham.

"That's not a bit like you, Tara, not with someone you just met."

"Since you seem to think I need a chaperon would you believe a wife and three kids are here in the house with me?" Tara tried to conceal her irritation with lightness. "An aged grandmother? Two aunts?"

"Not for a minute. Especially since Abbott found out that Dr. Shute's divorced."

Tara exploded. "My God, you've been conducting a real investigation."

"I forgave you for the scene with Abbott in March because I just came to understand you haven't gotten over him yet and you couldn't help yourself." Karen's voice was unbelievably smug. "I've been worried about you ever since, and now I find you've impetuously involved yourself with a man you hardly know."

Tara swallowed hard and counted to ten before she could get any words out. "Like you, I'm twenty-seven years old," she finally managed to say in such an even tone she hardly recognized it as hers. "Wouldn't you say that's mature enough to take care of myself? As for Abbott—"

"But you're such a child about men," Karen protested. "You always have been. It's just like you to try to deny how you feel by throwing everything away for someone who isn't worth it."

"I'm still working for Delta Two." Tara's voice was ominously quiet. "I'm here in San Diego as part of an assignment. Where I choose to stay while I'm here is nobody's business but mine. And for your information *and* Abbott's, any torch I carried for him was doused long ago."

Karen's sigh hissed in Tara's ears. "You never would face up to things," she observed sadly.

With great effort Tara held back her angry words. No. Karen mustn't be upset. "I have to go," she told her twin. "Stay well. Goodbye."

As she put the phone down she was startled by Brian's voice.

"Your sister?"

She whirled to see him standing in the doorway. How long had he been there? How much had he overheard?

"They—she and her husband—saw me on TV and called," Tara explained.

"The husband being your old flame Abbott?"

Good grief, she had run off at the mouth Sunday, hadn't she?

"I knew Abbott before he married Karen, yes." Her tone was warningly stiff. "They were startled by Pete Ulrich's mention of me as your assistant."

"Startled enough to call you here?"

She nodded. "I was surprised they managed to find me."

"I am, too, since I have an unlisted number. But then Abbott's a lawyer, isn't he?" His tone indicated he considered lawyers capable of violating any privacy.

Her face flamed. "I'm sorry if my being here has inconvenienced you. It was a mistake all the way around to come here."

Brian stared at Tara's flushed and angry face, trying to deny the jealousy twisting his guts when he thought of another man, of this Abbott who'd married her twin, touching Tara, holding her in his arms, making love to her.

He had no right to feel that way and, besides, jealousy was a dead end.

"They've been kidding me about that damn TV program all day," he said, hoping to avoid conflict.

"How's Mr. Palomar doing?" she asked, her voice cool.

"Improving. Against the odds. He's a tough old bird." He dropped onto the settee, pulling off his shoes and socks before sliding down on his spine and stretching out his legs. "Sorry if I snapped at you. I tend to be mean when I'm tired."

She took a deep breath and let it out slowly, then smiled lightly. "Would you like a cup of coffee? Something to eat?"

He shook his head. "Sit down." He gestured to the settee, but she chose the chair across from him.

He wanted to touch her. He wanted to feel her softness against him, to hold her quietly, to close his eyes and know she was with him, that she'd be there when he woke up. He searched for the right words.

"Karen tells me I'm making a mistake being here with you," she said.

"Is it her business what you do?"

"She's always thought so."

"And do you ask 'how high' when she says 'jump'?"

Tara sat straighter in the chair. "I lead my own life. Karen *is* almost due to deliver, though, so I don't want to upset her any more than I have to."

Brian felt tenseness contracting his muscles. Don't react, he warned himself. Stay cool, relax. Instead he heard himself saying, "Is that why you tried so hard to convince her you're no longer carrying a torch for her husband?"

Her eyes widened. "You were the one who mentioned privacy. Did anyone ask you to interpret what I said to my sister on the phone?"

"From what you told me on the beach Sunday—of your own free will, I might add—I got the impression you don't make many moves without consulting your sister."

"You don't understand Karen. She needs to feel wanted."

He shrugged. "Sounds unhealthy to me. She's married, isn't she? Doesn't good old Abbott want her?"

Tara glared at him and he raised a hand. "Okay, so I'm telling you what you don't want to hear," he said. "The truth is usually unwelcome, but my advice is to do what you want and to hell with Karen and Abbott."

She sat so stiffly her spine could have been a surgical steel rod. "Apparently you consider your life so well organized you feel free to advise me about mine. From the outside looking in, I'd say you could use some counseling yourself."

He bristled. "About what?"

She waved a hand at him. "Look at you!"

"What the hell's wrong with me?" he growled.

"You're obviously exhausted. You haven't had more than two hours' sleep, if that, since Sunday night. If this is the normal work schedule for your surgical group, then something's wrong with the scheduling."

He scowled at her. "I do work longer hours than I'm scheduled for," he admitted finally. "So what?"

She nodded as though she'd anticipated his answer. "Dr. Manning told his wife you were working too hard."

"If I am it's my own business!"

She looked at him in mock surprise. "So you can only give advice, you can't take it."

He straightened in his seat, feeling his anger spiral out of control. "Damn it, Tara—"

Her tight, angry laughter cut off his words. "Is it true, Doctor, that you're using the demands of your practice, keeping yourself busy sixteen hours a day, to avoid the unresolved problems of your private life?"

Brian sprang up from the settee and yanked her off the chair, gripping her by the shoulders. "That's enough!"

She stared at him, her eyes defiant. Under his hands her bones felt as fragile as the wing bones of a gull. Her breasts heaved with her fury, almost touching his chest and a shard of memory pierced him: the Cape and caressing those breasts, gloriously bared for him. Her scent, fragrant as a flower, filled his nostrils, triggering a massive wave of desire that swamped his rage.

He pulled her savagely into his arms and kissed her with all the pent-up passion he'd stored since that March. She stiffened, struggling, and he murmured her name against her unyielding lips.

"Tara," he urged hoarsely, "let's not fight."

Her lips softened under his, opened to his seeking tongue and he tasted what he'd hungered for, the incomparable sweetness of her mouth. The tenseness that had plagued him for most of the day uncoiled when she pressed close to him of her own accord and her fingers stroked the hair at his nape.

He closed his eyes, deepening the kiss, yearning to merge with her completely, in all ways, never separating, like he'd seen one-celled organisms do under the microscope. Together they were whole.

As his lips gentled on hers Tara felt a radiant bridge begin to form, tenuous as the mist, a linkage she'd wondered if she'd imagined before and hadn't expected to feel again. The fragile bond showed her his need as clearly as though it was her own. In a way it *was* her own, mirrored.

She was too caught up in the magic of his embrace to fear the mystery binding them together. Never had she been so aroused, and never had she felt desire so acute she thought she might die if it wasn't satisfied. Clothes were a burden she resented; they separated her from Brian. She slid her hands under his shirt to caress his warm skin, to draw him closer.

His fingers slipped under her sweatshirt and stroked the sides of her breasts, making her breath catch. She had to feel his touch all over; she couldn't bear to wait. As though reading her mind, he eased her away from him, grasped the bottom of her sweatshirt and in one rapid motion pulled it over her head.

He touched her bared breasts with his fingertips and she moaned with needful pleasure. His gaze swept from her breasts to her face, and when she looked into his eyes she saw the wonder and desire in their smoky blue depths.

He tore off his shirt and pulled her against him, her breasts to his chest, the curl of his chest hair delicious agony as it rubbed against her passion-peaked nipples. His hands cupped her buttocks, thrusting her against his arousal as his lips closed over hers in a kiss that left her helpless with desire.

Brian swept her into his arms, strode into the hall and entered the master bedroom where he eased her onto the waterbed before flicking on the lamp on the nightstand, and stripping away the rest of his clothes. When he stood naked before her, the beauty of his body and the intensity of his need took her breath away.

Deftly he removed her jeans and panties, looking down at her for a long, throbbing moment. His mouth shaped a word.

"Lovely."

She understood it as clearly as if he'd spoken aloud. They had no need to speak. The link between them told her he found her beautiful, just as he knew she thought he was. She was urgently aware of the wild need bringing them together and both were eager to fulfill that demanding desire.

Nothing in the world but Brian had any meaning for her. She held out her arms and he came to her, his body settling lightly, teasingly, atop hers as he rested his weight on his elbows. She closed her eyes to savor the indescribable feel of him as they lay skin to skin.

"Look at me," he whispered.

Tara opened her eyes and met the brilliant blue of his. Everything she'd ever wanted, ever dreamed of, glowed there in his eyes. We belong together, they told her. Forever.

He shifted to lie beside her, taking her into his arms. His kisses trailed down from her lips along her throat to her breasts. His hands stroked the curves of her hips, the softness of her thighs. He journeyed with her beyond thought, and they became beings of pure sensation, rising on a great wave of rapturous wonder evoked by the meeting of lips and flesh.

Beneath her the water of the bed shifted like a caress, accommodating each movement. The hot scent of their mingled desire swirled in her head. She tasted his mouth, the intoxicating salt flavor of his skin and knew she'd never have enough of him.

He was inside her, she surrounded him, they were part of each other. They rocked to the sea's eternal rhythm, the sea of life. They celebrated life by joining together. He would take her, and she would take him where neither could go alone, to the golden and shining place that belonged only to them.

The wave crested, foamed into shattering beauty and slowly, slowly subsided, carrying them to a shared peace.

Before she slept, Tara, curled beside Brian, his arm holding her against his side, realized that until now she'd never known the true meaning of making love.

Chapter Twelve

Sand gritted underfoot as Tara crept along the deserted corridor. Parts of the roof had crumbled away and fog slipped in like a temporary guest. She passed room after room. All the doors were missing. All the rooms were empty.

She knew what building she was in—a ruined, deserted hotel, the hotel in the painting above Brian's bed. Why was she here? Where was Brian?

Sand lay in drifts inside the rooms where windows had shattered. Tendrils of fog shaped like ghosts stretched out gray fingers to keep her from finding Brian. She called his name, but the fog swallowed the sound of her voice.

Panicky, she began to run, but the ubiquitous sand made the tiles slippery underfoot and she was forced to slow her pace to keep from falling. If only she could find a room with a door. Somewhere behind a golden door, Brian waited. But this nightmare hotel had no doors, and the corridor was endless.

"Brian!" she cried. His name echoed desolately back at her.

Grief twisted her heart. She'd lost him. She was doomed to wander alone forever in this nowhere place, searching but never finding.

A sudden gust of wind swept along the corridor spiraling the fog into a gray funnel that blotted out the light, covering her, covering everything in darkness. . . .

Tara woke with a start, her pulse racing from fright. She sat up and hugged herself.

"A nightmare," she whispered. "Just a nightmare." But the dream shreds clung to her, reminding her of her childhood dream of the black whirlwind sweeping away her brother Mike and how, soon after, death had truly taken Mike away forever.

No, she thought, this isn't the same. Nothing will happen to Brian, I've had a bad dream, that's all. She reached for the warm reassurance of Brian's body.

He wasn't in the bed. Prickles of fear raised the hair on the back of her neck.

Stop it! she urged herself silently. You're all worked up over nothing. The dream came from that horrible picture over the bed—you didn't like it to begin with.

Tara slid from the bed and, without bothering to turn on the light, padded to the door and looked along the hall toward the bathroom. Brian wasn't there. She ducked into the guest room and pulled on her robe, then walked into the living room where moonlight flooded in through open curtains. No Brian. He wasn't in the kitchen, either.

Back in the living room, she noticed for the first time that the front door was ajar. Frowning, she asked herself if she'd missed hearing the phone and decided she hadn't. She ventured outside onto the porch to see if Brian's car was gone.

A cool ocean breeze stroked her hair. The fog had dissipated entirely; moonlight shimmered on the water and outlined two figures embracing on the beach in front of the cottage. She hurried down the steps. Brian's car sat next to hers and a third car was parked in back of his, a Mercedes. She glanced toward the couple standing near the waterline, saw they were no longer in each other's arms and caught her breath.

The man's silhouette looked like Brian's!

Tara stood on the slatted wooden platform at the foot of the stairs, staring at the man, trying to make up her mind whether it really was Brian or not. The grit of sand under her bare feet reminded her of her nightmare and she decided she *had* to know, one way or the other.

"Brian?" Her voice was tentative.

He turned and saw her. "Tara!"

Numbly, she watched him urge the woman—who'd been in his arms only moments before—toward the house.

"I didn't want to disturb you," Brian said when he reached the platform. He wore nothing but a pair of jeans.

Tara could only stare at him.

"This is Ursula," he added, his hand on the woman's arm. "Ursula, Tara Reed."

Tara couldn't find words to acknowledge the introduction. In the pale moonlight she tried to assess Ursula. Red hair? The silvery glow showed a high-cheekboned face with eyes exotically slanted. Ursula's wraparound dress—silk jersey?—emphasized a slender, well-proportioned figure.

"Charmed." Ursula's voice was low and husky, and her quick glance took in and dismissed Tara. She clung to Brian's arm, gazing up at him. "Promise me you'll come by before you go to the office," she begged him.

"I promise."

Ursula let go of Brian and started toward the cars. She stumbled and he caught her in his arms.

Holding her, he said, "Maybe I should drive you home."

"I'll make it by myself. I—I feel a little better now." Ursula's husky voice quavered. "You *will* stay with me, won't you?"

"You know I will." The tender reassurance in Brian's voice and the way he patted his ex-wife's shoulder knotted Tara's stomach. "I'll take care of you, Ursula."

He led her to the Mercedes and helped her into the driver's seat. "I'll follow you to make sure you get home okay," Tara heard him say to Ursula.

Brian watched the Mercedes back out of the drive before turning and striding to Tara. "Sorry you were disturbed," he said. "Go back to bed. I'll be along in twenty minutes or less." He kissed her lightly and sprinted to his car.

She stared after him in disbelief. Go back to bed and wait for him? Despite what had just happened? How insensitive could a man be?

It gave Tara little satisfaction to slam the front door when she reentered the house. The door made a poor substitute for Brian. The digital clock in the master bedroom flashed three-thirty as she collected her clothes and brought them into the guest room. By quarter to four she'd showered and dressed, and by the time she heard Brian's car pull into the drive she was sipping freshly brewed coffee at the round glass-topped table in the kitchen.

Forty minutes. She tapped a forefinger on the glass top of the table as she waited for him.

"Good idea," Brian said, smiling as he came into the kitchen and unhooked a mug from the tree. "I could use a cup of coffee."

She couldn't deny he was good to look at, his blue eyes bright, one strand of auburn hair slanting over his forehead. Couldn't deny, either, the physical thrill that shot through her at the sight of him standing over her, naked to the waist, his jeans stretched tightly over the rest of him.

What was Grandma Fallkirk's old saying? Handsome is as handsome does? Under the circumstances, Brian didn't make the grade.

"Is Ursula's hair the same color as yours?" she asked him.

He blinked, then said, "Lighter. Red, though."

"I've heard redheads always stick together."

Brian frowned. "Look, Tara, she was hysterical when she got here. I took her outside because I didn't want you to wake up. I didn't see any need to involve you in her problems."

"Her problems?"

"Ursula was told she needs to have surgery and she fell apart. Eventually she pulled herself together enough to rush over here to tell me about it."

"Even though you're no longer married and, according to you, the divorce was far from amicable."

"She knew I'd help her. After all, I *am* a surgeon."

"Yes, of course." Tara did her best to quash the angry jealousy that soured her stomach, to try to imagine how frightened Ursula must be at having to face being cut open.

"Well, as you saw, I was able to calm her down."

I'll be reasonable about this, Tara told herself. Certainly I'd be scared if I were Ursula.

"Is her condition serious?" she asked.

"We won't know for sure until the pathologist gets a look at the tissue."

He'd held Ursula in his arms on the beach to comfort her. He was gentle and tender with her because he knew she needed that from him. Tara swallowed a sip of coffee, thinking she ought to admire Brian for his willingness to let bygones be bygones when his ex-wife came to him in need. Tell him so, she urged herself.

Instead, she said, "I hate that picture over your bed!"

He raised his eyebrows. "I've never paid much attention to it. An old barn or something?"

"Didn't you choose the painting?"

"No. Very little in this house belongs to me. Leon's in my group, and he rented it to me furnished when he left for six months study at Massachusetts General because he knew I needed a place to stay."

"The furnishings aren't yours, then."

Brian shrugged. "Ursula got the house and everything in it as part of the settlement."

"Up on a cliff somewhere," Tara said, putting out her arms to either side. "Soaring. The house I mean. The one that used to be yours."

He nodded. "I like it better here on the beach. I don't miss living there."

But how much do you miss Ursula? Tara wondered. Was there more to it than a doctor's reassurance when you held her? More than a friend's?

"She's very attractive," Tara said.

"I take it we're back to Ursula? She's a model; being attractive is her profession."

Tara pictured the elegant woman she'd seen an hour ago, exquisitely dressed, perfectly groomed despite what Brian had called her hysteria. She glanced at her own jeans and shapeless green sweatshirt and sighed inwardly.

"What do clothes matter?" he asked as though he knew what she was thinking. "Clothes don't make a woman beautiful."

They sure help, Tara said silently. She wished she could feel more charitable toward Ursula but she couldn't erase the image of her on the beach in Brian's arms.

"When is she having the surgery?" Tara asked.

"As soon as it can be scheduled. About a week from now, probably. She'll need a lot of support in the meantime."

"Then it's lucky I'm leaving tomorrow, isn't it?" She couldn't disguise the bleakness in her voice.

He leaned toward her. "Tara, this has nothing to do with us." He reached for her hand, but she picked up her mug to avoid his touch. The coffee was cold and bitter to her tongue.

"I told you it didn't matter!" The harshness of his voice startled her. He pulled the mug from her grasp and slammed it onto the table so hard she winced, fearing the glass top would crack.

Brian reached for her, forcing her to her feet as he rose. He put his hands on her shoulders, and she tried not to look into his eyes. The light from the overhead globe turned his chest hair to gold. She could smell his sharp masculine scent and willed herself not to be aroused.

"Tara." Her name on his lips was compelling.

She took a deep breath and raised her eyes to his face. His gaze was stormy, his mouth set.

"Would you expect me to turn Ursula away?" he demanded.

She shook her head, his reasonableness making her feel spiteful and mean. And annoyed because he made her feel that way.

Brian put his palm against her cheek. "I'll admit her timing was lousy. It wasn't her fault, though."

His touch ameliorated her annoyance. Tara longed to turn her head so her lips would brush his palm, longed to have his arms close around her, longed for his kiss that would banish everything except the two of them.

"No," she said, her tone conciliatory, "Ursula couldn't have known I was here."

"As a matter of fact, she did. Rita Manning told her."

Tara's eyes widened. "How did Rita know?"

"She noticed a strange car parked in my drive and was overcome with curiosity, so she parked and walked down to the beach. She saw you sunning yourself in front of the house."

Tara bit her lip. The privacy she thought they'd had was an illusion. Not only Karen and Abbott knew, but probably Brian's entire group knew. Plus Ursula. It shouldn't matter, but it did.

Another thought struck her. If Ursula was aware Tara was staying at the bungalow, did that partly explain why she'd arrived at Brian's door after midnight? It was hard to believe Ursula didn't have his unlisted number. Wouldn't it have been more natural to call him? Ursula was undoubtedly genuinely upset about her surgery, but was she also playing dog in the manger?

What's the matter with me? Tara asked herself. I'm reacting like a jealous shrew, questioning poor Ursula's motives. Except it was difficult to think of that lovely, chic woman as poor Ursula.

Brian cupped Tara's face in his hands, his eyes dark with desire. "Rita's nosiness doesn't matter. Nothing matters when we're together."

He bent his head to kiss her softly, insistently, and her hot surge of response burned away all thought of Ursula. She swayed toward him, her body needing the comfort of his. His arms locked around her, holding her close. She pressed against him, wanting to be even closer, wanting to be a part of him.

He tasted of coffee and of himself, an erotic mix. His skin was warm under her stroking hands, and he groaned when she eased the tips of her fingers under the waistband of his jeans.

"If you'd gone back to bed like I asked you to, we'd be there now," he said hoarsely, his hands cupping her buttocks to mold her to his hardness.

A chill filtered into her desire-dazed mind. That damn picture hung over his bed, the nightmare picture. She couldn't return to that bed.

She could tell him she preferred the guest room bed, couldn't she? Tara waited to be submerged again in the swell of passion swirling between them but, for her, the spell was broken.

She tried to pull away. He tightened his grip.

"No," she said unevenly. "Brian, please—"

He let her go. "What's wrong?"

How could she explain about the picture, how remembering her nightmare had changed the way she felt?

"Nothing's wrong," she said, turning from him.

Brian took a deep breath and let it out slowly, doing his best to hang onto what patience he had left—damn little by now. He knew some of his irritation came from lack of sleep. He wished Rick had told him about Ursula's problem. If I'd known ahead of time I could have kept her calm, Brian thought. Besides it would have prevented tonight's confrontation. What a hell of a time for Ursula to show up. It wasn't her fault, however.

Why couldn't Tara understand? Why did she draw away from him?

He badly needed to hold her, to lose himself in the magic between them. Earlier it had been like the Cape all over again. Only Tara had ever made him feel an uncanny sharing of that intense passion.

He watched Tara walk into the living room, growing angrier with every step she took away from him. He strode after her.

"How soon will you be able to let me know about the design?" she asked, facing him with her arms folded across her breasts.

"Damn it, I don't want to discuss the design now," he growled.

"I do." Her eyes had taken on that metallic gold sheen he was learning to distrust.

He stopped himself from reaching for her, aware he'd better not touch her in his present mood. Instead he kicked the stool by the settee and tumbled it over. Tara glanced from the overturned stool to him, her disapproving frown clearly telling him she thought he was being childish.

His control snapped. "My diagnosis is jealousy," he said.

"Jealousy?" Her voice rose. "I'm not jealous!"

"Doesn't the lady protest a bit too loudly? If you had any sense you'd know there's little reason to be. But, no, you have to get on your high horse—you spend a lot of time up there, it seems to me."

"You—you insensitive clod!" she cried. "I thought Abbott was bad but you're the most arrogant male I've ever met!"

He felt his blood was actually coming to a boil in his veins when he heard her compare him to Abbott. He didn't want that name mentioned, couldn't bear to think of her with any other man.

He glared at her, clenching and unclenching his fists, and she took a step back. Brian gritted his teeth and strode toward her, past her, and out the front door into the predawn grayness.

Chapter Thirteen

Tara caught a 7:00 a.m. flight to Sacramento. Brian hadn't returned to the bungalow by the time she was ready to go. She'd left a note asking him to call Delta Two and let D.D. know when he decided about the design. She couldn't help wondering if he'd gone to Ursula's.

As she watched the barren peaks of the Tehachapi Mountains pass below the jet, Tara told herself it was obvious he wasn't over Ursula. How could he commit himself to her when he was still emotionally involved with his ex-wife? If she'd had any idea Brian was still in love with Ursula she'd never have stayed with him in the beach bungalow. She should have had more sense, anyway.

She didn't really know Brian. As Karen had pointed out on the phone, he was practically a total stranger. Yet when the bond formed between them she'd felt she knew Brian better, more intimately, than she'd ever known another person.

Had she only imagined the bond? Brian hadn't mentioned feeling anything of that sort.

She sipped the airline's lukewarm coffee, thinking its taste was no more bitter than the ache in her heart. She'd walked into this affair with her eyes wide open so she had no one to blame but herself. Hadn't she foreseen returning alone to Sacramento, never to return to San Diego, to Brian?

His image swirled into her mind: his bright hair aglow in the sun, his sea-blue eyes beguiling, his strong and beautiful body inviting her into his arms.

How could she bear not to see him again? Not to touch him? Never to feel the thrill of his embrace?

Yet if it had to end, wasn't this abrupt cutoff better than the agony of watching love die slowly and painfully?

Love. Neither she nor Brian had mentioned the word. Didn't she mean passion?

She didn't know what she meant. She only knew she hurt terribly. Like a wounded animal, all she wanted to do was crawl into a dark and secret place and suffer until she died or became whole again.

No, she wouldn't die. As Shakespeare pointed out centuries before: "Men have died from time to time, and worms have eaten them, but not for love."

She'd go on somehow; she had no choice.

"You were gone so long I thought maybe you'd gotten permanently lost on those crazy southern California freeways," Roger told Tara when she walked into the Delta Two office later the same morning. "You know, going around and around on cloverleafs forever."

"No, I survived the freeways." She managed a smile.

"And returned in triumph, instrument order in your pocket, I've no doubt."

"Not quite. How was Tahoe?"

Roger shrugged. "Crowded. The condo anyway. Too much togetherness. San Diego and Dr. Shute was the better choice."

Not for me, she said to herself.

D.D. called her into his office late in the afternoon.

"Dr. Shute phoned me to approve your design," he said. "Roger told me you couldn't be beat in the medical field and, by George, he was right. We'll start work on the prototype as soon as we get Dr. Shute's signed agreement. Good work, Tara. I knew you could handle him if you just hung tough."

"Thank you." She wondered what D.D. would think if he knew what had gone on in San Diego.

"Quite a surprise to see you on TV," he said.

"I was in the right place at the wrong time."

"Too bad you weren't able to work in a mention of Delta Two."

At first she thought he was kidding, but when she saw he was serious she nodded.

"But a lot of people saw Dr. Shute and will remember him because he saved Palomar's life," D.D. went on. "If the doctor doesn't demand an exclusive on the instrument, we'll market it as the clamp used by the famous surgeon, Dr. Shute. Could be a real little money-maker."

So at least Delta Two would prosper, she thought wryly. Brian, too, for that matter. She was the only one likely to go into a decline.

Tara came home from the office exhausted. She dropped onto the couch but was too tense to relax so she finally got up and fixed herself a bowl of minestrone and a cup of tea. She stared at the TV without really following the programs until ten-thirty, then got ready for bed.

At first she tossed and turned, fighting her memories, but eventually oblivion overtook her.

* * *

She felt sand under her bare feet first, then the long dark corridor stretched before her, and she shuddered with the realization she was once more in the deserted hotel. She could barely make out every empty, open doorway in the gloom. Though there was no fog, it was night, and the moon, a waning quarter visible from time to time through holes in the roof, gave a grudging, ghostly light.

"Brian!" she called hopelessly, over and over, tears running down her cheeks. The echoes of her voice mocked her.

Somewhere another corridor existed, the right one, but not in this nightmare place. In the other corridor was a room with a golden door but how was she to find it?

In desperation she stopped running and stood sobbing in anguish and fear. A dark night wind swirled sand around her, covering her toes. She had the horrible foreknowledge that if she stayed still long enough the sand would drift higher and higher until she was completely buried.

"Brian!" she screamed in despair.

Only a far-off bell answered her plea, a shrill demand that grew louder and louder.

Tara woke with a start to the ringing of the phone on her nightstand. She groped for it, still half in the dream.

"Tara!"

"Brian?" She sat up in bed, uncertain she was awake, not quite believing Brian was actually at the other end of the line.

"Did I wake you?" he said.

"Uh—yes."

"What were you dreaming?"

Tara came fully alert. She reached for the lamp and turned it on. "Why do you ask?" she temporized.

"Because I just had one hell of a nightmare."

"I don't want to—" she began, but he cut her off before she could tell him she didn't want to hear.

"You know that picture above my bed—the one you said you hated? An old ruin of some kind. I dreamed I was in that ruin. It was like a hotel, with corridors and many rooms. All doorless, all empty."

"No," she whispered, the phone trembling in her hand. He ignored her.

"Sand was everywhere, drifting into the rooms, swirling around me. I was looking for you, I knew you were in a room somewhere, but I couldn't find you. I couldn't find you because this damned ruin was the wrong place, but I didn't know how to get to the right place. All I could do was call your name and go on from one empty room to another. Why did you leave so quickly, Tara? I'm going out of my—"

"Please, Brian, I can't talk to you." She couldn't speak above a frightened, breathless whisper. "Don't tell me any more."

Tara slammed down the phone, then reached over and jerked the plug out of the wall socket. She slid down in the bed and stared up at the ceiling. The sight of the fake stars on the midnight blue paint reminded her of looking at the night sky through the holes in the ruined roof of the dream hotel. She curled onto her side, huddling under the covers, numb with terror.

It wasn't safe to love. She and Mike had dreamed the same dreams. Her little carrot-topped brother Mike whom she'd loved from the moment she'd seen him yawning at her through the newborn nursery window. She and Mike had shared dreams and Mike had been taken from her. Mike had died. Now she shared dreams with someone else. A man with red hair.

It's not the same, she tried to tell herself. I loved Mike and I don't love Brian. I don't, I don't!

Then why are you so miserable without him? Why can you think of nothing else except him?

No. It's not the same. Nothing will happen to Brian. I won't talk to him, I won't see him ever again. He'll be safe because I won't let myself love him. He'll forget me and go back to Ursula. Then he won't dream with me anymore and nothing can happen to him if we don't share dreams.

Afraid to close her eyes for fear of dreaming again, Tara stayed awake for the rest of the night and dragged herself wearily in to work the next morning.

"You look beat," Yvonne told her at lunch. "You've been working too hard, over last weekend and all. What you need is a relaxing Saturday. There's a pool at my condo complex. Come on over and we'll laze the day away in the sun."

Tara felt too miserable to face anyone. At the same time she hated to be alone. If she went to Yvonne's, at least she wouldn't have to worry about Brian trying to phone her on Saturday.

"Thanks," she said, "I'd like to, though I'm afraid I won't be very good company."

Yvonne shrugged. "I had enough company in Tahoe to last me a lifetime. Never again. Believe me, quiet will be welcome."

Tara planned to get through Friday night by unplugging the phone, leaving the bedside lamp on and reading until she dozed off. She could only pray she wouldn't dream. She stacked several paperbacks on the nightstand and, once she was comfortably propped up on pillows, picked up the top book and opened it.

"Hamilton Driver ran a worried hand through his untidy red hair," she read, "as he eyed the long-legged blonde seated in the client's chair next to his desk."

Tara slapped the book shut and stared at the cover. Why this was one of the old mysteries from Grandma Fallkirk's house. She must have inadvertently packed it with her things when she left. She'd begun to read the book in Chatham, she remembered now. Remembered, too, how she'd stopped reading because the mention of red hair reminded her of Brian.

Long ago she'd convinced herself she didn't care for men with red hair. She'd never dated a redhead, never became emotionally involved with one. Not until Brian.

She saw now she'd been trying to protect herself because of what happened to Mike, that she'd believed red hair might have something to do with the shared dreaming. Did it?

Tara shook her head. How could she tell? Yet Brian and Mike both had red hair....

She took a deep breath and let it out slowly. Don't think about it, she warned herself. All you have to remember is not to see or speak to Brian ever again, and nothing bad will happen to him.

Tossing the detective story onto the floor, she picked up the next book and noted with relief the hero's hair was "as jet-black as squid's ink."

But, as she tried to read, the image of Brian's face kept interposing itself between her and the printed page. At least he'd be too busy, between taking care of Ursula's fears and his practice, to arrive in Sacramento in person. She could avoid talking to him on the phone, and she certainly wouldn't return to San Diego under any circumstances.

He was safe.

"I have a hunch, Tara," Yvonne said to her the next day as they lay side by side on lounge chairs near the pool, soaking up the sun. "I hope you won't get mad if I say so, but you're behaving like a gal who's lost her man. I recognize the symptoms from having had a god-awful case of those same blues myself two years ago."

What was the point in lying? "Something of the sort, Yvonne," Tara admitted.

"It's a bad scene. Plain low-down depressing. I don't say it's easy to recover but you will. I sure thought I never would. Time works wonders, though. A new man helps, sometimes, too." She glanced sideways at Tara, one eyebrow raised.

"I'm not ready to try that cure." Tara managed a twisted smile as she spoke, yet in her heart she knew no other man could ever take Brian's place.

"Roger, for instance," Yvonne went on. "You could do worse. Roger doesn't take anything seriously, and you don't want to at the moment. You two are a perfect match."

The thought of being paired with Roger brought a genuine smile to Tara's face. "We don't even like each other very well."

Yvonne shook her head. "You mean to say you've never noticed how Roger hangs around you? Why do you think he bothers?"

Tara frowned. "Oh, you must be wrong. Roger enjoys nothing more than putting me down."

"It's his way of getting even 'cause you refuse to notice him. I tell you he's had the hots for you ever since you joined us at Delta Two."

Tara stared at her unbelievingly. "He talked me out of going to Tahoe at the same time he set me up for San Diego with D.D. That doesn't sound like an infatuated suitor."

"Roger didn't want you at Tahoe 'cause he knew very well I planned to have you meet this fantastic hunk from Frisco."

"I don't think I could ever take Roger seriously."

"That's my point. You don't have to. He isn't the type, anyway. Just let yourself go with the flow. You'll feel better, I guarantee it."

"Even if I could, it wouldn't be fair to Roger because I really don't care for him at all."

"Fair, schmair. These attractions never last long with him once he gets the gal to notice him. You intrigue him 'cause he can't have you."

And I can't have Brian. Not ever again. All thought of Roger fled from Tara's mind as the achingly familiar picture of Brian formed in her mind. She imagined him in swim trunks standing on the diving board, his body poised and ready, muscles taut, the suit low on his hips, a snug fit.... Oh God, she thought, I couldn't bear life without him.

Late that afternoon, at home once more, she attached the phone answerer she'd bought and plugged the phone back in. It rang while she was trying to choke down a pear with cottage cheese for supper that she was eating only because she knew she should. She let the machine take the call. Afterward she checked the recording. Brian, asking her to call him. She shook her head.

Another call came in around eight. Again the machine answered. She was sure it was Brian and was taken aback to hear her mother's voice on the recording.

"Surprise! We're home five days early. Call when you can."

Tara immediately dialed their Virginia number. Her father answered and the sound of his laconic tones brought tears to her eyes. If only she could be a little girl again with the kind of childish problems her father always fixed. He couldn't solve the one she had now, and she had no intention of even mentioning it to her parents.

After exchanging a few words with her, he put her mother on.

"Well, we wanted to be sure to get back before our first grandchild was born," her mother said.

"How was New Zealand?"

"Spectacular. I'll write you because if I start talking about it you'd hate me when you got your phone bill. How are you, dear? Karen seemed to think something was wrong."

"Karen worries too much. I'm fine. I'm glad you've come home. Karen will need you once the baby's born."

There was a short silence. "Abbott's hiring a nurse," her mother said at last. "Didn't Karen tell you? So I won't be staying with them. Of course your father and I will be on hand for the great event. Karen insists you come, too."

"I won't be able to. I've used all my vacation time."

"She'll be very disappointed. You know how she always wants to share with you."

Sharing, her mother called it. Tara felt that wasn't the right word, but she couldn't think of another to express what Karen wanted from her. She and Mike had shared; she and Brian had shared. With Karen it was something else entirely, something not as intimate.

"She'll have Abbott and the nurse and you and Dad," Tara said lightly. "Karen doesn't need me."

"I'm not so sure you're right." Her mother paused again, then said tentatively, "If there's anything I can do for you—"

"Don't *you* start worrying about me." Tara forced a laugh. "Everything, including the weather, is great here in California."

"We'd fly out to see you after the baby's born, but your father has a July assignment in Scotland so we'll be off again. 'Figure six months,' they told him."

Her father was an industrial machine consultant, and her mother traveled with him, so her parents were often out of the country. Tara was sorry to miss seeing them before they left again but at the same time glad her misery would remain hidden from her mother's shrewd eye. She was no longer a child and her parents couldn't help her. It was best they didn't know.

"July sounds like a good month for Scotland," she said brightly. "Be sure and call me the minute Karen's baby's born. It's supposed to be a boy."

After she hung up, Tara started thinking about Leda Umak's predictions. "An oak tree wound with mistletoe," she'd foreseen in Tara's life. Too vague to mean much. The house and the man were, too. Didn't most women have a house and a man in their lives, sooner or later? Brian appearing when she stayed in the Chatham house was a coincidence, no more.

And the double dreams Leda had sensed? Could that be reasoned away?

Don't dwell on the dreams, it's dangerous, she told herself.

The phone answering machine solved Tara's problem of Brian calling her at home. When she went to work on Monday, it occurred to her he might try to reach her at Delta Two since she'd resolutely refused to reply to any of the messages he'd left on the machine. After Monday, Tuesday and Wednesday passed and he hadn't phoned her at work, she decided he didn't intend to.

He'd also stopped leaving the messages at her apartment. He'd given up. What she should be feeling was relief, so why was she so depressed? Because it hadn't taken him long to put her out of his mind?

If only she could forget him.

The week went by. She mall-hopped with Yvonne on Saturday and biked with a backpacking group on Sunday, picnicking on the UC campus at Davis.

May ended and the heat of June warmed the Sacramento Valley, bringing the first air-conditioning weather of the year. One workday blended into another until the end of the second week when D.D. called her into the office.

"We have a glitch," he told her.

Tara, who'd just finished working on a design for a stamping machine, thought that's what he meant. "I'm sure I can handle whatever it is," she said confidently.

"Good. Because Dr. Shute asked for you specifically."

Tara felt the thrum of blood pounding in her ears. No, she thought in panic, I can't get involved again.

"He's tried to use the model in surgery and apparently there's some difficulty," D.D. went on. "You'll have to fly down and take a look."

Chapter Fourteen

Muttering under her breath, Tara climbed up from the canyon parking structure toward UCSD Medical Center. She was in San Diego again, this time against her will. Once more she'd obeyed Dr. Shute's instructions, taking the Friday afternoon flight he'd suggested plus driving directly from the airport to meet him at the hospital.

"Have Ms. Reed ask them to page me when she gets to the lobby," he'd told D.D. At least this time she knew—only too well—who Dr. Shute was.

The heavy throb of a low-flying helicopter distracted her and she looked up to see it dipping down over the medical center, lower and lower, until she lost sight of it behind the buildings. She knew a helicopter pad for what Brian had called Life Flight was on top of the outpatient center. An emergency must be coming in.

She wondered how doctors and nurses in emergency units coped day after day with the constant need for quick decisions and quick action. She didn't understand, either, how Brian could go on working as he was doing, sixteen hours most days with inadequate time off. Where was the time for a private life?

Not that it made any difference to her. What Brian wanted to do was his own business and no concern of hers.

In the lobby she stopped at the information desk to ask them to page Dr. Shute. Will I have to observe in the operating room today? she asked herself uneasily. Once had been more than enough, and she wasn't looking forward to it again.

Brian appeared in the lobby before she had time to find a seat in the waiting room. He wore street clothes, a tan suede jacket with darker brown pants, his athlete's body moving with unconscious grace as he strode toward her. Her heart skipped a beat and her breath caught despite her determination not to be affected by him.

"We're going upstairs," he told her, taking her arm to guide her.

Not even a hello, she thought indignantly, trying to ignore the frisson of awareness along her spine when he touched her. Caught up in her annoyance, she wasn't certain of the floor where they left the elevator, though she noticed with relief it wasn't the second floor, where the operating-room suite was located.

When she realized they were passing patients' rooms, she glanced at Brian questioningly, wanting an idea of where they were going. He wasn't looking at her. He was checking his watch. She hoped he had so little time to spare she wouldn't be with him long. She'd given him the benefit of the doubt, but she still suspected his claim of problems with her design model might be only a ruse to bring her to San Diego.

"Here we are," he said, stopping in front of a half-closed door to a patient's room.

Tara heard a woman's light laughter as Brian pushed open the door and, hand on her arm so she had to go with him, he stepped into the room.

Ursula lay propped in the bed of a private room that was bright and fragrant with flowers. She wore a peach bed jacket over a lacy nightgown of the same shade and not only was every red hair in place but her makeup was flawless. A dark-haired man, who'd been leaning over her, straightened when they came in.

Tara tried to stop, but Brian wouldn't let her so she was forced to Ursula's side. "You're looking well," she managed to say, dredging up a smile.

Ursula smiled graciously. "Tara, isn't it? So nice to see you again." She held out her hand to Brian. "Darling, how wonderful of you to drop by."

He nodded but didn't move to take Ursula's hand. "Rick told me all your results were negative," Brian said, "and you'll be going home tomorrow."

Ursula reached out to the dark-haired man, and he grasped her hand, his thumb stroking the back of it. "Lance," she said, "you remember my ex-husband. And this is Tara."

Lance, his chiseled face a blank, made polite noises at Tara while he avoided looking at Brian.

Tara murmured a greeting. Brian nodded again and turned to leave.

"Not going so soon?" Ursula's husky voice held a hint of mockery.

"We're in a hurry." Brian lifted his hand in a quick wave, grasped Tara's arm with the other and propelled her from the room.

Just outside the door an idea struck her. What could she lose? She wrenched away from Brian.

"I have something I want to say to Ursula," she told him.

Tara hurried back into the room. Ignoring Ursula's obvious astonishment she leaned over the bed and said in a low tone, "What's the *E* stand for?"

"The *E*? Oh, in Brian's name, you mean." Ursula shrugged. "Who knows? Or cares, for that matter."

"What was that all about?" Brian demanded when she rejoined him.

"Nothing important," she told him, wondering what had possessed her to ask Ursula. What did Tara Reed care what the *E* stood for, either?

Brian strode so rapidly she had to trot to keep up with him. Were they now going to the O.R.?

The down elevator stopped at the main floor, so apparently not. With Tara in tow, he headed for the cafeteria.

"Look, Brian," she began, determined not to waste more time on anything unrelated to the instrument model, "If you intend—"

"Don't talk, just hurry."

She sighed and resigned herself to drinking a cup of coffee. But while she did, she'd insist he discuss his problem with the model.

They walked to the rear of the cafeteria and there Brian led her through a door into a room where several men and one woman sat drinking coffee. She recognized Rick Manning. He ran a hand through his graying hair, nodded to the man next to him and stood up.

"Ready?" he asked Brian.

"All set," Brian replied.

"I'm pleased you could make it." Rick smiled as he spoke to Tara. "Rita has mentioned several times how much she enjoyed meeting you."

Tara smiled back at him, not quite sure what was going on. "Your wife is very friendly," she told him.

"Well, then, let's get going before one or the other of us gets paged." Rick clapped Brian on the back and grinned at Tara. "Or before this workhorse changes his mind."

She felt she was missing cues. Rick ushered them through the door. They crossed the cafeteria and strode toward the lobby. Then they were outside and walking briskly.

"You've brought good weather," Rick said to her.

What on earth was he talking about? She glanced around Rick to try to catch Brian's eye. She couldn't.

"No fog, even," Rick went on. "Couldn't be better."

"Yes, the weather *is* nice," she said slowly. Were they going to the office?

A lean and tanned fortyish woman waved from beside a bronze Ferrari. Rita Manning. "Tara!" she called. "You made it. Good!"

"Rita's going to ride with you," Rick said to Tara as his wife approached. "Okay? We'll see you there." He walked on toward the Ferrari.

Tara turned to Brian but he was already hurrying away.

"I'm a bit confused," Tara said to Rita. "What's going on?"

"Well, you'll never find the place if I don't show you how to get there. I imagine you're parked in the visitor area—right?" At Tara's nod, Rita started downhill toward the canyon where Tara had left her rental car.

"But where are we going?" Tara asked as she double stepped to catch up to Rita.

"The marina, of course. That's where the boat is."

"Wait a minute. What boat?"

Rita's pace slowed as she stared at Tara, eyebrows raised.

Tara sighed. She'd been right—Brian was up to something. "Look, Rita," she said, "my boss sent me here to work the bugs out of Brian's instrument model. Brian insisted I meet him at the hospital, and I thought perhaps he wanted me to see what the problem was while he was actually using the clamp. Instead, he dragged me up to Ursula's room, then—"

"Complete with admirer, I'll bet," Rita broke in. "Which one did she have in attendance?"

"A man named Lance was with her. But that isn't the point. Brian—"

"Lance Disbrow. She ditched him ages ago. Must have called him in for Brian's benefit. She played this whole operation to the hilt, you know. Poor little me and all. It was only a benign cyst, a small one at that, in her left breast."

"Did they know what it was before the surgery?"

"Pretty much so. Rick told her it was a million to one the lump was anything but a benign cyst. She was the one who insisted it be taken out immediately."

"Ursula told Brian another story."

"I'm sure she did. She can't stand it because he's not a Lance Disbrow who comes running when she beckons, no matter how she's behaved. Would you believe she even wanted Brian to do the surgery? When she knows his specialty is abdominal surgery and Rick does the breast operations."

"Did Brian operate on her?"

"Of course not. He wouldn't have anyway, even if Rick hadn't told him how minor Ursula's problem really was. She must be mad as the devil because her little ploy to reattach Brian didn't work. Otherwise I doubt if she'd have bothered to dig up charming Lance after all this time." Rita shook her head. "Ursula always did have a mean streak."

"I don't follow you."

"When they were married, Brian must have realized she was running around, because all the rest of us knew. If he needed proof he finally got it when he came home and found Ursula with Lance in the master bedroom hot tub, both sans clothes. Brian's too damn nice. In the dissolution he gave her a 60/40 split in her favor when the usual is 50/50. Actually, under the circumstances, she should have gotten zilch. Because he behaved like a gentleman, Ursula's never really understood he's through with her once and for all."

Was Rita saying that Ursula had arranged for Lance to be visiting her hospital room when she knew Brian would be coming by to see her? Trying to twist the knife in Brian's wound?

"Brian didn't seem particularly upset," Tara said. "Today, I mean."

"He probably wasn't. With Brian what's done is done."

"But why take me to her room?"

They'd reached Tara's car and Rita stopped, turning to face her. "Well," she said, "since you've told me he got you down here on false pretenses, I'd say he promised to stop by and see Ursula before she was discharged, and he hadn't gotten around to it before he was due to meet you. So he took you with him to make certain you didn't disappear before he got back. I realize you and Brian are none of my business, but have you any idea of the way he's been acting since you went back to Sacramento? Cross as a bear and working harder than a medieval peasant."

Tara didn't want her defenses to fall any lower. She may have been wrong about Brian's feelings for Ursula. Apparently, as far as he was concerned, there was no chance of them ever getting back together. Was it significant he'd never told Ursula his first name? Somehow she thought it was.

So, write off Ursula. It still wasn't right for Brian to use a ruse to bring her here from Sacramento.

"What's all this about boats?" she demanded.

"Rick convinced Brian he had to take the weekend off and come with us to Catalina. I remembered you telling me you liked to sail, and so I told Brian to invite you. I thought it would do him good to have you along." Rita shrugged, smiling wryly. "He said you'd accepted. So naturally when I saw you I thought that's why you were here." Rita put her hand on Tara's arm. "Brian must have his reasons for behaving like an idiot. Please forgive the guy and join us."

Brian knew I wouldn't accept the invitation even if he could have gotten in touch with me to ask, Tara mused. A healing warmth spread through her as she realized how desperately he must have wanted her with him to involve Rick and Rita in his scheme. Had his nights been as lonely and miserable as hers?

"After all," Rita added, "you don't usually work weekends, do you? You must have Saturday and Sunday off."

And an empty two days they'd be in Sacramento, alone.

Maybe she'd overreacted about the dreams. Their discussion about the gloomy picture above his bed might have triggered Brian's dream. Especially if he really had missed her, as Rita seemed to be saying.

If she went she wouldn't be alone with Brian anyway—Rick and Rita would be there. How could it be risky to be part of a foursome? More than anything in the world she wanted to spend the next two days with Brian. Her eyes were starved for the sight of him, and her ears longed to hear his voice. Just to be with him...

"Thanks, I'd like to sail to Catalina with you."

Rita hugged her. "I knew from the moment we met you'd be the right medicine for Brian," she said. "He needs to learn life can be fun."

Brian and I had fun at the Cape, Tara thought. We had a wonderful time. Yet one thing after another has gone wrong between us ever since.

Rick and Rita, planning not to leave for Catalina until early the next morning, had invited three other couples to the marina for an informal dinner aboard their cabin cruiser, the *Cut It Out*.

"Her name comes from the surgeons' so-called motto," Rick explained to Tara as they waited aboard the boat for the guests to arrive. "One old Hippocrates didn't think of: When in doubt, cut it out! If I get to feeling I'm overworked and underappreciated, I apply the motto to myself and head out to sea. The cruiser is the best medicine anyone could prescribe."

"She's a beautiful boat," Tara said. After a moment she added, "Your group *does* seem to work hard. I'm glad to hear you realize the need to relax."

Rick shrugged. "We put in a good week's work, but don't judge us all by Brian. He doesn't know when to stop. I had to insist, as a senior member of the group, that he take this weekend off. Now it's up to you to get him to relax." He grinned at her and gave her a little push toward Brian, who was standing alone on the port side of the boat, looking down at the water.

You have to talk to Brian sooner or later, she told herself, knowing she'd been putting off a tête-à-tête. She walked slowly toward him.

The sun, low in the west, cast a golden light over the water. Brian's hair gleamed in the muted glow. He'd changed to jeans and a collared knit shirt of navy-blue that stretched over his broad shoulders and revealed his powerful torso. Her mental pictures of him were never as stimulating as seeing him in person. She couldn't imagine ever tiring of looking at him.

Conscious of someone behind him, Brian swung around. Tara stood staring at him, her eyes as green as her loose-knit shirt that hinted at the provocative rise of her breasts. The shirt fell below the waist of her slim white mid-thigh pants and underneath the shirt was the warm perfection of her soft skin, skin he longed to touch.

He sighed. At least Tara had agreed to go to Catalina. Thanks to Rita's persuasiveness, he supposed. He hadn't at first been at all sure of the outcome.

Tara stepped to the rail, and he caught a whiff of her personal fragrance, the scent that haunted his nights. He leaned on the rail and turned to face her.

"I didn't know how else to see you again," he said softly, "and I had to."

"You could have told me what was going on once I got here."

"You wouldn't have gone along with it."

She glanced sideways, smiling slightly. "No."

"Have you ever been to Catalina Island?"

She shook her head.

Unable to be so close without touching her, he reached over and stroked her forearm with his index finger. "I'd better warn you—Catalina's a romantic never-never land."

"Maybe I'm immune."

The trouble with touching her was it increased his appetite for more. He could feel the speedup of his heartbeat.

"No one's immune," he said. "The island infects young and old alike."

"Struck down by romance?" she replied. Brian's pulses leaped at the laughter in her voice. He still had a chance. They had a chance.

"What better disease to lay one low?" he asked, savoring her reluctant grin.

He took her hands, turning her toward him. "I've missed you."

Drowning in her eyes, green as the depths of the sea, would be a pleasure. He was learning that when they changed to amber he'd better put on the brakes because there was trouble ahead. Green, on the other hand, promised wonders he could find with no other woman.

"I missed you, too." She spoke so softly he could hardly hear her.

"Why did you leave me? Was it Ursula? I thought you understood she's no longer important to me in any way except for the help I'd give any upset patient."

"Rita told me Ursula overplayed her condition a bit."

"Sometimes I think Ursula couldn't be honest even if she took lessons."

"Speaking of honesty—maybe *you* could use a few lessons!" Tara eased her hands from his and raised her eyebrows.

"How else can I cope with a stubborn woman who disappears every time I turn around, a woman who hangs up when I call, who won't return calls when I leave a message? Anyway, I do want you to take a look at the clamp. I'm very satisfied with its gentle pressure on friable tissue, but I think maybe the shaft to the handles needs a slight angle adjustment to be perfect. So it wasn't a complete lie."

Her smile was rueful. "Why do I always wind up believing you against my better judgment?"

The lowering sun gilded her hair and her face. He wanted to gather her into his arms and never let her go, to taste the sweet promise of her lips forever.

They had to talk first, though, had to have nothing left festering between them. Something was bothering Tara besides Ursula's melodramatics, and he was determined to find out just what it was.

"Let's get off the boat and take a walk while we wait for the others," he suggested.

She hesitated, then said, "Rita might need help."

"Rita's as capable as any other five women. I'm sure she's completely organized and ready and, besides, she's got Rick to help. He claims he's the greatest hors d'oeuvre concocter in La Jolla." He turned toward the stern where Rita had joined Rick.

"We're going to take a walk," he called. "Okay?"

Rick waved a languid hand. "Go. With our blessings, if you need them."

Brian led Tara along the dock to the boat house. They climbed an incline, then crossed the road to a path running along the bay. Palm fronds rustled overhead in the late afternoon breeze, and pink blossoms fluttered like butterflies on the glossy green foliage of oleander bushes.

Here and there a fisherman cast into the golden-tinted water, but for the most part the waterline was deserted. When they came to a white bench, Brian steered Tara toward it.

"San Diego's beautiful," she said as they sat side by side. "It has a more manicured look than the Cape, but lovely."

He hadn't brought her here where they could be alone to discuss San Diego.

"I called you in Sacramento," he said without preamble. "In the night. Something I said about the dream disturbed you so much you couldn't talk to me. What was it?"

She bit her lip. "I'd rather not discuss it."

"Did it have something to do with the dream I had?"

Tara's hands clenched in her lap. She didn't answer.

He reached over and took her hands in his, gently massaging her rigid knuckles. "Hey, ease up. What's wrong?"

"The dreaming. I'm afraid of the dreaming." Her voice sounded stifled.

She'd been upset about the erotic dream they shared in Chatham. Upset about sharing it with him. His nightmare, though, had been far from erotic. He stared at her, willing her to go on, but she remained silent.

"Did you have a nightmare, too?" he asked finally, taking a shot in the dark.

She gasped, jerking her hands from his and bringing them up to cover her face. He put his arm around her, drawing her close, stroking her hair, her clean and flowery fragrance firing his senses. "Tell me," he urged.

"I dreamed about the ruined hotel, too," she whispered. "I searched through it but couldn't find you."

He was momentarily startled at the coincidence. But was it really so odd?

"I don't wonder." He used his soothing-the-patient tone. "We parted angrily. That damn picture had hung right over our heads, and both of us really wanted to be together again. Isn't that true?"

Her yes was barely audible.

"Why does it upset you so that we had a similar dream? Under the circumstances, I don't find it unusual."

She raised her head and took a deep breath. "I'm afraid of shared dreams." Her voice shook.

"Why?"

At first he thought she wasn't going to tell him but after a few minutes she leaned back against his shoulder and sighed. "When I was eleven I dreamed with my little brother," she said sadly. "Mike and I shared dreams. At Grandma Fallkirk's house in Chatham. And they came true."

She'd told him Karen was her only sibling. "Your brother Mike?" he asked.

"Mike was killed in an accident when he was seven."

He could feel her trembling and he tightened his hold, waiting, remembering now she'd said something at the Cape about dreaming with someone else.

"You see, I dreamed about Mike's death," she whispered. "I saw a dark whirlwind whip down and swallow him up. I knew it meant something terrible, but I was afraid to tell anyone. And then, a month later, when we were back home in New York . . ." She paused to take a deep, sobbing breath.

"Tell me the rest," he urged gently when she didn't go on.

"I was on my way to a dancing lesson. Alone. Karen wasn't with me because she'd hurt her ankle the day before. I was walking along humming the tune we danced to when all of a sudden this dreadful fear stopped me in my tracks. Then came an awful, piercing pain, like someone had shot an arrow right through my head. Then—nothing.

"When I could see again, a man was helping me up from the sidewalk. He was talking, but I couldn't make myself understand what he was saying because I knew something terrible had happened to Mike.

"I ran home. By the time I got there the ambulance had come and gone, but I saw Mike's smashed bike thrown up onto the curb halfway down the block. I think I understood he was dead before anyone told me. Eventually I realized what I'd felt was what *he* felt when the car hit his bike and killed him. Worse, I've wondered all my life if I could somehow have prevented his death by telling my mother and father about my dream."

Chapter Fifteen

By Saturday noon *Cut It Out* was anchored in the crescent bay that provided Avalon with a sheltered harbor. Tara, still distracted by Catalina's beauty, paid scant attention to Rita's talk of how they might spend the afternoon.

Avalon, the only town of any size on the island, seemed to Tara to belong in the Mediterranean, with its red-tiled Moorish-type buildings looking down from the hillside above the bay. Sunshine shimmered on incredibly blue water and highlighted the white stucco houses until the scene held the unrealistic clarity of a picture postcard.

Somewhere, faintly, a man's voice sang the words to "Avalon" while a guitar thrummed the tune. The sweetness of mock orange tinged the cool sea air. She felt that if she closed her eyes, when she opened them again the scene before her might have vanished like a vision in a dream.

"I told you Santa Catalina wasn't real." Brian's voice spoke in her ear.

She turned to him. "*Santa* Catalina?"

"The real name of the island," he said. "Cabrillo discovered it originally, but Viscaino named the island in a later rediscovery on St. Catherine's Eve."

"Wow. I'm impressed with your knowledge."

He brandished a small pamphlet. "It also says in here the island's twenty-two miles long and eight miles wide, and it's really a drowned mountain. Catalina's famed for its glass-bottomed boat cruises over the scenic California State Marine Preserve."

She frowned in mock outrage. "Here I am praising your erudition and you're only reading from a tourist brochure."

"Neither of you has heard a word I've said," Rita complained. "What are your plans for the afternoon?"

"Are there really glass-bottomed boats?" Tara asked.

Brian and Rita chimed in together assuring her there were.

"Shall we take a cruise in one?" Brian asked.

"You and Tara go. Rick and I have done that undersea wonder tour before." Rita smiled at Tara. "It's worth going the first time, but my problem is once I've seen one fish, as far as I'm concerned, I've seen them all. We'll meet by the dock around five and decide where to have dinner. Okay?"

Tara was entranced by the underwater sights in the marine preserve. Brilliant blue and green fish drifted lazily underneath the boat's glass bottom, and once a goldfish over a foot long approached the glass, seemingly as interested in staring at her as she was at him.

When a brownish something undulated below, at first she thought it might be an eel, but then more and more strands appeared, and she realized she was looking at seaweed. The kelp forest waved in the sea currents like the branches of trees in the wind, reminding her of her bad dreams about being lost in a seaweed jungle, lost and unable to find Brian.

She turned to him, needing to touch him to reassure herself.

He put his arm around her. "Tired?" he asked as she leaned against him. "I can't say my bunk last night was the world's most comfortable bed."

The Manning cruiser slept six in rather close quarters. A thin partition separated her from Rita and Rick, and another partition came between her bunk and Brian's. She'd been too aware of him on the other side of the flimsy plywood to fall asleep immediately.

It wasn't lack of sleep that bothered her. It was remembering Brian had told her about *his* kelp dreams. Had they been the same as hers?

No. She wasn't going to worry about dreams. She didn't intend to allow any fears to intrude into this fantasy island interlude.

She felt safe with Brian's arm around her. Protected. Loved.

She recalled his gentle hands as he carried Larry the gull in Chatham, his tenderness when he comforted her yesterday on the bench by the marina. She'd never told anyone else how Mike's death had affected her and, despite the anguish of reliving the experience, it was a relief to have shared the secret with Brian, who understood her pain.

A bond linked them. She may have tried to deny it, but she'd known it from the moment she first saw him. Though the linkage enhanced their lovemaking, creating an overwhelming empathetic eroticism, the bond had nothing to do with the physical.

Was it a sharing of spirits? She was uneasy thinking in such terms, but she didn't know how else to describe it. Brian was everything she'd ever wanted, ever would want. She loved him.

Tara sat up abruptly. No, not love—not the most dangerous emotion of all! It wasn't wise, wasn't safe to love anyone. She didn't love Brian, couldn't love him.

Brian's brow furrowed in concern when Tara jerked herself free of his arms. "What's the matter?" he asked.

She stared down through the glass bottom of the boat instead of facing him. "Nothing," she muttered. "Nothing at all."

Would he ever understand her? He'd hoped, after she'd chosen to confess the dreams shared with her brother and to admit her feelings of guilt over the boy's tragic death, that she felt what he did—a new closeness between them. Now here she was rejecting him again, running away from him in spirit if not in reality.

"Don't you ever meet problems head on?" he asked.

She turned toward him, and he noted with dismay how golden her eyes were. It meant trouble.

"Who said anything about a problem?" she demanded.

"There are no problems on Santa Catalina, remember?"

He watched her relax slowly until she finally managed a small smile. "Right. How could I forget?"

He reached for her hand and she hesitated a brief moment before offering hers. A strong and capable hand, he knew, and yet it felt fragile within his grasp. A strong urge washed over him to shelter her from all disappointments and sorrows. So her eyes would always shine with the soft green of happiness.

After the glass-bottomed boat brought them back to Avalon, Brian showed Tara the sights of the town: the columned casino, the bougainvillea-entwined cottage where Zane Grey had once lived, the quaint old house with the open tower that perched on a promontory overlooking the harbor.

"What's the rest of the island like?" she asked as they waded in the warm shallows of the bay.

"Definitely not as romantic. Mostly uninhabited—rocky hills, yellow grass, wild goats. There's a shortage of water on the island that limits building. Of course there's the old Wrigley mansion. We could ride the tour bus up into the hills to see it if you'd like."

She shook her head. "I like where we are."

He watched as she retrieved a beach ball for a toddler and saw how tenderly she smiled at the little boy as he ran on chubby legs back to his mother. She was so lovely, so completely unself-conscious about the breeze tousling her hair, or the water splashing onto her mid-calf pants.

She didn't live for how she looked but for what she was doing. He loved her naturalness, her unvarnished beauty. He loved—

Brian's eyes widened as he realized what he'd been about to say to himself. He'd been betrayed once before by what he'd believed was love. It hadn't been. He knew that now, but he hadn't known it at the time. He'd learned love wasn't a diagnosis to be made without lengthy interior consultation. Without analyzing every symptom, testing every response. Without careful consideration of all the aspects of the disease.

When in doubt, cut it out.

Rick and Rita were waiting for them on the dock and, Tara saw with some surprise, they were holding hands. Rita seemed to have shed ten years. Her thin face held the glow of youth rather than the gauntness of middle age, and Rick was smiling down at his wife as though they were newlyweds.

Apparently Brian noticed, too, because he murmured, "Catalina strikes again."

"Oh, Tara, Brian," Rita exclaimed as soon as she saw them. "You'll never guess what happened! We've found old friends here. Imagine. We haven't heard a word from them in years and here they are living in Avalon. They met at our wedding. He was Rick's best man and she was my maid of honor. Seeing them again really took us back." She glanced up at her husband.

Rick put his arm over Rita's shoulders. "Maybe that's a road we ought to travel more often."

"So I hope you'll understand if we desert you," Rita continued. "Pam and Chuck invited us to have dinner with them and to spend the night at their villa. I thought of asking them to include you, but Rick convinced me you two would prefer to be on your own." She smiled at them. "I'm sure he's right."

Later, after Brian and Tara had enjoyed a leisurely dinner at The Flying Fish, they stood together on the wharf waiting for a water taxi to take them back to the Manning boat.

"Alone at last in Avalon," Brian said.

Though the sun had set, traces of deep red tinted the darkening blue of the evening sky. Tara spotted a solitary star and remembered how she and Karen used to vie to see who'd find the night's first star and chant:

Star light, star bright,
First star I see tonight:
I wish I may, I wish I might,
Have the wish I wish tonight.

If she still believed wishes came true, she'd wish—for what? For Brian to love her? Tara shivered though the jasmine-scented air was warm. No, she wouldn't make such a dangerous wish. Wishing on stars was for children; besides, she needed no wish tonight.

Tonight she'd be alone with Brian on the boat, and she both feared and eagerly anticipated it. Everything they'd said and done since leaving Rick and Rita had been a prelude to the rest of the night. Each time he'd touched her the delicious tension mounted.

"Did you wish on the star?" Brian asked.

"No."

He ruffled her hair. "What are you, a skeptic? I made my wish. They come true on Catalina, you know."

"We'll see."

He put his arm around her, pulling her to his side. "What if I told you I was psychic? After all, I spent the afternoon sending secret mental messages to Rick and Rita, telling them to leave us alone, and it worked."

His joking about being psychic sent a chill through her, but she forced a laugh. "Hidden talents!" she teased.

"Just you wait. Tonight I reveal all." He leaned to her, but the water taxi pulled in and he straightened. "Just you wait," he repeated softly.

Aboard the *Cut It Out* Brian fixed them both a crème de menthe on the rocks, and they sat in deck chairs by the stern rail looking at the lights of Avalon reflecting in the dark water. Beneath them the boat bobbed gently and from somewhere distant a trumpet wailed "The Blues in the Night." Tara savored the sharp peppermint taste of the liqueur on her tongue and the warmth of Brian's hand holding hers.

She admired the strength and capability of his surgeon's hands. For all his massiveness he was a graceful man, and she never tired of watching him perform the simplest actions. Away from the concerns of his practice he'd become more like the easygoing Brian she'd met on Cape Cod.

"You know what that seaweed bed we saw today reminded me of?" he asked.

Tara tensed, withdrawing her hand from his under the pretense of pushing her hair back from her forehead.

"Remember those crazy dreams I told you about?" Brian went on. "The tangled-in-seaweed ones I was having before I called Delta Two and found you again. My subconscious knew what I didn't—that I'd never be satisfied until we were together."

"Please don't," she said.

He turned in his chair to stare at her, his face a white blur in the gathering darkness. "You're not worried about dreams again, are you? There's no reason to be."

"I dreamed about seaweed, too." Tara forced the words out. "Before I was summoned to San Diego by Dr. E. B. Shute. I didn't know you were in San Diego, and you didn't know I was in Sacramento. Yet we shared dreams. It scares me."

He rose and grasped her hands, pulling her to her feet. With his hands on her shoulders, he gazed down at her. "I'll admit I was a little uneasy at first about this, well, psychic understanding between us, but there's nothing to be afraid of. You and I communicate on a different level than either of us is used to, that's all. Haven't you sensed an interlacing between us that goes beyond the physical?"

"Then you *do* believe we've shared dreams."

"Let's say we influence each other in some way I don't really understand."

"And it doesn't frighten you?"

He hesitated, finally saying, "Not frighten, exactly. How can I be afraid of you? And this is part of you, part of me. But I'm not sure I would have asked for it to happen if I'd had a choice."

His hands cupped her face. "We're in it together, for better or worse."

She couldn't see his expression in the darkness, but she was acutely aware of the desire that emanated from him, surrounding her in an erotic aura, triggering her own desire and banishing her dread of the future.

This was now. He was here; she was here; they were together. Nothing else mattered.

His lips were gentle on hers, his tongue tasting, exploring.

"Mmm," he murmured. "Peppermint and Tara. My kind of flavor."

She gave herself up to the pleasure of his kiss, feeling herself open to him, offering him all that she was and feeling him open to her in the same mystically wonderful blossoming. They shared the heat of each other's arousal and the throbbing need for fulfillment that drove them to mold themselves ever closer to one another.

Brian was past thinking. He acted instinctively, carrying Tara under the shelter of the stern awning where they couldn't be seen by anyone on a nearby boat, throwing down the terry-covered pad used for sunbathing and easing them both onto it.

His heart beat out her name. She was a part of him in a way he'd never imagined was possible. He pulled off her shirt, feeling her thrill of pleasure as his hands closed over her breasts, the sensation fueling his passion so that he trembled as he bent to savor the taste of her engorged nipples.

She was more beautiful than any other woman, with an inner loveliness only he was privileged to see, and he gloried in being the chosen one. The need for her was an erotic ache coursing along his nerves like sweet fire.

He removed her pants and the slither of her satin panties beneath his fingers drove him wild.

"Brian," she whispered, moaning as he caressed her soft womanhood.

"I want you." His voice was hoarse with need. "I've never wanted a woman the way I want you."

Her fingers tugged urgently at the belt of his jeans, and he eased away from her, letting her undo the belt and unzip the jeans. He yanked them off and removed his shirt. The acute stab of their mutual pleasure when skin touched skin made him gasp.

She writhed beneath him, urging him to come into her but he resisted. When she touched his hardness he groaned in need and found her most sensitive spot with a caressing forefinger. She cried out, arching to him, her entire being telling him of her intense yearning to feel him inside her.

He poised himself over her, meaning to enter slowly but her hands pressed hard against his buttocks, plunging him deep within her while she rocked under him. With the wonder of her hot softness surrounding him he was no longer able to control his violent surge of response and drove rhythmically toward the release of their passion.

They whirled in a golden spiral of togetherness, united in body and in spirit, experiencing the turbulent, orgastic sorcery a man and woman create between them when they make love. They spun faster and faster as their passion crested until all was molten gold, then slowing, slowing as they drifted down the spiral, satiated but still together. Always together.

Tara stirred and opened her eyes when Brian's tongue caressed the whorls of her ear. She stretched languorously and reached for him, putting her arms around his neck and drawing him closer.

"Promise me something, Tara," he said, his lips almost touching hers.

Anything, at this moment: she'd promise him anything. "Yes," she whispered. "Yes."

"Promise you'll never leave me again without telling me you're going."

Her glow of happiness thinned, fading. With the magic of their coming together still potent, she hadn't gone so far as to think of their eventual parting. But he had.

"I promise," she said sadly. "I promise, Brian."

Chapter Sixteen

Tara snuggled against Brian on the rattan settee in his bungalow, trying not to remember that it was Sunday night and she had to catch an early flight to Sacramento in the morning. She smiled a little, imagining D.D.'s disapproval if he knew Dr. Shute had demonstrated to her what he meant about revising the angle on the design model by using the clamp on the soap while they were together in the bathtub.

On the other hand, maybe D.D. wouldn't mind at all, as long as the client remained satisfied. And Brian had certainly seemed to be.

So was she. Blissfully satisfied. Except for having to leave him. They'd be separated for longer than she wanted to think about. Between Brian's call schedule and committee meetings and her Monday through Friday working days, it would be a month before they'd have another weekend free to spend with each other.

Then in September he'd be in Texas for two weeks at a surgeons' seminar, and she hadn't enough vacation time left to go with him. Her only consolation was that Brian was as upset as she about their being apart.

"You work too hard," she told him. "Too many hours."

He didn't reply for a while. "When I was a med student," he said finally, "I saw myself as one day becoming a family physician in a low-key, small town practice where I'd get to know my patients well."

"Instead you're in a fast lane surgical group practicing in California's second largest city. What changed your mind?"

"I found I had a talent for surgery. I figured, why not specialize in what I was good at? I did, and one thing led to another."

"And, presto, the world famous E. B. Shute, surgeon."

"Do I detect a hint of mockery?"

"Is the *E* for Erskine?" she asked. "Eustace?"

He squeezed her up against him until she yelped. "I'll never tell," he whispered in her ear.

"But you *do* put in too many hours a week," she persisted. "Even Rick thinks so."

"It comes with the territory."

"Don't you ever long for the low-key practice you once dreamed of?"

He shrugged. "Most med students are idealists. I consider it a youthful fantasy."

"You could still do it if you really wanted to."

"It's impractical to change what I'm doing. I'm beginning to get a name here and—"

"And soon you'll be working even harder?"

He pulled away to stare down at her. "Are *you* living the kind of life you planned when you were younger?"

She straightened. "Well, you might say so. I always wanted to create from what was around me and design engineering is creating."

"Design engineering is a compromise. I compromised, you compromised. That's the reality of growing up."

A part of Tara violently rejected his words, but before she could formulate an objection, he continued.

"If you were doing found-object sculpture, your time would be your own, and you could be with me on my Wednesdays off instead of putting in your hours at Delta Two."

"I couldn't support myself doing that!"

"How do you know? You've talent enough."

"But I—but that—" She waved her hands. "You don't quit a good job to experiment."

"That's what I pointed out a few minutes ago. Compromise is the name of the game."

A heavy weight settled in her chest as she pondered the truth of his words. She liked design engineering well enough, but it would never give her the same satisfaction as creating her own vision of the world around her. She *had* compromised. She couldn't deny it, and the realization saddened her.

"Don't look so forlorn. You're good at what you do and I'm good at what I do, so the world rewards us. Isn't that enough?"

She wanted to shake her head but instead sighed and nodded. "I suppose so."

"Only a child believes he can have everything."

She didn't want everything, but Brian had made her, for the first time, question what she'd chosen. Looking back down the corridor of the years to college she saw the art courses she might have taken and did not, even though they'd intrigued her.

They're impractical. I don't have enough talent, she'd told herself at the time.

Yet she'd never tested her talent, never challenged herself to try. Was it only because she'd believed Karen was so much better? Or had she been afraid of failing?

Now Brian was telling her it was too late, and he was probably right. Again she sighed and he gathered her into his arms.

"I'd say you're in desperate need of some E. B. Shute special therapy," he murmured. "Something I've been saving for a really tough case." He shifted her onto his lap and then rose, carrying her toward the bedroom.

She clung to him, responding to the warm surge of desire his touch summoned. He'd replaced the horrible picture over the waterbed with one of a farmhouse shaded by a huge tree crowned with brilliant autumn foliage. For some reason she didn't care for the replacement, either, even though it was a well-executed watercolor.

The picture didn't matter, the lost visions of early youth didn't matter—not when she was in Brian's arms.

His kisses and the passion and strength of his beautiful body ignited her smoldering desire into a wild flare of need, a fire created by Brian and one that could only be quenched by their joining.

All the intensity was there, all the hot glorious madness of uniting with him, and it wasn't until she luxuriated in the afterglow that she realized the special harmony between them was missing and had been missing all through their lovemaking.

Why? She told herself it didn't matter, that it might be all to the good. It might mean they'd no longer share dreams, either.

* * *

Sacramento was lonely without Brian but not as dismal as when Tara thought she'd never see him again. Her spirits were noticeably higher, so much so that Yvonne commented on the change.

"It's either a new man, or the last one discovered he couldn't live without you after all," Yvonne said as they ate lunch on Tuesday. "I'd guess the lost lover resurfaced."

"Something like that," Tara admitted.

Yvonne eyed her appraisingly. "Don't get taken in twice, that's all I have to say. Otherwise I'm happy for you. For myself, too. Now I can date the Frisco hunk I was trying to save for you without a guilty conscience."

Yvonne was busy over the weekend but Tara didn't mind being alone. She relived the night on Catalina with Brian over and over in her fantasies. But fantasies weren't the same as being with him, and by the end of the month she was restless and edgy from the need to see him again.

The weekend they finally shared in San Diego was all too brief. Tara returned to Sacramento reluctantly but glowing. If a sliver of disappointment pricked her occasionally because they hadn't regained that special closeness they'd shared in Catalina, she successfully ignored it.

By the end of September, Tara and Brian had only been able to get together twice more. Once he flew to Sacramento, and once they met in Santa Barbara for a marvelous few days.

Abbott called her on the first of October.

"You haven't come east to meet your nephew yet," he said.

"I know. He's a darling. I love the pictures you and Karen sent me. But I just don't have any vacation time due." She didn't add she'd used the couple of days she'd accrued to meet Brian.

"Karen really needs to see you."

"Is something wrong? Is she ill?"

"No. The doctor says everything's fine. But she's depressed and you'd cheer her up."

Guilt nagged at Tara. "How about Christmas?" she asked. "I'll have a few days then."

"I wish you'd come sooner."

"Abbott, I just can't. May I talk to her?"

"I'm calling from the office. Please think it over, Tara."

After she'd hung up, Tara sat beside the phone, frowning. For Abbott to beg anyone for a favor was unheard of. And why had he called from the office? Was something the matter with Karen? Yet he'd assured her the doctor said she was fine.

Tara bit her lip. During Thanksgiving she'd have extra time. She and Brian had planned to fly to Mexico but maybe she'd better reconsider. In the meantime she'd call Karen and talk to her and find out what she could.

Karen was uncharacteristically curt on the phone.

"I'm fine," she snapped. "Why wouldn't I be?"

"Well, I heard sometimes new mothers get the blues, something like that," Tara said soothingly.

"Why on earth would you think I had the blues?"

"Karen, I don't think anything of the sort. I'm sorry I haven't been back to see you and my new nephew, and I promise I'll come as soon as I can."

"We wouldn't want to drag you away from the famous Dr. Shute." Karen's voice was tart. "After all, I'm only your twin, hardly as exciting as a new lover."

Karen's irritability reassured Tara. She decided nothing was really wrong with her sister. Karen was only pouting because becoming a new mother wasn't as important to everyone else as it was to her. Her sister always seemed to reach for more than Tara could willingly give. Thanksgiving would be soon enough to go east and maybe she could even put it off until Christmas.

Not that she wasn't attached to Karen and concerned about her, but "the famous Dr. Shute" *was* first and foremost in her thoughts and on her calendar. And, after all, Karen did have a husband of her own.

Tara flew to San Diego on the third weekend in October. Brian was waiting for her at the airport, and she all but flew into his arms.

"We can't go on meeting so seldom and so briefly," he said into her ear after a long, passionate kiss. "Not seeing you is driving me out of my mind."

"Me, too," she admitted breathlessly.

"Thank God Thanksgiving is coming. Six wonderful days with you in Acapulco—no beeper, no phone, no interruptions." He kissed her again and released her.

No, she told herself, she was definitely not going to give up those wonderful six days. Karen would have to wait until Christmas.

You know one permanent way to keep her with you, Brian told himself as he drove toward La Jolla with Tara beside him in the Porsche. Much as he needed her with him, that was a step he wasn't ready to take. Marriage created more problems than it solved, if his experience with Ursula was any example.

Hell, Tara might not accept anyway. She'd given no indication she was eager to marry him. As for living together...

He shook his head. Ask her to give up her work at Delta Two and move in with him? How unfair could a man get? If he knew Tara, she'd treat that suggestion with the contempt it deserved.

He'd hinted she might look for a design job in the San Diego area and move down here, but she'd taken the remark lightly, merely saying D.D. would never forgive her. Obviously there was no way for him to move to Sacramento.

He put a hand on the sensual warmth of her thigh and she slanted a smile at him. Their unusual closeness on the boat in Avalon Bay had never been repeated, but making love with her was still incredible. He couldn't believe he'd ever want any other woman.

But he didn't want to get married, either.

"The weather's good so I thought we'd cook and eat on the beach tonight," he told her.

"Great. We haven't had a picnic since Chatham. Sometimes our days together at the Cape seem no more than a beautiful vision."

"You call that storm beautiful?"

She grinned at him. "Which one? Inside or out?"

Her eyes glinted green, and he saw his own desire mirrored in their jade depths. He wanted her right now, this minute. He wanted her most of the time, and her living so far away played hell with his needs.

"I hope Jake's taking good care of Larry," she said.

He nodded. The gull's courage and his will to survive had given him a personality not easy to forget.

"Old Larry will do all right," he assured her.

"Do you miss the Cape sometimes? I do."

"Living permanently on the Cape's filed away among my youthful fantasies."

"Wouldn't it be wonderful!" She glanced at him. "Don't remind me—I know—compromise is the world's revenge."

"Why revenge?"

"I've decided the world hates idealists, like many of us were in our teens and early twenties. Didn't you tell me we had to change or not survive?"

He frowned. "I didn't put it quite like that. It's not a matter of survival but of being practical."

She didn't reply and after a few minutes he glanced at her, taking in the loose-knit pink sweater she wore with a wine skirt. Very attractive. But his strongest visual memory of her was in jeans and green T-shirt, standing on top of a dune at the barrier beach, a golden girl looking out to sea.

Chatham had been a place where they'd both stepped out of reality as they had in Catalina. His breath quickened just remembering the warm silken feel of her when they made love on the boat.

How was he going to wait until they got to the house to hold her?

"Do you think," he asked her, "that the Highway Patrol would overlook it if I pulled off the freeway and made love to you right now?"

"We can only try it and see," she said solemnly.

He swerved into the right lane, pulled onto the shoulder, stopped the car and leaned over to kiss her. The warm satin of her lips, the taste of her, aroused him almost past the point where he cared where they were.

"Damn, these cars aren't made with lovemaking in mind," he muttered as he reluctantly let her go. "I guess we can't challenge the CHP after all."

Her smile was sultry, inviting. He made himself look away, restart the car and pull back onto the freeway. She reached over and slowly began unbuttoning his shirt, stopping after each button to run her fingers over his chest hair and caress his nipples.

He felt his breath rasp in his throat as she continued to tantalize him by pulling the undone shirt out of his pants so she could stroke his upper abdomen. He groaned as her fingers edged under his waistband.

"You don't know what you're doing to me," he said hoarsely.

"Then you'll have to tell me, won't you?" Her soft, seductive tone made the blood pound in his temples.

"Tell you, hell, once I get off this damn freeway I intend to show you!"

Brian all but dragged her out of the Porsche and into the bungalow. He pulled off her sweater as soon as he shut the front door behind them, then stopped and raised his eyebrows. Tara giggled at the surprised look on his face.

"What, may I ask, is this?" he asked, smoothing a finger over the very sexy silk and lace champagne-colored bra she'd bought just for him, his touch making her shiver and her nipples rise with delighted anticipation.

"You haven't seen anything yet," she told him as she eased out of her skirt and half slip.

The bikini panties matched the bra. The pair had cost a fortune but watching the admiration in Brian's eyes as he looked at her made it worth every cent.

"You are some sexy woman," he murmured, caressing her breasts through the fragile, see-through fabric.

She'd never had the nerve to wear wispy undergarments like these before but Brian made her feel sexy and beautiful enough to wear anything.

Under his touch, she pressed close to him and she felt his arousal, hard and urgent against her.

"With surprises like that," he said against her lips, "you're going to be lucky if we even make it to the bedroom."

His tongue explored her mouth, his enticing taste increasing her own urgency. He cupped her buttocks, his hands hot through the flimsy bikini, lifting her, holding her, rocking her against his hardness, until she longed to tear away the cloth separating them.

His mouth sought her breast, his tongue circling her nipple through the bra, and she moaned.

"Brian," she whispered. "I need you. Now."

He set her feet back on the floor and began to unbuckle his belt, his eyes smoky-blue with desire.

A knock on the door froze them both. Brian swore, rebuckling his belt.

"I'll get rid of whoever it is," he growled. "Fast."

Tara grabbed up her belongings and fled to the bedroom. When Brian didn't join her after a few minutes, she started to get dressed. She was pulling on her skirt when Brian tapped on the closed door before opening it far enough to stick his head inside.

"Our caller is here to see you." He spoke without expression, and before she could ask who the caller was, Brian closed the door with a bang.

Tara put on her sweater, ran a brush through her hair and left the bedroom wondering who on earth would appear at Brian's door asking for her. Rita? No, she'd call first.

As she stepped into the living room, Tara stopped abruptly, her eyes widening.

"Abbott!" she exclaimed. "Whatever are you doing here?"

Chapter Seventeen

Tara had time to see Abbott was as impeccable as always, in a navy-blue blazer and pants, a white shirt and striped tie, before he reached for her hands. He must have noticed her attempt to withdraw because instead of hugging her, as she thought he meant to, he merely squeezed her hands and let her go.

"You're looking very good, Tara," he said.

"But why are you here?" she asked him again, aware of Brian glowering behind Abbott.

"I was in Los Angeles for a meeting," Abbott explained. "When I called your place in Sacramento, the phone machine gave me a number I recognized as Dr. Shute's. So I flew to San Diego. No one answered, but I was able to discover where Dr. Shute lived and I drove over here."

"You seem to have a talent for ferreting out unlisted numbers and addresses," Brian said coldly.

Abbott glanced at him. "I felt this was an emergency."

Tara cringed inwardly, knowing Brian wouldn't appreciate Abbott's who-are-you-to-question-me? tone. Then Abbott's words registered.

"Is something wrong with Karen?" she demanded.

"Yes. I told you when I called earlier this month how depressed she was. She's worse. Sits and cries all the time. The doctor calls it postpartum depression and admits he's worried about her. I'm worried, too. I wouldn't be here if I wasn't.

"If my mother hadn't offered to stay with Karen for the time I was gone I would have had to cancel the L.A. meeting because, frankly, in her present state, I wouldn't want to leave her alone overnight."

Karen would never have agreed to that arrangement unless she was past protesting anything, Tara thought, because she detested her mother-in-law.

"I talked to her doctor about how close Karen has always been to you," Abbott continued, "and he agrees with me that a visit from you might go a long way toward curing Karen. Twins, he said, share a special closeness, an intuitive understanding of one another."

But *we* don't, was on the tip of Tara's tongue until Brian said it for her.

"Tara told me she and her sister aren't identical twins." Brian wasn't cool now. He sounded actively hostile. "Fraternal twins aren't known to share intuitive relationships."

She stared at Brian, trying to catch his eye but he was glaring at Abbott, who ignored him.

"Karen's problem's affected the baby, too," Abbott said to her. "The pediatrician blames his colic on his mother's depression. Michael's healthy enough, it seems, and the doctor can't find any other cause. Babies sense stress and react to it, is what he told me."

"You still have the nurse caring for the baby, don't you?" she asked.

"No. She told us when we hired her she was strictly a newborn nurse and would leave after six weeks, no matter what. I've hired nursemaids but they don't stay." He shrugged. "Little Michael screams most of the day and half the night, and Karen just sits and cries. Frankly, I dread coming home evenings."

"And you expect Tara to solve all this?" Brian demanded.

Abbott turned to him. "I fail to see what business it is of yours, Doctor."

To Tara they seemed like two angry tomcats facing each other, fur ruffled, each growling a challenge at the other.

"Brian," she put in hastily. "I've always been able to handle Karen. I may be able to help."

Brian transferred his stormy gaze to her. "You're going? With Abbott?"

"Well—" her eyes pleaded with him to understand "—what else can I do? She's my sister and she needs me."

"I hoped you'd say that," Abbott said, gripping her shoulders. "In fact, I knew you wouldn't let me down."

She eased away from Abbott and crossed to Brian, whose arms were folded across his bare chest. He gazed at her stonily.

"I arranged for your ticket from L.A. to Kennedy," Abbott said from behind her. "We'll fly back together. Tonight."

A muscle twitched in Brian's set face. Tara bit her lip. She glanced over her shoulder at her brother-in-law.

"Look, Abbott, would you mind waiting in your car?" she asked.

He smiled at her. "Of course not." At the door he paused and said, "My apologies if you feel I've trespassed, doctor."

As the door closed behind Abbott, Brian said through clenched teeth, "Are you going with him?"

Tara took a deep breath and let it out slowly. "Stop it! This has nothing to do with Abbott. Yes, I *am* going to Karen. She needs me."

"This is the sister who, from what you've told me, has been exploiting you all her life, all your life. Don't you think this is another example?"

"I never said Karen exploited me!"

"Not in so many words. Maybe you don't listen when you talk about your twin. The message comes through loud and clear."

"You're twisting what I've told you."

He shook his head.

Tara, who'd been hanging onto her temper, lost control. "I'm not any happier than you are about having to leave but I've no choice. There's no reason for you to be angry at me."

"No? Why are you in so much of a hurry that you have to fly back with Abbott? Do you jump every time he tells you to?"

She stared at his scowling face. "Just what are you implying?"

"You can't tell me that you're not going east partly because of him. Because *he* asked you."

Tara was speechless with fury.

"I knew you wouldn't let me down." Brian mimicked Abbott's voice.

"I'm not responsible for what he says. I'll tell you one more time and that's all. I feel responsible for my sister. She needs me, the sooner the better. I'm flying east to try to help her. Abbott has nothing to do with it."

He grunted, a sound of total disbelief.

Tara stomped into the bedroom to retrieve her shoulder bag. On the way back she stopped in the living room and glared at Brian.

"You asked me once to tell you when I was leaving," she said icily. "Well, I am. Now!"

She strode to the door, opened it and, fighting her impulse to slam it behind her, gritted her teeth and closed the door gently. She yanked her suitcase out of the Porsche and the waiting Abbott stowed it in his rental car.

"Your Dr. Shute has a short fuse, doesn't he?" Abbott said as he backed the car from the drive.

"I don't care to discuss him!" she snapped, as angry for the moment at Abbott as she was at Brian.

Of all the insensitive, wrong-headed men in the world, Brian took the prize. Insinuating she still carried a torch for Abbott! Abbott was the past for her as much as Ursula was for Brian. Over and done with. Once she'd thought she was in love with Abbott, but now she knew her feeling had been no more than infatuation. Love was another emotion entirely. A terrible, frightening one. An emotion she didn't want to experience.

She had to admit, though, she'd been jealous of Ursula. Without cause, maybe, but jealous anyway. So she understood, in a way, Brian's being upset over Abbott. What she couldn't forgive Brian for was turning what she'd told him about Karen into something perverted and ugly. She could never forgive him for that. Never.

New York was cold and rainy. Tara was thoroughly tired of Abbott's company, though at least he'd behaved himself, apparently cured of any tendency to come on to her. She was looking forward to seeing Karen.

On their arrival, she found Karen shut in her bedroom, and Mrs. Dade, holding a fretful Michael, looked as tired as Tara felt.

Tara barely had her jacket hung in the entry closet before Mrs. Dade thrust the baby at her.

"I'm all packed and ready to leave," she told her son.

Abbott promptly took off to drive his mother home to Delaware, announcing he'd stay overnight at her house, leaving Tara with a crying baby she didn't have the least notion how to care for. There was no choice but to wake Karen, who Mrs. Dade had said was "resting."

Tara tapped on the bedroom door, then opened it. Michael wailed loudly and Karen sat up in bed, took one look at her sister and her son and burst into tears. It was some time before she quieted enough to tell Tara what to do for Michael.

Tara, unused to handling small babies, tried to cope but felt awkward and uneasy. Little Michael, seemingly aware of her inexperience, wailed louder than ever when she changed and bathed him, and she thought she'd never get the nipple of the bottle into his mouth properly. When he finally slept she breathed a sigh of relief.

She was up for almost two hours in the night with him and found she had full responsibility for Michael again the next day.

"I just can't cope," Karen pleaded fretfully. "You don't understand. No one does."

By seven that evening Abbott still hadn't returned. If Karen wasn't resting in her room when the baby cried she'd look at him hopelessly and cry herself.

"I'm dead on my feet," Tara announced once she finally put Michael in his crib for the night. "I think I'll go to bed. The time difference—"

Karen put her hands over her face and sobbed.

Tara touched her sister's shoulder. "What's wrong?" she said.

"You look so great and I look like an old frump," Karen said between sobs.

Tara found no quick reply since the truth was Karen had let herself go. Her hair needed cutting and a new permanent. She'd either not lost all the weight she'd gained with the pregnancy, or she'd gained weight after she delivered. Whatever the cause, her clothes didn't fit.

"I wouldn't say that," Tara finally answered cautiously.

"Then you're a liar!" Karen wiped her eyes with already damp tissue.

Tara sighed. "Look, I'm so tired I don't know which end is up, much less what I'm saying. Why don't we both get some sleep while Michael's quiet?"

Karen began to sniffle again. "Abbott's not home yet. What if he isn't going to come home? Maybe that's why he brought you here, so he could leave and never come back."

"Karen, that's—" Tara paused. *Crazy* wasn't the best word to use. "You're overreacting," she went on. "Probably because you're tired, too. Neither of us got much sleep last night because of Michael's colic."

"You don't like him," Karen accused. "You're upset because I named him after Mike, and you're cross with both me and the baby because of it."

"He's a darling. I love him already." That was stretching it a little. Both she and the baby needed to get used to each other, but he certainly was cute enough when he wasn't crying. "As for his name, I'm glad you called him Michael."

Karen stared at her suspiciously.

"I think he looks a lot like your baby pictures," Tara went on. "Blond and blue-eyed. You know you were a beautiful baby. He is, too."

Karen's face softened. "He's so sweet. I used to hold him and feel as though I was melting with love. But now he cries all the time. I'm afraid something's wrong with him and no one will tell me. The pediatrician, Dr. Trump, claims it's all my fault, so if there isn't anything wrong with Michael maybe he cries because he doesn't like *me*."

Tara wanted to take her sister by the shoulders and shake her until Karen's common sense filtered back into her head from wherever she'd mislaid it.

"On Monday I'll find a woman to come in and help take care of the house," Tara said. "After she's been here a few days and we can tell she's reliable, we'll leave Michael with her and go shopping for a few hours. Buying new clothes will cheer you up."

"You think I'm fat," Karen wailed.

The door opened and Abbott walked in. Tara thought she'd never been so glad to see him in her life.

"Here's Abbott now," she told Karen firmly. "I'm going to bed. We'll both feel better in the morning."

By the end of the following week Tara was at her wit's end. Nothing was ever any better any morning. She'd tried two women; one was impossible and the other hadn't suited Karen. Michael cried so much Tara insisted on taking him to Dr. Trump for an exam. He pronounced Michael a healthy, normal infant and lectured Tara about reducing the stress in the home.

Karen alternately wept or found fault with everything Tara said or did, and Abbott came home late and left early. When he was home, he shut himself in his study.

The skies stayed cloudy with intermittent rain. Tara pictured Brian relaxing on the beach in front of his La Jolla bungalow under the California sun and hated him.

She also missed him acutely. He hadn't phoned or written and she wasn't about to contact him. After all, whose fault was it he'd been so unreasonable about Abbott and so cruel about her sister? Certainly not hers.

She called D.D. in Sacramento and told him she'd have to take an indefinite leave of absence since she didn't know when her sister would be well enough for her to return to California.

"I can't say I'm happy," D.D. said, "but, considering your excellent work record, I'll okay a full month's leave. Keep in touch with me."

Tara had been at Karen's house ten days before she found an older woman, Carla Bell, she thought would work out. Unfortunately Carla could only come half days during the week and not at all on weekends but her presence allowed Tara to get some much needed rest during the day.

Now I'll get somewhere with Karen, she told herself optimistically. We'll go shopping, maybe have lunch at a fancy restaurant. She'll feel better once she's wearing clothes that fit and is out in the world again. Once she's feeling more like herself, she won't be so unreasonable.

Karen wouldn't budge from the house.

"How well do we know Carla?" she demanded. "Maybe she's just waiting for the chance to kidnap Michael."

"Okay, I'll stay here with Michael and Carla," Tara said. "You go and at least get your hair done."

"What's wrong with the way my hair looks?" Karen demanded.

Tara held her tongue with difficulty.

Each day, despite Carla's help, the tension in the house increased. Tara crawled back into bed at two on a Friday morning, after walking the floor for an hour with a wailing Michael, and lay awake thinking of Brian. She relived the last time they'd made love and wound up more restless than ever.

What was he doing at this moment? Was he sleeping in the water bed under that picture of the house shaded by the big oak? Or was he at the hospital taking care of some emergency?

The watercolor stuck in her mind and she wondered again why she didn't like it. The artist had talent. The tree, especially, was beautiful with the leaves in colorful autumn dress....

The tree loomed over her, larger than any tree she'd ever seen, bigger than a redwood or sequoia. The leaves flared like fire, threatening her, and she backed away. A wind rustled through the branches and the leaves began to fall like embers. Tara turned and ran, fearing their touch.

Suddenly she was inside a house, looking from a window. Not the house the tree belonged to. She was in Grandma Fallkirk's house and could see a man standing on the beach outside the window. He held out his arms to her, and her heart pounded frantically when she recognized Brian.

She tried to call his name but no words came. Hurrying to go to him, she flung open the door, only to discover a tree growing directly in front of the door, between her and the beach. Between her and Brian. The huge trunk of the oak blocked the exit so she couldn't squeeze past.

Afraid of the burning leaves, she stared up into the branches and saw with a shock that the tree was wound about with mistletoe, so much she could scarcely see any of the bark or the leaves because of the parasitical growth.

Though the tree blocked her way, at the same time it was dying because the mistletoe had sucked its life away. The knowledge terrified her. Again she tried to call to Brian but could not. She was trapped....

Tara woke crying. As she calmed herself, recovering from the nightmare, a name popped into her mind.

Leda Umak. Leda had told her about an oak wound with mistletoe. Had her words lingered in Tara's subconscious all this time and triggered the dream? That must be it.

During the rest of the day the dream haunted Tara. Finally, late in the afternoon, when Karen was resting in her bedroom and not likely to overhear, Tara called Leda Umak.

"Tara Reed? Why, yes, I remember you—I never forget a sensitive. There are so few of us."

Tara told her about the dream.

"That was my vision, too," Leda said.

"But what can it mean?" Tara couldn't control the tremor in her voice.

"You have a sister, don't you? A twin?"

"Yes. Karen."

"I had a feeling that day when the two of you visited, a feeling so nebulous I hesitated to mention it. Even now I wonder if I should."

"Tell me," Tara pleaded, "what did you feel?"

"I sensed an unhealthy color where your auras overlapped. That's all. It may mean nothing."

After Tara had thanked Leda and put down the phone, she sat on the couch pondering the parapsychologist's words. The mistletoe wound around the tree, Brian's angry insistence Karen was exploiting her, Karen's misery that was making everyone around her equally miserable—were they connected?

Tara was distracted through the evening meal and when she went to bed she couldn't sleep, despite her fatigue. What if Brian is right? she asked herself. Am I the oak and Karen the mistletoe?

The more she thought it over, the more convinced she became that Karen *was* taking advantage of her. And she was allowing it to happen. Why?

Tara shook her head, unable to answer. Guilt, she supposed, but why should she feel guilty about Karen? It should be the other way around. Karen ought to be feeling guilty because she'd hidden the fact she and Abbott were seeing each other for months, while they both allowed Tara to believe Abbott was still interested in her.

Not that it mattered any longer. She found less to admire in Abbott with every passing day. Why couldn't he take some responsibility for Karen and his son?

Toting up Abbott's weaknesses wasn't going to solve the basic problem. What was wrong between Karen and her?

Tara sighed and turned over in bed for what seemed like the thousandth time.

Since I've been here Karen seems to resent everything I say or do, she thought. Yet she gets panicky if I mention leaving. It can't go on like this. I have to force the issue.

Tomorrow, she decided. It's high time Abbott was inducted into service. Tomorrow's Saturday so he can take Michael for a walk in the stroller, leaving Karen and me alone to thrash this out between us.

And I won't be satisfied with anything but the truth.

Chapter Eighteen

Is he or is he not your son?" Tara asked Abbott on Saturday afternoon, her voice sharp with annoyance.

"Really, Tara, what kind of a question is that?" Abbott tried for an injured tone but had trouble concealing his irritation.

"Well, from the way you're acting, I thought you might have disowned Michael. All I asked you to do was to take him for a walk in the stroller. The sun's finally shining and he needs fresh air. He's been fed, he's not crying, he's clean and dry and he's dressed warmly. If you need a demonstration of how to push the stroller, I'll be glad to provide one."

Abbott put on his best supercilious glare. "Is that meant to be amusing?"

Tara ignored his words. "You have to get used to Michael sometime," she pointed out. "Today's the day to start. I mean it, Abbott. You take your son for this walk or I'm going to walk out! I don't mind taking care of him, but

I'm damned if you're going to sit around watching college football on TV instead of doing your share."

"All right, all right. No need to overreact. That's always been a problem with you, Tara, this tendency to—"

"Don't talk. Just do it. Now."

Once she'd finally seen Abbott off with Michael in the stroller, Tara tapped on Karen's bedroom door.

"I'm resting," Karen said petulantly.

"Sorry, time's up." Tara pushed open the door as she spoke.

Karen lay propped against pillows, her blue eyes wide with surprise. Tara crossed to her, kicked off her shoes and sat at the foot of the bed, Indian fashion.

"Abbott and Michael are taking a stroll," Tara said, "so we won't be interrupted. I think it's time you and I had a serious talk."

"You let Abbott take Michael out alone?"

"He's his father and a perfectly capable adult."

"But Abbott doesn't—"

"Shut up." Tara spoke quietly, without rancor. "This is our discussion, yours and mine. I refuse to let you distract me."

"Whatever's gotten into you?" Karen demanded.

"We have to clear the air between us." Tara tried to keep her voice calm and even while her stomach roiled with apprehension. "Last night I was mulling over the problems we're all having right now, and I realized I've been knocking myself out since I came here trying to placate you. Suddenly I understood it was a continuation of a lifelong pattern. I've *always* tried to placate you.

"I searched for a reason and I think I've found it. My behavior's a reaction to yours. You act as though you resent me; you have for years. Why? Why do you resent me so much?"

"Resent you? What a strange thing to say when we've always been the best of friends."

"Don't avoid answering. You do resent me. Since I've been here you've not only refused to cooperate with my efforts to improve things, but you've done your best to make me do all the work. The more I try to please you, the worse you get. Your doctor says you're suffering from a postpartum depression. Okay, I won't argue about that, but your behavior toward me goes back to our childhood."

Karen sat straighter, crossing her arms over her breasts. "You're crazy!"

"No, I'm not." Tara paused a moment to try to still the tremor in her voice. "Why do you dislike me, Karen? I don't dislike you."

"You're imagining things. Why, we're twins. Twins love each other."

"We're fraternal twins so we're no closer than sisters might be. Many sisters are very close. Others hate each other." She gazed challengingly at Karen.

Karen's lower lip trembled. "I don't understand why you're being so mean. I'm trying to get my strength back and here you are picking on me."

"You're doing it again!" Tara cried. "Putting me on the defensive, hoping to make me feel guilty. I won't tolerate it any longer, do you hear me?"

Tears welled into Karen's eyes as she looked piteously at her sister.

In desperation Tara grabbed Karen by the shoulders and shook her. "Be honest with me for once in your life!" she demanded.

Karen jerked away from her, dropping her defensive pose. Her eyes glittered with unshed tears as she pointed a shaking finger at Tara. "You never loved me!" she cried. "No one's ever loved me and it's all because of you. It's all your fault. You were born first. You were always the first."

Her voice took on a child's high pitch. "First with Mom and Dad. First with Grandma Fallkirk. When Mike was born he smiled at you first. He liked you best. I tried to make you like *me* best, so someone would, but then you had to go and dream with Mike. Why not with me? I'm your twin. You should have dreamed with me."

Tears ran down Karen's cheeks and she brushed at them angrily. "When you shared dreams with Mike I knew you'd never love me best. No one has ever loved me as much as they did you. Not even Abbott. And now you're taking my baby's love away from me, too."

Karen flung herself onto her side, sobbing convulsively. Tara, her eyes blurring with tears, reached for her sister, putting a hand on her shoulder. Karen tried to shrug her off, but Tara threw both arms around her, crying as she hugged her twin, and they wept in each other's arms.

"I never knew," Tara finally said brokenly. "I didn't realize how you felt. To me you were always the prettiest, the most talented. I never felt I was first in anything."

Karen pulled away, reaching for a box of tissues on the nightstand. She took a handful and offered the box to Tara.

"In a way you're right about me," Tara said as she mopped her wet face. "I'm afraid to love anyone—even you."

Karen paused in wiping her eyes. "Why?"

Tara curled her legs under her. "I was too upset to tell you or Mom and Dad, but the moment Mike died in that accident I knew it. I felt his death inside me—because of sharing the dreams with him, I guess. I loved Mike and he died.

"I suppose my fear of loving anyone started then. I didn't consciously think it through, but I must have decided that if I loved you, then you might die, too. I knew I couldn't bear it if you did, so it was safer not to love you. Or anyone else."

Astonishment flooded Karen's tear-washed eyes. "I didn't have any idea you felt like that! No wonder Abbott said—" She broke off, covering her mouth with her hand.

Tara managed a wry smile. "You can tell me. I'll survive."

"Well, Abbott said when you two were, well, going together, he never felt close to you because you always kept your distance. 'Sometimes she treated me like a stranger,' he said."

Tara nodded slowly. "He's probably right."

"I felt rotten about seeing Abbott behind your back," Karen went on, "but I loved him so much and I, well, I didn't believe you did. He needed *me*, not you."

"It hurt," Tara admitted, "but I felt betrayed more than anything else because you waited so long before you told me what was going on. As for loving him—no, I didn't. Any more than Abbott loved me."

Karen sighed. "I'm not so sure about him. He came on to you last March, if you'll recall. I know I yelled at you then, but I really knew it was Abbott's fault. You'd never behave underhandedly. You never have and you never will."

Tara made a face. "It was a misunderstanding all the way around. Abbott had a misplaced surge of lust when I came out of the bathroom not realizing he'd arrived home early. You walked in before I managed to extricate myself, and you were justifiably upset. I don't excuse his behavior but lust isn't love. Far from it!

"Abbott was never in love with me. He needed someone like you and he was smart enough to recognize it even if I wasn't." Tara smiled. "I once thought I'd never be able to mean this, but I'm glad you found each other."

"We seem to have lost the way since then." Karen turned her head to glance at herself in the mirror over the dresser. "I look positively awful!" she wailed. "No wonder he shuts himself in the study all the time."

"Your hair needs cutting and styling. New clothes will take care of the rest."

"I'm afraid I need a new me!" But Karen smiled ruefully as she spoke, and Tara felt a surge of hope and happiness.

On Monday, Karen and Tara went shopping in New York City, leaving Carla to look after Michael. Tara could hardly get over the change in the baby in just two days. His colic had all but vanished—he'd actually slept through last night—and he smiled so much she realized for the first time he had an engaging dimple in his right cheek.

On Tuesday Karen went off alone to have her hair done while Carla and Tara got everything ready for a special supper for two that Carla had agreed to stay late to serve.

Karen arrived home at five looking, Tara thought, absolutely gorgeous. Partly because of the hairdo but also because her face had regained its customary animation. Karen hurried to take a quick shower and put on a periwinkle-blue wool dress she'd bought the day before.

"Stunning," was Tara's verdict.

"Do you really think so?" Karen's blue eyes, their attractiveness enhanced with carefully applied makeup, widened in apprehension. "I feel so nervous."

"You've never looked more calm and poised. If it's enough to fool me, you can certainly fool a mere man." Tara grinned at her, feeling a closeness to her sister that had been lost for years.

As soon as Abbott pulled into the drive, Tara began to dress Michael in his snowsuit. By the time he entered the house she had Michael ready and was putting on her jacket.

"Where are you going?" Abbott asked her.

"Michael and I have a date this evening," she said. "Karen's waiting in the living room to tell you all about it."

Abbott stared at her. "But where—?"

She held up her hand. "My lips are sealed. You'll have to find out from Karen." She picked up the baby, who was strapped in his infant seat, and was out the door before Abbott could question her further.

Tara, who'd been apprehensive as to how Michael would like being pushed through the nearest mall in his stroller, was pleasantly surprised when the baby seemed to actively enjoy the outing, gazing wide-eyed at the brightly lit store windows and at the passing people.

"What a beautiful child!" a grandmother shopper commented. "You must be very proud of him."

"Oh, yes," Tara replied. "I am."

I wish he *was* mine, she thought. Not Michael, really, but a baby like him. Only her child wouldn't be blond. She or he would have auburn hair....

Tara shook her head sadly. If Brian cared anything for her, he'd have called by now. That imaginary auburn-haired child would have to be put aside with her other discarded dreams.

Glancing at her watch, she decided Karen and Abbott must be eating their candle lit dinner by now. They'd be alone in the house because Carla would have left as soon as the meal was on the table.

Abbott better have the sense to appreciate the change in Karen, she thought. If he doesn't measure up to her expectations, she'll be crushed. If he's capable of loving anyone besides himself, though, it's Karen. Let's hope he proves it to her tonight!

Michael smiled and cooed at Tara while she sat in a Friendly's having a cheeseburger and a vanilla shake.

"You're trying to entice me to stay on at your parents' house, aren't you?" she said to him. "Trying with that dimple to charm Aunt Tara into not going back to California. Well, kid, much as I'm going to miss you, it won't work. I'd just be in the way if things turn out like they should. And if your thick-headed father picks up on his cues, everything *will* turn out well."

Karen really does love Abbott, she mused. She'll never threaten his image of himself as all-powerful. I'm sure I did. Abbott and I would have been miserably unhappy together. Thank heaven we *didn't* marry!

Tara fed Michael his evening bottle shortly before the mall closed at nine, then bundled him into his car seat and drove back to the house. He was sound asleep by the time she got there and didn't rouse when she carried him in through the back door.

Abbott and Karen weren't in the living room. The study door was open and no one was inside. When she headed for the nursery with Michael, she saw the door of the master bedroom was closed, and she smiled triumphantly.

Tiptoeing down the corridor, she entered the nursery and carefully closed the door behind her. When the baby was in his crib and she was certain he wouldn't awaken, she left the door ajar and went to her own room. Everything was going to be just fine.

Except for her.

What was Brian doing at this moment? Was he thinking about her as she was him? Missing her? Of course he didn't miss her. She probably never even crossed his mind, and she'd better remove him from hers. There was no use in dwelling on Brian. It got her nowhere and only made her miserable.

Tomorrow she'd make her reservations for Sacramento and, with luck, be there before the weekend. Depression settled over her like a La Jolla fog. What, after all, was she returning to? Only a job.

Sometime in the night Tara believed she saw Grandma Fallkirk's tall, spare figure bending over her bed. I'm dreaming, she told herself.

"Tara," Grandma said, "you must choose wisely."

"How do I know what's wise?" Tara asked.

To her distress, the figure began to fade. She sat up and reached for her grandmother's hand, touched nothing but air. Grandma Fallkirk was gone and only her words lingered in the darkness.

"Go home, child, go home."

In the morning Tara assured herself it *had* all been a dream. She deliberately waited in her room until she knew Abbott had left for his office and then came down to the kitchen. She heard Karen singing before she got there.

"*A* is for an apple red," Karen sang, "*B* is for a baby's bed..."

Tara stopped, tears stinging her eyes, remembering their mother singing the same song to Karen and herself when they were little. In the kitchen, Michael was on the table propped in his infant seat, smiling at his mother as she sang to him while she loaded the dishwasher.

"Okay?" Tara asked, though the answer was obvious since Karen radiated happiness.

Karen raised one hand, putting her thumb and forefinger together to form a circle. "Abbott said he'd been so afraid he'd never get back the girl he married. Wasn't that sweet?"

"Well..." Tara lifted her eyebrows.

"I knew you'd have problems with it." Karen grinned. "So I said to him, '*Woman* you married, dear.'"

Tara laughed and threw her arms around her sister. Michael chortled with delight.

After she'd eaten breakfast and was drinking a second cup of coffee with Karen, Tara told her she was leaving.

"Oh, I wish you'd stay for a while longer," Karen said.

"No, you don't. Three's a crowd now. We won't count Michael, he belongs."

"California's so far away," Karen said wistfully. "You've been wonderful with Michael. I can see you adore him. I wish we lived closer together so you wouldn't miss him growing up. I'd like him to know and love his Aunt Tara."

"I can hardly bear to leave him. I didn't realize babies were so addicting. Especially Michael. But I can't just leave my position at Delta Two. It's really a very good job."

Karen smiled. "You're omitting California's other attractions. I *do* understand, and I'm sorry I was so bitchy about you and Dr. Shute."

"I won't be seeing him anymore." Tara kept her tone carefully emotionless.

"That's a shame! I had the feeling you really liked him."

Tara started to deny it, then stopped. She and Karen had started out afresh and her sister deserved the truth. "I did," she admitted. "But things just didn't fall into place for us."

When Tara picked up the phone to call Kennedy Airport, her finger froze above the buttons. What waited for her in California? Definitely not Brian. The feeling gripped her that she absolutely couldn't go back to work at Delta Two with her emotions still in a turmoil. D.D. had given her a month's leave and the month wasn't up. She couldn't stay here, but she could drive to Chatham.

A sense of peace eased the ache in her chest. In the dream her grandmother had told her to go home. That's exactly what she was going to do.

Chapter Nineteen

On the long drive to Cape Cod, Tara tried to keep memories of Brian from surfacing. She turned on the radio and the station, featuring fifteen minutes of what they called "music for grandparents," played "Avalon." She switched stations before she began to cry, but it was a close call. After that she made sure she tuned into news or talk shows.

She arrived at Jake Logan's to pick up the keys to the Chatham house, wondering if Larry would remember her at all. She knew he probably wouldn't. Even if gulls happened to have long memories, her acquaintance with Larry had been very brief.

"I'll take the gull with me, too," she told Jake when he handed her the keys.

"Well, Miss Tara, likely you won't." Jake spoke in his usual laconic drawl.

"Why not?"

"'Cause he ain't here. Ain't been here since the week after you left in March. He couldn't fly worth a darn, but he had enough gumption to get hisself over my ten-foot fence. I ain't seen hide nor hair nor feather of him since, and I been looking."

"He hasn't been around the Fallkirk house at all? Or on the beach nearby?"

Jake shook his head. "If a bird or an animal ain't able to fend for himself, why it's the nature of things that something finishes him off."

Tara felt tears threaten and blinked them away. If she once started crying, she might never stop. She'd counted on Larry's company to occupy some of her time. He'd been so persevering, so plucky. It was almost more than she could bear to think he was dead.

"Maybe I'll find him," she said with a hopefulness she willed herself to feel.

After two days of walking along the beach searching for Larry, she reluctantly concluded Jake was right. Only the tough, those with no disadvantages and those with a sense of purpose, survived in this world, she told herself as she ate her evening meal beside the fire. If *she* meant to survive she'd have to find a direction. She certainly couldn't spend the rest of her life huddled in Grandma Fallkirk's house aching with the misery of missing Brian.

Absently she noted that her old found-object sculpture she'd rescued from the attic was beginning to fall apart—probably from age and being handled—and she decided the grasses were too ancient and brittle for her to try repairing it.

She could make another one. Maybe it wasn't much of a direction, but sculpting would occupy her while she made up her mind what to do with her life.

The night passed restlessly. She was awake as much as she slept, but she was grateful not to have any dreams she remembered.

The next morning, alone on the cold November beach, she enthusiastically gathered flotsam and driftwood at low tide. The sound water glittered in the sunlight, a chill breeze ruffling its gray-blue surface. The scent of wood smoke from someone's chimney reminded her of the warmth of her own fireplace, and the pleasant acrid odor hurried her steps homeward.

There wasn't a bit of glue in the house. This was turning into more of a project than she'd envisioned. Now she'd have to go shopping.

At the craft shop, Tara asked what type of glue was best for what she intended to do.

"Driftwood and flotsam?" the thirtyish woman running the shop repeated. "That sounds fascinating. Do you have a place to sell your sculptures?" She flipped the long black braid over her shoulder so it hung down her back. "I don't mean to pry but I have a friend who rents space in her gallery, and I thought you might be interested."

"Well, I don't—" Tara began.

"Wait. I have her card somewhere," the black-haired woman said, digging in a drawer. "Here it is." She handed the card to Tara. "You never know, you might want to talk to her about it sometime."

Sell her sculptures? Tara thought with amusement. She hadn't even created one yet! But it was simpler to accept the card than to explain.

"I also have sand-smoothed glass pieces in the back if you'd like to see them," the woman said. "It sounds like sea glass would work well in what you're doing."

Tara left the shop with a package of various colored glass bits, the glue, a pamphlet on preserving weeds, flowers and grasses and the paraphernalia to do it. She'd also bought a stapler supplied with gray and tan staples that looked less obvious in wood. Plus she'd met a potential friend. Anne Rochelle, the shop owner, had invited her to lunch on Wednesday.

Using the kitchen table, Tara worked the entire afternoon on a sculpture, only to take it apart in the evening. She wasn't sure what she wanted to create, but she knew what she'd done wasn't right and she went to bed discouraged.

Nothing was right. She couldn't sculpt, Larry was missing, and she'd never see Brian again. How was she going to live without Brian? The tears began and she cried until she was exhausted.

Even then she couldn't sleep. Lines from "Avalon" went around and around in her head on a monotonous musical carousel.

Only she couldn't go back because there'd be no magic on Catalina without Brian. He was the magic and the wonder. He was everything she wanted.

In Brian's arms she was beautiful; in his arms she came fully alive. Without him she merely existed.

But he didn't want her. Hadn't he shown how little he cared by not trying to get in touch with her since she'd left California?

I won't think about him, she told herself firmly, turning over onto her other side. The next minute she was imagining they were on the boat in Avalon Bay exchanging sweet crème de menthe kisses and slow, sensual caresses while the deck rocked underneath them, rocked them to a shattering climax of passion....

Tara stood on the beach watching a flock of gulls winging over the water. Some wore speckled brown feathers on their breasts and wings, and she knew they were young birds, not yet a year old. Soon they'd be old enough to grow the spotless white breast plumage she sported. She preened her gray wing feathers and readied herself to join the flock.

Running along the sand with her clawed feet, she launched herself into the air. For a moment she was filled with the joy of rising, of flying, then she slipped sideways and tumbled back to earth.

What had happened? She knew she could fly, she'd been born to fly, like all gulls. Again she launched herself, and again failed. The gulls she'd been watching were almost out of sight, heading for the fishing boats in hope of a meal. They hadn't waited for her to join them; she hadn't expected them to. After it left the nest, each gull was on its own.

She wouldn't give up. She'd keep trying to rise into the air because she was a gull and gulls flew.

Then she wasn't a gull. She was Tara, and she stood on the beach watching a herring gull try to fly. Again and again it rose a few feet above the sand, failed, fell back. One of its wings was crippled. It would never fly but the gull didn't realize it was doomed. Again and again it launched itself until she could bear the sight no longer and turned away, crying....

Tara woke with a vision of the sculpture she meant to build in her mind.

All day she fought to realize her vision, choosing, discarding, placing a piece, moving it. By three in the afternoon she stood back and sighed. Not quite what she was aiming at but almost. She was succeeding. Her stomach growled, reminding her she hadn't had lunch.

She peeled a banana and ate it while she stared at the sculpture, considering what had to be added or changed to make it exactly right. Darkness had fallen when she finally decided what she'd made expressed her vision of a bird, a gull struggling to do what it knows it was born to do—fly.

Excitement spread through her as she gazed at what she'd done. I've finished, she thought. Finished my sculpture and my work says what I want it to. Brian was right. I *do* have creative talent. If only I could show the sculpture to him.

Brian would understand. Brian would be happy for her. But he'd never see it, never know.

Why not? she asked herself. Why can't *you* call *him*?

If he wanted to hear my voice he'd have called me.

Would he? Maybe he really does think you're carrying a torch for Abbott.

How could anyone be so stupid?

Jealousy is usually stupid. Remember how upset you were about Ursula?

Brian knows how I feel about him.

Does he? When did you tell him?

Well, he *must* know. After all that's happened between us.

Did you ever tell him how you felt?

No. No, I never told him I loved him.

There, it was out. She loved Brian. She couldn't help herself, never mind if it was dangerous or one-sided or futile. She loved him, and she would always love him. And, damn it, she was going to tell him, whether he wanted to hear the words or not.

How foolish she'd been to fear love because she feared loss. Love might be a risk but without love you had nothing. She was richer for having loved her brother Mike, even though she'd lost him.

How would she go about telling Brian? What would she say when he came on the line after she called him?

I can't just blurt out, "I love you!" she thought.

Then again, why not? Maybe the simplest way was the best.

What if he tried to cut her off? What if he told her he didn't care how she felt?

It didn't matter. She wanted to tell him, needed to tell him, was determined to tell him.

Tara, her heart pounding so hard she could feel the thump in her chest, dialed Brian's number and waited, holding her breath, for him to answer.

"E. B. Shute," his familiar voice said.

"Brian—" she began.

His words cut across hers. "If you leave your name and number when you hear the bell, I'll call back as soon as I can. Thank you."

An answering machine! He hadn't had one before she'd left California. He hadn't needed one, he'd said, because his number was unlisted and because the surgical group had an answering service that screened after-hours patient calls. Why had he bought one? So he wouldn't have to talk to her? She closed her eyes in pain.

That's a defeatist attitude, her inner self argued. At least leave your name and number.

She hesitated.

Go on, do it!

"Tara Reed," she said, her voice faltering. Her mind went blank and she couldn't remember the Cape Cod area code, but it finally came to her and she gave the number.

Her hand trembled as she put down the phone. Would he call back?

It was three hours earlier in California and he wouldn't be home yet. She'd have to wait and see.

Chapter Twenty

Tara, with one of her grandmother's quilts wrapped around her, got up from the couch to turn off the radio.

"...sunshine and temperatures in the high sixties," the announcer was saying. "Indian summer in November..."

She clicked it off and returned to the couch, where she stared at the fire, its flames dying to glowing embers. The last time she'd heard the time on the radio it had been four in the morning, and that had been over an hour ago.

She'd given herself all kinds of excuses. Brian was on call and hadn't gotten home. He'd come home but hadn't checked the answering machine. He'd gotten her message but was waiting until morning to call because he didn't want to disturb her sleep.

The truth was he wasn't going to call. Ever.

Face it, she and Brian were through. Finished. He'd never know she loved him.

How can I go back to California? she asked herself. She enjoyed her job but what else was there? And California was so far from New York, Karen and little Michael. She didn't want to be that far away from them. If she gave up her job at Delta Two, what then?

Tara watched the red coals on the hearth as though they'd give her an answer. She'd finished one sculpture she thought was good, but who knew if it would sell? She could do others. Would they sell? And if they did, would the money be enough to live on even if she kept expenses down by living in this house?

Of course there were other design engineering firms. A full-time job would limit her sculpting, though. Wait. What was it D.D. had said last winter after Roger had to fly to New York twice in one month to complete a project?

She pictured D.D. in his office, one hand rubbing his bald spot, glancing from one to the other of the engineers assembled for a staff meeting.

"I've thought once or twice it'd be to our advantage to have a representative on the East Coast. Not on salary, of course. On commission." D.D. shook his head. "The problem is he'd need to be someone operating out of New York City and I never met a New Yorker I trusted farther than I could see him."

"I'm a native New Yorker," Tara had protested. "Not from the City, though."

D.D. had grinned at her. "I have to admit I'd trust you. Okay, if you ever decide to leave safe and sunny Sacramento for that grimy mugger's paradise, we'll talk."

Well, she wasn't exactly in New York City, but Cape Cod *was* on the East Coast. It might be worth discussing with D.D. He did value her designing and he wouldn't be out any money by saying yes.

The more Tara thought about it, the better she liked the idea. She got up and threw another log on the dying fire. Sparks flew up, then flames licked at the dry wood.

It wouldn't be any easier to be without Brian on the Cape where memories of him lingered, but she felt better in Chatham, felt as though she belonged here. Though Sacramento was pleasant enough, it had never been home to her.

Here in front of the fire she and Brian had shared their first dream. Here they'd made love for the first time. She remembered the shining golden door in their dream and the wonder that waited for her behind that door.

Had he felt the same magical excitement? Yes, she knew he had because they'd been bound together and she'd shared his response. How could he forget what they'd had together?

The reflection of the fire had flickered in his eyes, tiny flames of desire in the ocean blue. His hair, soft and silky under her fingers, had been as deep a red as the embers. The warmth of his body had taught hers the meaning of spontaneous combustion. A man of fire and flame, igniting her until they both flared as brilliantly as comets.

Tara sighed. She could never forget.

Despite the ache of the memories, she wanted to stay in Grandma Fallkirk's house. No, in *her* house. She owned it jointly with Karen, but her sister had never felt about the house the way she did.

It must be almost dawn. In California it would be about three in the morning. Was Brian—?

No, stop thinking about him. About the past. Plan for tomorrow.

The day would be unusually warm and sunny for November. It was another beautiful day on the Cape—a good day to search other beaches for flotsam and driftwood for her stockpile of found objects. She'd call D.D., too.

And she had to decide when she'd fly back to clean out her apartment and drive her car east.

At the moment, though, what she needed was sleep. She hadn't changed into her nightgown. She still wore jeans and a sweatshirt. It was too late to go to bed, so she'd try to doze on the couch.

Half-asleep, she relived coming to Chatham last March: the long drive in the night, coming into the house, going to her bedroom and looking from the window. There on the beach . . .

Tara gazed up and down the empty beach. Confused, she didn't know if the beach was in Chatham or La Jolla, whether the water beyond, gray in the predawn light, was the Atlantic or the Pacific. Yet she was upstairs so she must be in the Chatham house.

Where was he?

The first rays of the rising sun tinted the water of the sound a pale gold.

He was late.

He belonged on this beach, a dark figure in the stillness of dawn. Why didn't he come?

He wasn't going to come.

Yes he would. He had to. . . .

Tara roused, her neck stiff from her awkward position on the couch, the dream vivid in her mind. Brian. The beach.

The windows showed the brightness of sunrise. She stood up and, as if drawn by a power beyond her control, climbed the stairs to her bedroom and pulled up the shade to gaze down at the beach.

A dark figure stood below looking up at her window. Tara closed her eyes, certain she'd created a vision from her desperate need. When she opened them he was still there.

He was real!

Okay, it's a man, she told herself, trying to still her wildly escalating hope. He must be an early-morning jogger curious about who's living in this house. You know he can't be Brian.

She stared at the unmoving figure, heart pounding. Now sunlight shimmered around him so he seemed to be standing in a golden shower. He held up his arms to her and her breathing stopped.

"Brian!" she cried.

Tara raced down the stairs, flung open the front door and ran toward him. He met her halfway and gathered her into his arms.

"Brian," she sobbed, her arms tight around him. "Oh, Brian."

He murmured her name, his lips against her temple. She felt his tongue taste the tears on her cheek and then his mouth met hers. His kiss restored her, renewed her, aroused her.

"How could you get here so quickly?" she asked when she could bear to break away long enough to speak. "I didn't call you until yesterday afternoon."

He shook his head. "I didn't know you called; I was gone by then. I came because I dreamed the night before last. I was here, on this beach, and I was a crippled gull, trying to fly. A terrible dream, a wonderful dream and I knew the dream was yours, too." He stroked her hair, touched her lips with his forefinger.

"It was hell, missing you," he continued. "I tried to hang on to my anger, tried to make myself believe I was better off free of any ties, but it was a losing battle. All I could think about was you. Then I dreamed and when I woke from the dream, our dream, I knew how much I'd lost when you left. I knew I'd never have any happiness without you. I was certain you were here in Chatham, but I called your sister to make sure. Do you know what she told me?"

Tara gazed up at him, thinking she was ready to explode with joy. "I can't imagine what Karen might have said."

"Well, let's call it plain talk. Something to the effect that I might think I was the world's greatest surgeon but if I didn't get my ass over to the Cape in a hurry, in her opinion, I was nothing but a damn fool."

She laughed. "Karen can be blunt."

"I took the first flight I could get." He pulled her closer. "Do you realize I never once told you I loved you? My God, how could I have been so stupid?"

"I love you," she whispered. "That's what I called to tell you."

He kissed her again, a long, slow meeting of lips and hearts.

"I've had a time adjusting to the fact we can dream together across an entire continent," he said, pulling away to look at her. "What about you? You're not still afraid of our shared dreams, are you?"

Tara hadn't properly taken in his words about the dream that had brought him to her, but now she realized the meaning of that dream. They'd dreamed together again, even though he was in California and she was in Massachusetts.

She remembered the dream, the crippled gull who knew only that he'd been born to fly. As she'd been born to share dreams with one special person, whether she wished to or not. The double dreaming was a wonderful happening, a gift to be cherished. What happened in the past had nothing to do with Brian. She was wrong to fear the dreaming, just as she was wrong to fear love. Nothing worth having was without risk.

How could she fear something that brought her closer to Brian? The marvel of communicating with him in dreams added another dimension to their love. How lucky they were to be able to experience this special closeness that belonged to only the two of them.

"I'll never be afraid of anything I share with you," she said.

"Let me tell you about the next dream we'll have together." He spoke softly into her ear, his warm breath exciting her senses. "First I'll build up the fire in the fireplace while you lie on the couch watching me. You'll have a quilt over you but underneath the quilt you'll be wearing nothing." His hand slid along her hip to pull her against him.

"Are you sure you can wait for the dream?" she teased, aware of his arousal and quivering with her own need.

"I've been waiting for so damn long an extra hour's nothing. After I finish with the fire, I'll kneel beside the couch and pull the quilt down—first to your waist. Then I'll kiss your breasts, first one, then the other until you moan and hold my head against you. Next, I'll pull the quilt entirely off and—"

"Brian," she begged breathlessly. "Stop talking, let's go dream!"

He released her, taking her hand as they headed for the house. Before they got there, she stopped and faced him.

"I have to tell you—I'd just decided not to go back to California," she said. "Maybe you can change my mind but nothing will ever make me like those long hours you work." Her gaze was defiant. Much as she loved him, it was better to have this out once and for all.

He nodded. "I was going to bring this up later, but I'll tell you now. Along with understanding we had to be together or life wasn't worth living, I realized if we *were* together I'd have no time to be with you. My soul-searching showed me how blind I'd been about what I really wanted out of life.

"How would you feel about me starting a low-key practice here in Chatham? After we get married, I mean. We can buy out your sister's interest in the house and live here if you want to."

"But you've made a name as a surgeon in San Diego. You'll have to start all over again here."

"I'll still be doing surgery, and that's all that matters to me. When I was a child my father told me I had to make myself into somebody because he hadn't and I believed him. But I'm not my father. I'm me, and that's all I want to be—non-famous Brian Shute. Despite my arguments with you to the contrary, I'm a small town doctor at heart and always will be. Could you be happy here?"

"This is my home!" she cried, throwing her arms about him.

Brian started to pull her closer, then held her away. "Look," he commanded, pointing, "my welcoming committee."

A sea gull flapped awkwardly to a landing in front of them. Tara stared in disbelief at the gull's damaged left wing.

"He flew!" she exclaimed. "It can't be Larry."

"Let's say he flew after a fashion. Another gull might find fault with his technique. And why can't it be Larry? It sure looks like him."

"Larry's lost. I've been searching for him but—"

The gull advanced, squawking loudly, stopping at Brian's feet. After a final, indignant squawk, he pecked at Brian's shoelace.

"Okay, Larry, I get the message. Food." Brian dug into a pocket and pulled out half a ham and cheese sandwich wrapped in plastic. "I saved this for you. I hope you don't object to airline food." He spread the plastic on the sand and placed the bread, meat and cheese on it.

Tara smiled as she watched the gull gobble the food. "No one but Larry can eat that fast. It has to be him."

"Of course it's him," Brian told her, putting an arm around her. "We're all together again, the way we're supposed to be. Here's how I see it: You want to live here, and I want to live here. Larry wouldn't dream of living anywhere else. All the omens are right." He smiled down at her.

"You, me and Larry," he went on, "we've all learned to fly in our own way. Obviously the three of us were meant for each other. Why fight destiny?"

"Who's fighting?" she asked.

"I'm glad we agree," he said as they started for the house again. "You can be pretty feisty at times. Now if you promise you won't run away from me before the marriage, I might even be persuaded to commit the ultimate sacrifice."

"You don't mean it!" She grinned at him. "I thought that was a deep, dark secret never to be revealed."

He pulled her against his side. "If I don't tell you what the *E* stands for you'll probably dream what it is anyway some night when I'm asleep and helpless."

"You don't need to tell me," she said. "Unless I guess right. It'll be more fun that way."

"Fun? You call that fun?" He stopped, lifting her into the air, then sliding her down his body and holding her tightly against him. "Let me show you what *I* call fun."

FORGIVE AND FORGET—Tracy Sinclair
Rand worked for the one man Dani hated—her grandfather. And though Dani knew it was just Rand's job to entertain her, she found herself falling in love with him.

HONEYMOON FOR ONE—Carole Halston
Jack Adams was more than willing to do the imitation bridegroom act, but he didn't want to stop with an imitation, and Rita wasn't willing to comply. She wanted someone serious and stable, and Jack was anything but.

A MATCH FOR ALWAYS—Maralys Wills
Jon was a player without a coach; Lindy was a coach without a player. They made an unbeatable team so it was only natural they would find each other. Suddenly tennis wasn't the only game they were playing.

ONE MAN'S LOVE—Lisa Jackson
When Stacey agreed to help Nathan Sloan with his daughter, she didn't realize that the father would be the biggest puzzle—and cause the most problems.

SOMETHING WORTH KEEPING—Kathleen Eagle
Brenna was unsure about returning to the Black Hills, but nonetheless she was excited to compete against Cord O'Brien. She was confident she could win the horse race, but she might lose her heart in the process.

BETWEEN THE RAINDROPS—Mary Lynn Baxter
Cole Weston was hired to prove that Beth Loring was an unfit mother. But how could he build a case against this woman when he found himself falling head over heels in love with her?

AVAILABLE THIS MONTH:

DOUBLE JEOPARDY
Brooke Hastings

SHADOWS IN THE NIGHT
Linda Turner

WILDCATTER'S PROMISE
Margaret Ripy

JUST A KISS AWAY
Natalie Bishop

OUT OF A DREAM
Diana Stuart

WHIMS OF FATE
Ruth Langan

Silhouette Desire

Available
January 1987

NEVADA SILVER

The third book in the exciting
Desire Trilogy by Joan Hohl.

The Sharp brothers are back, along with
sister Kit...and Logan McKittrick.

Kit's loved Logan all her life and, with a little
help from the silver glow of a Nevada night,
she must convince the stubborn rancher that
she's a woman who needs a man's love—not
the protection of another brother.

Don't miss *Nevada Silver*—Kit and
Logan's story and the conclusion
of Joan Hohl's acclaimed
Desire Trilogy.

DT-C-1